LOST IN THE HOLLER

A NOVEL

MICHAEL WEST

LOST IN THE HOLLER

For rights and permissions, please contact:

Michael R. West
320 Corporate Drive
Knoxville, Tennessee 37923
Michael.west864@gmail.com

www.Michaelwest-writes.com
www.michaelwestwritessubstack.com

Paperback ISBN: 979-8-9894753-3-9
eBook ISBN: 979-8-9894753-4-6

Cover design & typeset by riverdesignbooks.com

Also by Michael West

Mom's Diary

For Tiffiny, Ashley, and Thomas

*Not much happens in Gizzard's Holler
cept the rhododendrons blooming in the spring,
fog hovering below the tree limbs,
music wafting through settlers' souls, vittles
giving more than sustenance, and an unbreakable
bond forged in secrecy*

Prologue

Today, I know who I am and where I belong. I am the son of Nita and Frankie Burnette, the husband of Alice, my lifelong love, and the father of Caroline and Franklin. I am a farmer in Gizzard's Holler, a small mountain valley tucked amongst the Appalachian Mountains in the farthest corner of Upper East Tennessee, and the proud owner of fifty cows, sixteen pigs, a dozen chickens, and two homely dogs, Buddy and Leroy.

I am also at peace, comfortable with my life, finally; I haven't always lived with the confidence I currently possess. Twenty years ago, in the summer of 2001, I abandoned what I thought I wanted, what I believed I needed, to limp home and start over, only to learn home wasn't what I thought it was. Confused and hurting, I struggled to rationalize my existence; wondering, did I need to know the truth about my family's past to understand who I was?

I have heard it said that the passage of time dulls the intensity of previously painful emotions, gives space to forget, to move ahead and, if needed, compartmentalize that which you don't want to revisit; that sentiment captures my experience. For two decades I have spent little to no time revisiting how I ended up living in the house where I was born, farming like my daddy, and married to my high school sweetheart. In all those years, I never looked back nor felt the need to share with anyone the emotional struggles I navigated when I left my business career, hoping to fill a hole, only to realize my recent despair at work wasn't my problem. My problems were deeper than an abandoned career. I felt lost. Afraid to revisit the events from twenty years ago, I consistently avoided discussing the entire experience and washed it away from my consciousness. I didn't want to remember how devastated I was to learn of my new and unexpected reality; to relive the isolation and pain of no longer being RJ Burnette from Johnson County, Tennessee, but RJ the New Yorker.

My personal drama was deep. Whatever baggage and insecurity I collected and carried home from my time in the Northeast only magnified my personal despair when I learned: mystery shadowed my family, and they didn't want to include me in their tightly protected, closed web. What started as a chance to find myself became a question of my character and my value system.

Tomorrow, I will turn fifty, a day most people try to ignore. I will not hide away and pretend my life is only beginning. My wife has a surprise party scheduled, and, strangely, everyone seems to think I don't know what is in the works. It would be fair for them to assume I am clueless; people in Gizzard's Holler can keep a secret. I hear tell Alice expects thirty friends, our two kids, and my living relatives, of which there are a couple of dozen, to spend the day picnicking on our farm. Food will be the dominate feature of the day; it is at most country gatherings; as sure as mist settles in the mountains: weddings, birthdays, and funerals are certain to get locals cooking and comfort food on the table. My favorite dish is skillet-fried corn; nothing about it is healthy, and that's what makes it good; if the cook doesn't hold back on the butter, I am asking for seconds. I am also partial to mac and cheese; a southern staple that doesn't grow in the ground but counts towards our daily vegetable intake and is a part of every respectable meal. Who am I kidding? I could live off meatloaf, mac and cheese, fried corn, green beans, and fresh rolls and never want for anything else.

Even though I will enjoy the frivolity, it won't be all that is on my mind. The approach of this landmark birthday has privately stirred me to reflect on my life and, more specifically, the events of twenty years ago that forever altered my path. And yet, thinking about my past, and how I came to find peace, I realize I haven't shared my story with my kids.

Kids often see their parents' lives as grander than they are; well-managed and stable. My two children have never had a reason to believe their dad wasn't always in control; life in Appalachia in the twenty-first century is easier than it used to be. Even conversations about my family and our farm's history lacked the punch to grab my kid's attention. Today, on the eve of my big day, I have decided; I am going to share with them what happened to my family, and to me, and how it changed my life. They need to know my path wasn't straight or planned. They need to know my life hasn't always been perfect; more accurately, I want them to understand how I struggled. The need to hear the truth about my heritage, my Momma and Daddy, my siblings, and the secret this community kept and still holds. And with luck, they will decide their dad is honest, faithful, and true to his word. They will know I live my life with values learned in these hills, and finally they will gain an understanding of how we take care of each other and protect those we love from those we don't know.

My kids no longer need to wonder about my past; they need to hear it from me, every little detail.

PART I

1

Coming Home for a While

I HEARD WHAT GEORGE SAID. "IT WAS A GREAT ASSIGNMENT, a tremendous opportunity for the firm, a drop-everything-you're-doing kind of offer," I heard all that, but I wasn't listening. I was absent, thinking about anything but my role as a partner at a New York boutique investment bank. Actually, if I recall, I was wondering what would cause fireflies to synchronize their blinking when speed dating in the Great Smoky Mountains National Park, a fair line of thinking, given, it was June and the annual pilgrimage of tourists, with lawn chairs in tow, were on buses bound for the Elkmont Campground, with the sole intent of watching sexually aroused fireflies perform for prospective one-night stands.

This wasn't the first time I had failed to engage with my colleagues. It was just the first time I had specifically ignored the firm's senior partner. My emotional detachment was difficult for me to hide, as the lead banker for the manufacturing section at a recognized lower Manhattan firm. Maybe they noticed, or maybe their own careers occupied my colleagues, and they weren't interested in my professional detachment.

Regardless, no one in my area had said anything or challenged me. That is until George, a colleague of eight years, and my boss for the last four, noticed I wasn't jumping up and down at his offer to lead the sale of a worldwide manufacturing company to GE.

Not shy nor subtle, George looked up, glanced over the top of his reading glasses, and said, "What the hell is the matter with you, RJ? Did you hear anything I said?"

It was a fair question, and he deserved to know the truth. It was time to stop delaying the inevitable.

Weeks before I had considered sharing with George my growing anxiety. An idea that faded as fast as it surfaced. I couldn't talk to George. He was the boss, and his response would reflect his role. I don't know if he ever consciously chose his route or if it evolved, but I believed he would scoff at my seemingly soft, worrisome feelings. I took him to be hardened, and unapproachable. Maybe he wasn't always a hardass; maybe the job and his life pushed him to the limit and left nothing but an angry New York investment banker. Twice divorced, and the father of two kids who hated him, George's existence was the firm, our deals, and money. I don't recall ever seeing him smile, and he certainly never laughed. Any hint of joy he showed came from a twisted sense of manipulation he perfected when he became the senior partner. He loved harassing the aspiring analyst and eager junior associates; toying with their desire to succeed. As I watched his daily performances, my initial admiration for George faded. He was now symbolic of what could happen to a person who put the interests of his firm over living a normal life. I wanted no part of the world he had created for himself.

To be sure, I didn't want to hear what he said. It was predictable and self-serving. I wasn't interested in him telling me about how great my life chasing fees would be for me and my family of one, my four-year-old dog, Winston.

I was done, and there was no turning back. It was time to tell George. The blank look on his face as I told him I was resigning, said it all. George couldn't believe it. "Was I out of my mind? Did I remember I had a non-compete? How could I walk away from the financial opportunities in front of me?" were just a few of the questions posed.

He didn't get it; I knew he wouldn't. I didn't want to explain to him what I was thinking; it wasn't his business, more to the point, I wasn't sure I had completely processed my reasons. If I didn't know what I was doing, how could I explain my rationale to him? Honestly, there wasn't much either of us could say, and so the conversation was brief. It ended with his asking, "Where are you going to go?"

"I am going home to see Momma."

My answer surprised me. I had given little thought to what was next and even less time considering home. And with that, I turned and walked out the door.

It was a fitting end to my time as a New York banker. There were no personal moments, laughter, or emotions; it was transactional, just like every day before. I didn't expect to feel happiness or freedom, but I felt both. Before I made it to the street, a smile had developed on my face, and my pace picked up. I was out of there.

Relieved to have admitted to George what I had internalized months before; I grabbed my phone and called Momma. She picked up after five rings. "Hello."

"Hello, Momma, this is RJ," I said. My voice broke with unexpected emotion.

"I know who this is, RJ," Momma said in her sturdy voice. "You okay, RJ?"

"Momma, I am coming home for a while. Should be there tomorrow. I sure do look forward to seeing you."

"Boy, am I excited to see you. You travel safe… be hungry when you get here."

I closed my phone and put it into my jacket, tears filling my eyes. I was going home.

2

The Sad Mess

IN A FLASH, MY EUPHORIA CAME CRASHING DOWN AS MY pace slowed, and I considered what I had just done. A growing panic filled my body, and I bent over, not sure if I was about to scream with joy or throw up in the middle of the bustling Wall Street elite. I suddenly felt trapped in a vortex I couldn't escape; I needed to sit down, to slow down. Spotting a bench in Zuccotti Park, I scampered over and threw myself down onto the metal seat.

Slowly I regained my composure. With each rhythmic breath, my brain found its footing, and I remembered why I had sought to escape my career.

It had been obvious for a while that change was necessary. I no longer had it in me: the long meetings, sleeping at the office, cold Chinese takeout, and a never-ending competitive need to beat the other side in the negotiation, not just for the sake of winning, but to ensure they lost. I lived in a world where negotiating mutually beneficial transactional terms was a veiled attempt to appear reasonable. Fairness was the stated goal, but most of our clients wanted to claim victory by gaining a measurable advantage over the other party in the deal; and so, did I. We were keeping score, and you would win more if the closing terms had your client jumping for joy after the money cleared their account. It had all become too much.

Funny thing about knowing you want to do something different, but not knowing what it is: indecision, apathy, and uncertainty establish residence in your head, and you feel stuck; and it can linger. Without a powerful force pushing them, people can live in an emotional holding pattern for a long time. It is how workers stay in jobs for years, unhappy and underperforming. I was circling the airport seeking a place to land, running low on fuel, without a plan for figuring it out.

Sadly, I didn't have other colleagues who could offer counsel and a welcoming venue to allow me to talk out my options. I didn't have any friends — a hard thing to admit, but true. It was difficult to find time for someone else, and if I am honest, I could be as entertaining as a root canal. Given my less than charming personality, I didn't have a girlfriend or even anybody outside of work to go to dinner with. I was a sad mess.

The only person I considered chatting with was Jeff, a peer who focused on the firm's retail transactions. We had gone out for drinks a few times in the last five years. Maybe he could offer some brilliant, sage advice. Or maybe not, as I thought about calling him to see if he wanted to go to dinner, I remembered the total extent of our "friendship" was that he had gone to Vanderbilt University for undergrad and was the only person I knew in the city who had any connection to southern sports. He knew, even though he wouldn't openly admit it to colleagues, that the SEC wasn't a government agency to be feared, but the athletic conference that Vanderbilt and my alma mater Tennessee belonged to. However, the loose thread of commonality that might have held us together was flawed from the beginning. Despite our shared mutual love for southern football, we couldn't hang out together; his team hated my team and wanted nothing more than for us to lose every game, and I would rather drink glue than watch Vanderbilt play football. Hardly the basis for a close buddy you could hang out with on the weekend binging on sports; Jeff would not help me; I was on my own.

Unable to move from the bench that had become my afternoon home, I replayed the hopeless feelings of the last few months, a growing sense of desperation. I didn't know whether I could do anything else. I thought about operational roles but realized that just because I was good at giving advice — bankers love to tell executives tidbits that could make their business better, with no regard for whether it made sense or if it was possible; advising from the cheap seats was easy and rampant — I didn't know the first thing about running a business. And frankly, even if I did, I didn't want to do anything with for-profit companies; I found business boring beyond belief; a personal admission I had fought to acknowledge to myself, but I could no longer hide.

I knew my frustration had paralyzed me. There were countless nights staring out the window of my apartment with the obsessive thought that surely, I could rally from my funk, get my juices flowing again and rejoin my previous drive for professional wealth. The more I imagined a resurgence, a new energy, the farther removed I became from my New York persona; nothing could stop my need to flee.

There were frequent talks with Winston about my

dilemma; and why not? A dog is clearly your best friend, and Winston was the best, and only, friend I had. A cheerful Golden Retriever, Winston, had lived his entire life in a small apartment on the Upper West Side. His world was a narrowly framed landscape that included our building and the cross street we lived on. Occasionally we found our way to Central Park so he could feel grass and sit in the shade of a tree. Despite his concrete existence and no history exploring fields of grass, Winston never hesitated to mark his territory on things that grew. It was an unusual occurrence for him to explore nature, and so even in the park, he stayed close to my side; he was a city dog; he knew people, cars and noise; other dogs, although interesting, were to be avoided. I always felt guilty leaving in the morning to go to work, but Winston became accustomed to my long hours; he liked the building superintendent, and Jackson liked him. Jackson took Winston for daily walks, and I suspect much more. Even as a puppy, the neighbors in the building and the regulars on the block seemed to know Winston better than they should. I gather Winston spent most of his day hanging out with Jackson; there is no telling what they got into. Each night, Winston never failed to greet me energetically when I unlatched the deadbolt on the door; tail wagging, a gentle whimper, spinning in circles as though he hadn't seen me in months.

Lately, I noticed Winston sensed I was off-kilter, and he quickly became concerned about my looming crisis; dogs are smart that way. I guess he noticed I was coming home earlier and eager to spend more time walking around the city, ignoring all the surrounding distractions. Each walk was the same, my head down, keeping a quick pace. I appeared as if I was purposefully walking towards a destination, resolute and focused, like all the other people on the sidewalk. It was a mirage. The rhythmic sights and sounds of the city that never sleeps invaded my scattered mind; sounds that used to excite me no longer stimulated my mind; now they terrified me.

New York no longer sustained me, giving me a vault of energy; it was depleting my tank; I withdrew, rarely leaving my apartment. In a strange way, Winston internalized my distress and became enthralled in my secluded ramblings. He never hesitated to tilt his head when I would ask a profound question or explore a potential option. I appreciated his listening to me; I just got minimal feedback.

Thoughts of Winston calmed my emotions, and I laughed at the notion of what my life had become and what was ahead. Standing up from the bench I had spent the afternoon resting on, I mumbled to myself, "Wait till I tell Winston where we are off to."

3

Leeverage Their Neesh

T HE NEXT MORNING, WITH A SENSE OF URGENCY, I grabbed everything I thought I could fit in my car and called the garage attendant to start the hour-long process of getting my car out of the garage; parking in New York being fraught with its own unique set of challenges. With more cars than space, car owners were required to pay exorbitant fees to store their cars in a garage that used an elevator system to stack cars on various levels, tightly packed in neat rows, with no apparent way out. A successful result depended on the motivation and talent of the attendants to secure a car successfully in a timely manner. If you were like me, someone who rarely removed their car, you could assume that dozens of cars buried your car. It was equivalent to the airport security wait on Wednesday before Thanksgiving: you would get to the front eventually, if your car started. As I patiently waited for my car to navigate the route to freedom, I worried if the rarely used Wrangler could handle the trip; I guess I was about to find out. To my surprise and joy, my car arrived at the street level about forty minutes after I called; things were already looking up. My luck continued; I found a metered parking spot near my apartment. Grabbing the space, I ran upstairs, picked up my stuff, and Winston; with everything in hand I bounded towards my car. As I loaded Winston into the front seat of the car, I realized he had never been in a car before. He was in for some new experiences.

Working your way out of the city is a process that takes time and can be stressful; except I was unaffected by the stress I normally felt. My decision was final, and I was leaving, and no matter how long it took to get on the other side of the Hudson River, my thoughts were already on my drive south. I hurried south on the west side of Manhattan, hoping the Lincoln Tunnel wouldn't be congested. I was in luck; it was still early in the day, and the tunnel traffic was moving. It seemed fitting to leave the city through a tunnel. It was a means to an end, unremarkable and uninteresting, but it got the job done. Exiting the tunnel, I laughed to myself. I couldn't recall a time I was so excited to see the city limit sign for Weehawken, New Jersey.

As I left New York behind, I thought about how I wound up in a cramped car with my dog and a shattered sense of self. Immediately my mind was fully engaged. I needed to process why this had happened. Not to enable an explanation for others, but to reaffirm for myself the choice I just made.

Once I got onto I95 south, it hit me. I remembered the exact moment I stopped caring about my job. We hosted the executive team of a two-hundred-million-dollar company who were on the street looking for an advisor to work on their deal; our team had prepped for the meeting and, at least from my perch, we looked like the logical choice to represent the company. As we neared the end of the final meeting, our prospective client began asking David, the team leader and guy who would handle most of the heavy lifting, summation questions that signaled we had won the business: "How do we get started? What is the process for communication, etc.?"

And then it happened. The CEO of our newest client-to-be said, "Finally, what do you guys look for in a company you represent?"

This was a gimme, and David could have gone in any direction, but he chose; "We look for companies that can effectively leeverage their neesh."

What? Did this young banker from Ames, Iowa, just tell the CEO of a company from Madison, Wisconsin, we wanted them to "leeverage their neesh." Yep, that's what he said. It was a response the CEO didn't expect. He sought an answer that provided assurance he was in expert hands. What he got was a glib attempt from the banker to convey sophistication. Unsure how to respond but wanting to fit in with his new partner, the CEO responded with a hopeful, eager smile, "Then we are a perfect fit."

The absurdity of two Midwesterners attempting to speak some advanced form of Ivy League English was more than I could take. Unable to hold my emotions, I laughed out loud. The room's energy evaporated, and everyone immediately glared at me. I felt like a twelve-year-old who broke wind at Sunday Bible school: embarrassed, yes, but also secretly taking joy in being the class clown who thought my noisy contribution was funny. Even as they peered at me, I didn't respond verbally. The scene was too comical, and I had no desire to join in the silliness.

After the client left the building, handshakes, high fives, and occasional shouts of joy filled the air. The team was thrilled, and I was happy for them. However, I struggled to show it. I sat quietly, fully aware my team thought I was smoking weed and had lost my mind. In that moment, I felt like the old uncle at Thanksgiving who is in the room but doesn't get the joke.

It wasn't my age catching up with me. A newly minted partner at thirty, I was at the beginning of my peak earning years. I just couldn't get past his blatant attempt to sound more sophisticated than he was. I just kept thinking to myself: yes, the work we provide is a valuable service and our expertise matters; it just didn't matter to me.

From that day forward, I concluded I too had pretended to be something or someone I wasn't. As I reflected on my brief career, I recalled that, day after day, my life was a game; everything was a game. I had reached a point where my desire to chase deals and drive fees had stripped my passion to provide value. My desire for the kill and the financial rewards were all I cared about. In my professional pursuits, I channeled my inner Ivy League-assumed history to impress; and I was ashamed.

It hadn't always been that way. I hadn't always felt embarrassed about who I was.

With the gloominess of Newark adding to my dark mood, I instinctively reached for the radio, hoping music would lift my spirits. It did. I set the dial to a classic country station. Ricky Skaggs crooning about the hills of Eastern Kentucky caused my left foot to tap and me to turn my attention to how my journey to the big city started.

Twelve years ago, when I left home for college, I didn't know what I wanted to do; I only knew I wanted to get beyond the small holler I grew up in. My high school teachers encouraged me, so I applied to the University of Tennessee, which accepted me with a small scholarship. That aid, and the little money Momma and Daddy had, covered most of my costs, so it would be up to me to fund the rest with a job scheduled around my classes. With a little apprehension, I rode with Daddy down to Knoxville; it was the farthest I had ever been from home. For the better part of two hours, we both stared blankly at the passing countryside. We hardly spoke. Daddy was proud of me, but this was foreign to him. No one in his family had ever tried to go to college; with no history to draw upon, Daddy was short on advice. His only words were, "RJ, remain true to yourself, how you were raised, and don't forget your roots."

Wise words from a humble man.

With no money, I quickly got a job washing dishes in one of the on-campus dining halls. It wasn't glamorous, but they worked with my schedule, and I could eat for free; flexibility and food — it was a good deal.

I was immediately surprised because I didn't know how other students lived. Most students did not have to work and seemed carefree. Their carefree approach to life captivated me, and I quickly pursued a career that would give me all the rewards that money brings. Something I had never considered before.

For four years I excelled in the classroom, I studied, and I worked. Occasionally, some guys living in the dorm, who came from a similar background, would get a little crazy with cheap beer. It was as harmless as my days back home, drinking beer with my friends on the tailgate of a pickup truck. We didn't bother anyone, and no one bothered us.

My success in the classroom caught the eye of my finance

professor. Dr. Simpson, a campus veteran for the last two decades, was legendary. He was both feared and loved by the students in the finance department. He had a reputation for being brutally challenging, opinionated, and abrasive. A transplant from Connecticut, he never seemed to fit into the laid-back style of a southern university.

Unlike my classmates, I found him fascinating, and he noticed me. I think I garnered his attention because he could never get under my skin, no matter how hard he tried. His attempts humored me. His accent made me smile; he could sound authoritative and smart saying the simplest things, and I always sat on the edge of my seat waiting for him to deliver a harsh quip or unexpected zinger when he thought a student wasn't meeting his expectations. He was unlike anyone I had ever met. He opened a world to me I didn't know existed.

During my last two years on campus, Dr. Simpson became a mentor. We were an odd pair and perfectly suited for each other. As much as he fascinated me, I intrigued him: an unassuming country boy who never seemed befuddled and always wanted more. In the fall of my senior year, out of nowhere, he asked me, "RJ, what are you going to do after you graduate?"

"Honestly, I don't know. I don't think there is anything for me back home." I responded.

"I guess I will stay around here and see if I can land a good job."

He was unimpressed with my passive response and, with classic Dr. Simpson aggression, said, "Damn, RJ, that is the worst answer I have ever heard. After all you have done to rise to the top of your class, don't you think you should aspire to do something special, something important?"

His comment wasn't a question; it was a challenge.

"What do you suggest?" I asked.

"RJ, I think you should go to New York and compete with the big boys. You have what it takes. You owe it to yourself." He said with little emotion.

Excited and falling for the idea of something big, I took his bait. "I don't know anyone in New York; I wouldn't even know how to find a job."

"Don't worry, I've already spoken to an old college friend who's a partner at an investment banking firm, and he'd love to give you a shot. He found it intriguing that I believed a country boy from the hills would succeed in Manhattan, because I had never suggested that he hire any of my students."

After that discussion, I set my path. Immediately following graduation, I packed up what little things I owned and, without stopping home to say goodbye, drove to New York.

When I started my professional journey, I didn't feel overwhelmed or scared. In retrospect, my hubris was silly: I had neither the pedigree of my cohorts nor a historical role model I could channel. From my colleague's perspective, my path to early success didn't seem plausible. Having no experience prior to moving to New York, and little real-world sophistication, created hurdles and caused some more well-healed insiders to look down on me. Their condescension and tendency to take me for granted opened a lane for me to fill. My country, common sense, overshadowed my lack of hereditary credentials; I knew how high corn should be on the Fourth of July: I understood what a watermelon festival looked like, and I knew when supper was. After I learned to hide my Southern accent, I found an effective ability to relate to and befriend clients with a charm that was one-part heartland and two parts private school. In time, that combination worked for me, and I built my brand and reputation. With success, I quickly became more detached from my core upbringing and my history that had allowed me to exercise my down-home style to open doors and find deals. No longer was a third of my effectiveness driven by my approachable charm: I was all confidence, bravado, and certain about everything I said or did.

I became obsessed with closing deals and the prominence that came from it; so much so that I ignored my prior life and the people who inhabited my first two decades. Truth is, I looked down on my past; I was a little embarrassed about where I came from and thought the people back home, who grew up like me, were incapable of understanding the important companies I represented. Just as the establishment harshly judged me, I judged my old friends and family. My kinfolk, I decided, had isolated themselves and were stuck in the past. They weren't progressive in their thinking; they just didn't get it, and the world was passing them by. I loved them, but it was a detached love. In my mind, I couldn't allow myself to value their existence and pursue my self-driven goals.

I increasingly lived my life through the prism of Wall Street. I was successful, but when I considered my most productive days, I was lonely and missing something; candidly; I was arrogant, opinionated, and miserable and as a result had little to no social life; I was becoming George.

Even with my professional success, my awareness that I had faked who I was to get a leg up was always in the back of my mind, but it didn't bother me. The imposter syndrome didn't apply; nothing could slow me down. Eight years is a long time to suppress your upbringing and its impact on who you are; long enough that any semblance of the real me seemed lost and buried.

And then, David, from Ames, Iowa, showed me the absurdity of pretending to be refined.

4

Mountain Folk Ideas

THE VIRGINIA STATE LINE MARKED A NEW BEGINNING. Whatever need I had felt in the prior five hours to replay my life in New York was gone. I headed south, almost home and eager to breathe mountain air. And yet, unsure of what lay ahead. It was natural I was apprehensive about my return. It had been three years since I had been home; an embarrassing admission, any son worth a damn would have made it a point to visit his momma more than that. Not me. The last time I saw Momma was the day after we buried Daddy under the tulip poplar tree out back of the house. I remember telling her I would be home soon to check on her. I remember the promise, but not enough to take the time to show up.

Not that we had a poor relationship. I loved my family and thought the world of Momma. My view of Johnson County, Tennessee, was a little more complex. Mountain folk with mountain folk ideas inhabited Johnson County, which was tucked in the northeast corner of Tennessee, on the border with Virginia and North Carolina. It was all I had known until I went to Knoxville for college.

I was born in the summer of 1971 and raised in a house my Papaw built on a two-hundred-and-fifty-acre pig farm at the bottom of Gizzard's Holler, two miles up Stinking Creek Road, off State Road 91. The youngest of four children and "the mistake" - Momma had me when she was forty - everybody was out of the house when I came along. Therefore, I had the upbringing of an only child. My oldest sibling, James, was born nine months and two days after Momma and Daddy were married — a precise recounting of the days was no doubt important to the Laurel Bloomery Presbyterian Church pastor and concerned congregates. Ralph followed James, and he was the rascal of the bunch; he gladly took on the role as the wild one in the family, and I heard tell, was a handful from the day Momma laid eyes on him. A few years passed before she had Sue Ann. I never met Sue Ann; I was told she had passed away from meningitis before her thirteenth birthday. They buried her under the tulip poplar next to Papaw and Mamaw.

I arrived after James and Ralph had already grown up and left, so they didn't help raise me. We weren't close growing up; we never have been. By the time I was an infant, James and Ralph were well on their way to establishing their lives. Momma and Daddy were in their forties and carried themselves more like grandparents. It wasn't anyone's fault, but my childhood lacked the energetic youthfulness found in burgeoning families. Momma and Daddy had raised their kids and knew the routine; they were less worried about every little detail in my life. They had seen it all before. Everyone around me was old, and I quickly developed an old soul. I wasn't bored; I was comfortable being alone; I was also inquisitive and adventurous. I had to entertain myself, and

I lived on a large farm with lots of activity. With freedom and little structure, I developed a creative imagination that I fed with constant questions. Momma grew weary of my never-ending inquiries. I don't know if I touched on sensitive subjects, or if she lost the energy to keep up with me, but she frequently cut me off. I remember her guidance: "RJ, some things are best left alone."

My childhood taught me independence, gave me the freedom to choose my path, and through observation, provided a framework for establishing my values. It also spawned my urge to abandon home for other pastures. Years later I was repeating my desire to flee; having reached the end of my failed attempts to take the next step in New York, and with nowhere to go, home seemed like a logical place. I could see Momma, recharge my batteries, and figure out my future. It shouldn't take more than a month; the question would be, could I make it a month in a place that I had worked so hard to leave.

As the miles passed, I grew excited to see Momma. After the death of Daddy, I assumed she had lost a step or two, but figured she still possessed the toughness that came from bearing four kids, raising three boys, running the house, and helping Daddy with the farm. I imagined her joy. Her baby boy was coming home, and I expected to smell her excitement the moment I stepped onto the front porch. Momma greeted people, like most country folk do, with a hug and a hearty meal. Fixing supper for family and guests isn't a tradition for Southern people; it's a way of life.

In the country, recipes are never recorded; that would be too formal. People pass down recipes from generation to generation. Each new offspring might add a unique touch or two, but the core of the recipe remains, no reason to make changes. As my daddy would say, "If it works, I don't see no reason to fix it." Of course, he was talking about some cobbled-up contraption he built to solve a problem he was having with the tractor and not cooking, but the logic applies to fried chicken just the same.

Even though recipes rarely use different ingredients, how the food tastes depends wholly on who cooks it. Each cook might sneak a little more salt, or pepper, or butter into their version, much like the preacher sneaks a nip of whiskey when no one is looking. The skillet impacts how it tastes; older cast iron skillets create a flavor that is hard for a new skillet to replicate (a skillet must be around longer than your oldest dog for it to be considered anything but new). Momma uses a cast-iron skillet that is older than me and may have a few years on Ralph.

Unknown intangibles also seem at work in how food tastes from one kitchen to the next. I don't know what it is, but food takes on the personality of the cook. Aunt Emily's house always smelled like antiseptic; unsurprisingly, no matter what she cooked, it tasted like it had a cleaning solution as part of the gravy. Our neighbor — she lived roughly three miles up Highway 91, Mrs. Davis — was the sweetest person I ever met. Her melodic voice instantly made you feel better, and she smiled a smile that would cause butterflies to sit on the clothesline and watch her. She was honeysuckle sweet. And her desserts were the best-tasting desserts in the county; it couldn't be a coincidence.

Momma's food conveyed a hard day's work with a touch of love dropped in to add to its heartiness. Food tastes better when you're tired, having worked up an appetite, and living on a pig farm qualifies as hard work.

Hearty food is also important when your day hasn't started. I'm not sure how she did it; getting up early every morning to fix a breakfast worthy of the hard day ahead; homemade biscuits and gravy steaming next to eggs and bacon. "Gotta eat a good breakfast if you're gonna have a good day," she would say most days as she laid the overflowing plate in front of me. It took a long time to break the heavy-breakfast habit. After I moved to New York, breakfast became a time sink, and healthy, quick options were my only goals at the start of the day. I had a feeling my breakfast habits were about to change, and I was looking forward to it.

There was more for me in Gizzard's Holler than just Momma. I had high school friends who were still there. It would be good to catch up with them; I could use a good laugh. Maybe my old girlfriend, Alice, hadn't left town. It wouldn't be easy to get in her good graces after what I had done. Maybe she would give me a chance to explain.

Maybe I can go fishing with my cousin Frank; we always had a good time together. I hear tell he is quite good with a fly rod; known as one of the best fly fishermen in the county—a distinction that is no small feat. His trout-fishing prominence is ironic, though. Frank wasn't always known as a great angler. In fact, for years, he had a more inauspicious reputation; he was the only person anyone had ever known who couldn't snag a catfish on the summer noodling trips.

I don't know when folks in the South decided it was a good idea to catch a catfish with their hands or feet, but some good ole boy must have tried it, and it took hold. The key is to go in the late spring or early summer when the catfish are hanging out in their holes, tucked up against the bank. When an object, like a hand, enters, they have no choice but to bite it to protect their nest. It is a rather odd way to spend a day, wading in dirty water, feeling around for a hole that holds a catfish; but it works, and I am told it is entertaining, although it's not that hard to entertain a country boy.

Even the most awkward fella in the group could somehow pull a catfish out of its lair, but not Frank. Every time he thought he had one, it would dart between his legs with a violent splash, followed by a loud angry scream from Frank. To be fair, Frank was bowlegged, presenting a natural escape route made to order for the nervous catfish. From my vantage point, Frank had done well for himself, migrating from wading in the murky water, intending to pull a catfish out of a hole by hand, to the beautiful rhythms of fly-fishing. If only all of us could have evolved so well.

5

Another Lifetime

Unlike prior trips home, the Shenandoah Valley's sweeping beauty drew my attention. The countryside was looking like home: rolling hills, open pastures, beautiful farmhouses with wrap-around porches, and a clear sky without the layer of haze I had grown accustomed to. I81 south is a step back in time; Civil War-era houses dot the landscape, still standing tall a hundred and thirty-five years later.

Where I came from, the Civil War held little curiosity, unlike other parts of the South. Northeast Tennessee didn't rally around the rebel cause. It was a split allegiance, with many families supporting the Union. Without deep passions, there wasn't a lingering residual pain, nor much reference to what folks from Georgia call the War of Northern Aggression.

My last detour before Gizzard's Holler was a rest stop just south of Blacksburg, Virginia, for a break and to let Winston roam around. I instantly felt the warmth of home. I am not sure why; it was odd. Even though I hadn't been timely with my trips home, I had been back to East Tennessee a few times since college. I had driven this exact route and stopped at this rest area before but had never felt this way. Maybe it was my newfound freedom from: work, my cell phone, expectations, and the need to be back in the city; maybe my heart hadn't ever left Johnson County, and I was aware of that sensation for the first time in a long time. Maybe I was just relaxed, and the peaceful pace of home was easier to remember. I don't know why, but there was a skip in my step as I stretched my tired legs that were only outmatched by the vigorous enthusiasm of Winston's tail; he had never looked so happy; I could almost see a faint smile. If I didn't know better, I could have sworn he shared my sensation of smelling fresh biscuits in the oven.

For the last hundred miles of interstate, my mind reflected on my immediate family and how little I knew about their lives. James, with over twenty years of age on me, felt like an absent uncle, not purposely detached, but not present in my life. In fact, I could hardly remember him being there during important times that marked my youth in the mountains. I don't blame him, but I also didn't know him. When I was born, James was married and starting his own family; being my big brother wasn't his priority. Sad to think we were siblings who lived ten miles from each other, and we shared no intimate bond or connection. Admittedly, I don't recall trying hard to reach out to James. I guess I didn't think I needed him. That was then. Today, my heart is telling me I need a relationship with my brother. For the first time, I feel compelled to build something lasting. My goal in coming home wasn't about establishing a relationship with James, but it would be nice. It would likely fill a hole I have in my life.

If James served as an elder uncle, Ralph was a complete mystery. I have rarely seen him over the years. In fact, people rarely see him. Two years after high school, while still working on the farm with Daddy, he moved into a shack deep in the holler. I don't recall when he left. I was too young; in my mind, he was never a part of our house. It wasn't long before he stopped showing up to help Daddy. With nothing to cause him to leave his place, Ralph became a complete recluse, living off the grid and existing with what the land provided. As a teenager, I attempted to see Ralph, and would ask Momma about him, only to be told, "Leave him be; he has his reasons for staying up there."

That was an okay answer to give a kid. I'm not a kid anymore. There must be more to the story. How could someone who grew up in Momma and Daddy's home reject people and society? How could you exist in a loving environment and feel the need to flee people and the world? I can't help but ask myself, is he just weird or is he crazy? I'm not sure which would be better. Maybe Momma will give me better insight into why my brother lives alone and wants no part of society. Or maybe she will keep it to herself, a habit she seems to have perfected.

Thoughts of Ralph agitated me. It made no sense. But neither did the fact that my family shied away from talking about Sue Ann. Stories about her always carried sadness, and that is understandable, but it feels like there is something more than grief hanging over her story. She has been gone for over thirty years, and people hush whenever they mention her name. I can't judge what it must feel like to lose a family member at such a young age; I can only feel the resulting tension and unease. I was told she died of meningitis; I am wondering if that is true.

It wasn't long before Winston and I pulled off 181, turned

left and pointed the car towards Damascus, Virginia—a friendly, if not quirky, town recognized as one of the few stretches on the Appalachian Trail where the trail goes right through the heart of a town. Damascus is also famous as a point of access to the thirty-three-mile Creeper Trail that begins at the top of the mountain at Whitetop Mountain Station and travels north to Abingdon, Virginia. Damascus, sleepy as it can be, represents a rebirth for small Appalachian towns nestled against the mountains. In recent years, tourists flocked to experience the beauty of towns like Damascus in search of a myriad of activities, a slower pace, and local food. Growing up, we didn't make it to Damascus much, odd since it wasn't more than ten miles across the state line from our farm. When we did, we would go to the Dairy King (not to be confused with the national chain Dairy Queen). A mom-and-pop hamburger spot famous for its homemade custard, the Dairy King was a recognized stop for the weary Appalachian Trail hikers passing through town. I don't remember how old I was when I heard of Dairy Queen, but I recall thinking it odd a big company was copying the name of this little hamburger joint in Damascus.

As I wound through the mountains into Tennessee, I cried. I don't know why, nor do I remember shedding tears since Daddy died. It wasn't a gully washer of a cry, nor was I sad; my tears came from emotional releases of something that had hung over my head; something I could feel but not understand, let alone describe. I was still wiping tears off my face when I turned right onto Stinking Creek Road and crossed the wooden bridge over Laurel Creek to enter Gizzard's Holler. It had been a long drive, but the trip home was longer than the drive. All the years that passed since I left for college had taken a toll and, without me knowing it, had pushed me away from my home and the way I felt when I was there. I hadn't been out of New York and my former existence but for fifteen hours, and yet I felt like it was another lifetime, lived by a stranger who didn't know the joys of hearing crickets sing as the sun wanes in the night sky.

As expected, Momma was on the front porch rocking in her favorite white-stained rocking chair when I pulled up; she had a loving smile on her face, and I felt the warmth I always observed when I made eye contact. As soon as I opened the car door, Winston jumped out and started running around. Momma's smile faded as she realized I wasn't alone. After a lifetime with animals, I guess she wasn't keen on having a hairy dog running around her house. She said nothing, though. Her focus shifted back to me. "Come give your momma a big hug; you look hungry."

Yep, I was home, and a southern feast wasn't too far away.

Predictably, Momma made one of my favorites, meatloaf. Not the kind of meatloaf fancy restaurants put on their menu, but the kind people in these parts eat: simple, with farm raised meat, a small, chopped onion, and a ketchup-based glaze that always included molasses to give it the sweetness. Of course, she cooked green beans with bacon fat, and she made creamy mashed potatoes with homemade gravy. Momma's gravy always started with the drippings from whatever she was cooking, followed by a spoon or two of Martha White flour and a dab of butter; it was never the same but was always rich and smooth. I swear it was the best meal I had ever had. Oh yeah, I forgot. She also had homemade buttermilk biscuits with honey. I couldn't stop shoving my face, and Momma couldn't stop topping off my plate. She never sat down; she was busy feeding her boy. She wasn't in a hurry to catch up with talk; feeding was the first step in reconnecting. Talking would come after supper, when we gathered on the porch.

The house had changed little from the last time I had seen it. In fact, I doubt it had changed much since my papaw built it in 1910. A two-story craftsman-style farmhouse with a brick foundation and a shingled exterior, the house had a wraparound porch, and a simple oak front door covered by a screen door. Under the house was a cellar that Momma used to store her canned vegetables. I never enjoyed going down there to get jars for Momma… too many spiders. On the first floor, there was a parlor with a still-functioning fireplace and a piano that had been a part of the family since before Momma was born. Next to the parlor was a reading room or what you would now call a living room. This room always felt too formal for me and my overalls to recline in. Daddy loved it though. If Daddy was home and not working, you could find him resting in his chair, a pipe hanging from his lips and his eyes fixed on the paper.

The hallway leading to the back of the house was dark, narrow, and creaked when you walked. The sound it made was the perfect clue someone was making their way to the kitchen. As you entered the kitchen, you immediately noticed a large, hand-crafted table that could easily seat twelve, surrounded by benches on each side and two upright chairs on the end. This is where Warren's and then Burnette's had gathered for more than ninety years, to say their prayers before digging into whatever was being served.

Today, the kitchen was more modern than in the days of my youth; Momma now had a dishwasher. She cooked on a gas stove with her large oven always ready to use; there wasn't a microwave oven, Momma wouldn't allow it. Above the wash sink, there was a window that looked out over the wheat field. She could also see the barn. This is where Momma kept an eye on her boys and Daddy. Momma had all the practical things she needed to make do in her kitchen. There wasn't anything fancy; and there was no need to buy her the latest kitchen gadget for Christmas; a toaster was as advanced as she would get. Stacked along the walls were shelves of her spices, baking items, and non-perishable food items she bought at the market. It looked like a disorganized mess, but she knew where everything was.

The only other room on the main floor was the "gathering room." That's what we called it, and that is what the people who lived in this house had been doing for almost a century. It was where stories were told, music played, and where everyone met to listen to the radio. From the Grand Ole Opry to news reports about the war, to Tennessee sports, three generations of the inhabitants of this home in Gizzard's Holler had spent their evenings glued to the words and sounds emanating from a radio Papaw bought after he built the house.

The upstairs of my family home was the living quarters. There were four bedrooms and two small bathrooms; Momma still called them washrooms. Indoor plumbing was added to the homestead thirty years after it was built. With a well in place, it was time for this modern indoor amenity. I am told that until his dying day, Papaw still used the outhouse.

Occasionally, the house would get a thorough cleaning, and a fresh coat of paint. Despite its age, the house stood tall and proud. Every time I see it, I am amazed at the creativity and ingenuity of Papaw some ninety years ago to build something that has stood the test of time.

Momma had also stood the test of time. She was now seventy years old, and I could tell her energy level had diminished. Her health seemed good and her mind sharp; she just didn't have the gumption to work like she had for the better part of fifty years. Despite her slow pace, her hug reminded me that Momma was tough. She was soft to the touch, but firm when she wrapped her bony arms around you. She no longer stood upright, and arthritis drew her fingers in. It looked like she should be in pain, but if she was, she wouldn't have ever said it. In her mind, there was no time for fussing about problems. "It wouldn't change anything anyway."

"Momma, how are you feeling?" I asked her as we finally settled into the outdoor rocking chairs.

"I'm good, honey, been canning most of the week and am just a little tired."

"Health good?" I tried again.

"Everything is great. Tell me about this little dog." She responded, ready to move on and talk about anything but herself.

We spent the next hour talking about Winston and the dogs we used to have on the farm. There were so many that we couldn't remember all of them by name; dogs came and went, the memorable ones left an impression; they were either especially loyal, or rotten. My favorite was a stray that wandered onto our property looking for anything other than what he had. He wasn't striking in appearance; in fact, he was a bit ugly. Not knowing what to name the homily dog, and short on creativity, I named him Davy in honor of Davy Crocket. Despite his appearance and uninvited arrival, he captured my heart from the beginning. His temperament and desire never to leave my side bonded us together, and we became inseparable. I went nowhere without him, except for church; we wore our best on Sundays, and no matter how many times I gave Davy a bath, he was never clean enough for respectable folks.

On a farm with livestock everywhere you look, dogs had a special place; they were there as companions, and, if they were talented, they could help herd the cows. Cows, pigs, and chickens didn't rise to the high level of regard that dogs possessed. Livestock existed to provide. Daddy had two quarter horses he used to move cattle and round up the occasional runaway cow; horses didn't warrant special names at our place. We called the two I remember, Brown and Spotted.

I hadn't thought about Davy for a long time. Funny thing about having a previously unloved dog as your pet, you're likely to experience a connection that may never happen again. As I retold stories of Davy, Momma sat quietly, rocked in her chair, and listened to me with no distractions or thoughts beyond our front porch. This was new to me. I wasn't used to people taking time to talk without interruptions. I usually saw the person I was talking to grab their cell phone or look around to see who else was there. On the front porch with Momma, for the first time in years, the world was tiny.

Rocking gently as the sun faded over the mountains, I noticed that the growing shadows, not the beeping of notifications on my phone, marked the passing minutes. As such, you felt like time passed slowly, and then you noticed you had been talking about a dog you cared for fifteen years ago for the better part of an hour. I couldn't remember when I had spent an uninterrupted hour with someone casually talking about nothing. Momma thought little of it, but I was keenly aware of the oddity of spending time engaged in meaningless conversation. I hadn't even settled into my room and was already aware that time, its passage, and how I spent it were going to be the biggest change for me.

6

She Was Beautiful

I T WAS PAST MOMMA'S BEDTIME, AND I WAS FEELING THE effects of a long day. It was time to go to bed. I was staying in my old room, with the same mattress and bed sheets; I was looking forward to wrapping myself up in that familiar blanket. It had been twelve years since I had called that small room on the second-floor home, but I expected to settle in nicely.

I gave Momma a hug and watched her slowly climb the stairs. She looked unsteady. I couldn't help but feel a tinge of guilt thinking of the gaps between being with her. It looked like I had missed her final vibrant years.

Before heading upstairs, I noticed an old mason-jar box beside Momma's favorite chair. It appeared to be full to the brim with old pictures. Not wanting to mess with Momma's organization, I decided not to disturb the box. I figured I would have time to talk with Momma about her memories and the stories the pictures told.

Before I could retire to my room, I needed to get Winston up and moving. He hadn't been here for a day, and he was already in the farm's rhythm. No need to move if you didn't have to.

I had been home a few times since college but had never felt emotion when I walked into my old room. This time was different. An overwhelming need to feel loved consumed me, and for the second time in a day, I cried.

My room looked the same as when I left for college, but different from what I remembered on my subsequent visits. I guess the few times I came home from New York I hadn't allowed myself to detach from my Wall Street life and career. Each time I was home, I was unwilling or unable to embrace my old life. I had obviously constructed a wall around my feelings and went through the motions.

As I laid my head on the pillow, a peaceful sigh left my body and a smile emerged on my face. Winston jumped onto the bed and curled up next to me, signaling it was time for me to turn out the light. Reaching for the bedside lamp, I noticed a framed picture of me and Alice. It was from our senior year. We were sitting on the tailgate of my truck, my arm loosely around her shoulders, and she with a big grin on her face. She was beautiful with her flowing brown hair and Daisy Duke cutoff jeans.

I hadn't seen or noticed this picture in more than a decade, but I immediately felt a charge through my body. I loved Alice before I left, and I loved her twelve years later.

Momma and Daddy loved her too. They, like everyone else, always assumed we would marry. It was what high school sweethearts do. That is unless one person leaves the other in search of something else. This picture still in my room caused me to wonder if my leaving Alice not only disappointed her but also disappointed Momma. Maybe most of what I have done since leaving home disappointed Momma.

Slowly I faded off to sleep, troubled by my growing unease with my life. I had a lot to process.

The sound of a rooster was a stark departure from the never-ending honking of taxis and the rumble of garbage trucks that greeted me in my New York apartment. As a boy, the rooster crowing was annoying, the first sign that chores lay ahead. On this morning there was an eerie, peaceful quality to the crowing rooster; I felt no need to get up. I had nowhere to go and nothing to do. Winston was, however, curious and disturbed to hear an unfamiliar sound outside the window. He didn't know what could make such a rhythmic screeching sound. "Come here, boy," I said to Winston as I motioned for him to come closer.

With a laugh I said, "That's a rooster. I'll show you what it looks like on our walk."

That explanation seemed to satisfy his interest; and with that, he laid down and went back to sleep.

Sunrise in the mountains comes later than its normal first peak above the horizon. The mountains looming over the farm meant that, on most days, it was a full hour into the day before sunlight hit our rooftop. That didn't stop farm activity nor the first order of the day. Not long after teaching Winston everything I knew about roosters; I caught my first whiff of bacon. Not store-bought bacon, but bacon from the farm; and eggs that Momma had collected from the coop, with a deep colored yolk that looked and smelled rich in flavor. Any thought I had of my normal breakfast of yogurt and grains was out the window, and I hurriedly got dressed.

I tiptoed down the narrow staircase and followed the smell that was drawing me forward — a clue to breakfast, the kind I had missed more than I realized. Standing at the door to the kitchen, I saw Momma standing over the stove in her white cotton gown, humming an old gospel hymn, *How Great Thou Art.*

"Then sings my soul, my Savior God, to thee,
"How Great Thou Art."

I paused for a moment and watched Momma singing peacefully. The sound of her voice, the smell of biscuits, gravy and bacon rushed through me; childhood memories flashed through my mind. Standing in the kitchen, I felt sixteen again.

Momma was born on July 31, 1931, with little fanfare in an upstairs bedroom, in the house she still calls home. She was kid number ten born to Betty Sue Warren, and thus a new arrival engendered little excitement; there was too much to do. Momma's daddy, Thomas Hudson Warren, was a farmer, and although proud of his flock of kids, viewed them primarily as additional helpers to keep the farm afloat. Mamaw Betty and Papaw Thomas were married when she was 14 and he was 23. When I asked Momma about the youth of her mother, all I got was, "I hear tell she was mature for her age."

Nothing else needed saying.

After cleaning the kitchen after a hearty breakfast, Momma shuffled into the parlor and sat in her favorite wingback chair. She bought this when I was in high school, and, unlike most of the furniture in the house, it wasn't an antique.

"Momma, I noticed you have a box of pictures there next to your chair. You've been stirring up memories of your family."

Momma smiled and nodded. "Yeah, I was walking down memory lane. I have had a good life."

Momma's comment about her life grabbed my attention. Did she mean more in what she said, or was it a phrase you would expect from someone in their seventies?

"Momma, what was Mamaw Betty like?"

Momma's face brightened, and she leaned forward. "She was a tough one. She had her first child when she was 15. It was your Uncle Henry; he was twenty years older than me."

Hearing Momma point out the age difference between her and Uncle Henry reminded me of the gap I had with my siblings. Knowing what I was thinking, Momma said, "A bit like you and your brothers."

One thing I knew from my youth was the name of each member of the clan. Estelle, Margie, Bubba, Alton, Sis, Tommy, Eddie, and Emily followed Henry. Not out of names, or I guess energy, Mamaw Betty named Momma, Jaunita Ann. A pretty name that was immediately shortened to Nita. As a last show of strength, Mamaw Betty delivered one more child two years after Momma. His name was Richard, but oddly everyone called him Jasper. Eleven kids were born to the Warren brood from 1911 to 1933, an impressive feat.

Momma was one of the youngest in the house, but she still recalled the days when most of the youngins lived on the farm. "It was a wild house; your Mamaw and Papaw had a room. There was a room for the boys, one for the girls, and a room for the babies."

Momma smiled as she thought back to her earliest days. "Bein the baby girl, I was sheltered, spoiled."

I enjoyed listening to Momma relay her position as the youngest girl and the "special" treatment she received. It made me wonder if my upbringing differed from James and Ralph's. I think it did. Being an only child in the house helped establish a unique bond between me and Momma. She treated me as older than I was, and I embraced the idea that I could handle things beyond my upbringing. Our connection is likely the genesis of my seeking to get out of the holler. Momma showed me more than most kids see, and I wanted more than my home could give.

"You know, RJ, there were nine of us kids in the house when the Great Depression began."

"Henry had moved out and married a scrawny girl. She might have been the origin of the phrase, bless your heart." Momma laughed.

"Estelle was also out of the house, having married some young boy at sixteen. In no time, she had twins. They lived in a two-bedroom cabin in Shady Valley."

The onset of the depression displaced millions and brought widespread poverty to America. At the depression's peak, the unemployment rate was almost twenty-five percent; but the worldwide financial meltdown had little impact on life in Gizzard's Holler.

"The Depression was hard." Momma said.

"But holler folks were poor before the rich in New York lost money in the stock market crash, and we was poor afterward."

Momma had shared this before. Regardless of world events, their life still revolved around subsistence farming, and it was hard work. The dirt in the holler wasn't the easiest to pull a good crop from, but they somehow did. Papaw kept chickens he "acquired" from a stranger passing through the area some years back—the former chicken owner having no choice but to hand over his chickens when faced with the consequences of getting caught trying to steal a horse, from Papaw's barn. Through extraordinary discipline and luck,

Papaw kept ten pigs. Papaw's cousin Jinks owned a boar hog, and it bred the sows (in return for the use of the boar, Jinks received one piglet he could later butcher). This was a fine arrangement for all parties involved except for the unlucky pig headed to Jink's place. Each year the family kept and enjoyed harvesting one pig. They sold or traded the others for whatever little they could get. Livestock was a valuable currency in the mountains; animals, like horses, that could help with farm productivity were the most valuable, followed by those that provided food.

"RJ, you remember when I told you I wanted you to go to college?" She asked.

"I do, Momma, but I didn't really know why you said that."

"It is because my family didn't have a formal education. Most of the Warren kids dropped out of school before entering high school. We just couldn't get past eighth grade."

"I wanted more for you, wanted you to do something no one in our family had ever done. I was confident you could do it," she said with a wink.

"What about you, Momma? You are smart."

She rolled her eyes at that comment. Finally, offering a response. "I was proud to graduate high school."

7

The Tulip Poplar

"RJ, I'M GOING TO TAKE A NAP. NEED ANYTHING?"

"No, Momma, I am good."

With no plan or idea of what I was going to do, I decided my next order of business was to take Winston for a long walk; there was so much for him to see, and I hadn't walked the farm in years. When I walked out the front door, the tulip poplar at the side of the house immediately drew my attention. Buried in the family cemetery were Papaw, Mamaw, Daddy, and Sue Ann. The sight of the four headstones stopped me cold. I am not much of a religious person, but without hesitation I prayed, my body trembling with suppressed feelings I didn't know I had. How could I have reacted so quickly and emotionally? Was it guilt? No, I didn't feel guilty because of things I had actively done, more like my awareness that I had emotionally disconnected from my family; blocked them from my mind and life. I couldn't remember ever spending more than a minute in the cemetery, but on this day, I sat down, leaning against the tree for the better part of the morning. Winston's walk could wait. I had never met Papaw, Mamaw, nor Sue Ann, but I felt a connection to them. We had each spent our lives on this farm; we were historically bound. Staring at her headstone, I recalled that Sue Ann and her life were a mystery to me.

It didn't take long for me to see signs that since Daddy had died, the farming activities had slowed. Momma kept Daddy's favorite farmhand around to manage as best he could, but gone were the days of a large pig farm. These days, they keep only five pigs at a time. They still had the chickens but had sold off most of the cows. They dedicated the meadow to growing hay for sale. It had been years since I had wandered the farm, but I still knew my way around; other than reduced activity, nothing seemed to have changed.

There was a tire swing hanging from the oak tree in the backyard. The fort next to the western edge of the meadow I built out of rocks and logs remained intact, ready for the sentry and his dog Davy to take up position to defend the property against strangers, Indians, or the law. The makeshift dam I stacked in Stinking Creek was still there; I spent many a day wading in the slow creek looking for crawdads and salamanders. I never heard why folks called it Stinking Creek. It smelled fine to me; maybe the still at the top of the creek gave off an odor. At the end of the property, I saw the overgrown path leading to Ramsey's Creek Trail; a favorite trail I would walk and a path that Momma forbade me to take. She never explained to me why this trail was off limits, and I didn't ask. I did, however, find it more interesting because it was off limits.

Naturally, if the path had drawn me as a kid, nothing would stop me today from taking Winston for a walk up to the caverns. Even though the entrance was overgrown, it appeared someone still used the trail often. It was well-traveled. I couldn't imagine who would walk along here, but someone clearly did so regularly. The trail was beautiful, with a mixture of rhododendrons, ferns, rock formations, a little babbling brook, and lots of wildflowers. Rich with fauna, the Appalachian Mountains could be dense and forbidden; it was easy to get lost, turned around with no obvious sense of where to go. I was not a wanderer by nature. I was perfectly content to stay on any trail that lay before me; even ones that are off-limits.

As I climbed, I noticed a stack of rocks on the right side of the trail as I neared the top of the trail. This was new to me. I had never noticed this before, but it was obvious it had been there a long time. As I approached the organized rocks, they took on the shape of a miniature monument, and then I saw it. Painted on the top rock was the symbol of a cross. Clearly, this display was purposeful, but for what reason? After a few minutes of speculation and no insight into what it meant, I moved on. I walked along the path, but I couldn't get the strange scene out of my mind. Was someone or something buried there? Who would have done this? Is this why, growing up, Momma said I wasn't to take the trail?

The rest of my walk was less relaxing, as I imagined all kinds of weird possibilities. I was determined to ask Momma if she knew anything about what I found on the Ramsey Creek Trail, but the moment I saw her, my plan changed. Even though I was a grown man; my childhood memories overtook me, and I remembered I wasn't supposed to be on the trail. I didn't tell Momma growing up I went up there, so why start now?

Momma had lunch ready when I walked into the kitchen. Chicken salad sandwiches and a macaroni salad waited on the table for me to sit down.

"Momma, if I eat like this every day, you're going to make me fat."

That was the best compliment you could give a Southern cook.

"You'll be alright," she smiled.

Interested in learning more about Momma's past, I asked her, "Momma, how old were you when the war ended?"

"I was fourteen. It was such an exciting time. Everywhere you looked, people were joyous, always smiling. It was as though we had come through the worst of it and the future was there for the taking."

"Everything settled down after that. That is until a couple of years later."

"What do you mean?" I asked.

"Well, I will tell you." She said.

And with that, Momma told me the story of how a Saturday night bluegrass jam on Papaw's front porch forever altered her future.

8

A Saturday Night Bluegrass Jam

BLUEGRASS MUSIC WAS A CORE PART OF MOUNTAIN FOLKS' entertainment; everyone could play something or sing a tune. It was only natural that families and neighbors would gather most Saturday nights on someone's porch to pick an instrument, sing, and dance. These joyful, understated sessions would sometimes go well into Sunday morning. You could count on hooting, and hollering, and laughter filling the valleys with happiness; you could also count on the evening shutting down with just enough time to sleep off any moonshine hangover and pray at church on the Lord's Day of rest.

To hear Momma tell it, as she sang her favorite song, a young, handsome stranger stepped onto the porch and walked quietly towards a distant chair at the end of the row. He wasn't completely new to her, but this was the first time she had seen him up close. She had watched him earlier in the week working out behind the barn, tending to a drainage ditch that was causing Papaw trouble, but she was busy and didn't pay him any mind.

A new farmhand, he had recently arrived in Johnson

County looking to start his life away from his upbringing in Newport, Tennessee. Born December 19th, 1927, in a shack along the banks of the Pigeon River, Franklin Stewart Burnette had an inauspicious start. His mom died during childbirth, leaving him to be raised by his grandmother; his father having skipped town on the news he was about to be a dad. She did the best she could, but by the time Franklin was eight, he was on his own with nowhere to go and no adults to protect him. Such became his reality, a nomadic lifestyle moving from house to house throughout Cocke County seeking help, food, shelter, and any hand-me-downs he could find.

Education was hard to get for a child without a home. Franklin rarely went to school and didn't receive formal teaching; but he was smart. A self-taught reader, he wanted to learn; he was curious and observant. When Franklin turned twelve, he caught a break. Cold and hungry, he stumbled onto the front porch of Lewis Kirk seeking somewhere to stay for a night, or at a minimum, a warm meal. It wasn't easy for him to walk up the stairs of Kirk's place. Kirk had a reputation as a curmudgeon with a dark side. Rarely seen or heard from, he lived alone, isolated on his small plot of land. Newport residents liked to tell stories about the creepy old man living at the end of Benham Road, to spin tales about children who had found themselves on his property only to disappear   no child had ever actually gone missing because of Kirk, but that didn't stop the stories from being told and the legend of crazy Kirk to grow.

Hungry, shaking, and scared, the scrawny homeless boy knocked on Kirk's door, afraid an evil man was going to answer. Kirk greeted him with a smile. "Hello, young man, what can I do for you?" Kirk inquired in a soft, pleasant voice.

Startled by Kirk's greeting, all the young boy could say was, "I'm hungry."

Thus began a friendship that would alter Franklin's life. He was no longer alone, begging for food or care; Kirk took him in. Franklin came to spend most days and nights in the spare room at Kirk's place, each evening reading selections from Kirk's impressive library; or sitting by the fireplace as Kirk told stories of his life and travels; tales of Cross-Atlantic journeys on steamers, or transcontinental rides across Europe on famous trains like the Orient Express.

Kirk spent weeks detailing the winter spent in India traveling from city to city, teaching classes in American history for a college exchange program. He talked of the Taj Mahal, the Ganges River and the outdoor crematorium in Varanasi, the pink palace in Jaipur, and the Bengal tigers in the brush.

Through his stories, and his love, Kirk broke the chains that Cocke County and his dysfunctional family had wrapped Franklin in. He gave him hope; he saved his life. In return, Franklin brought Kirk companionship, laughter, an audience for his storytelling, and peace in the remaining years of his life. They became family, each fulfilling a role the other never had in their lives.

They were inseparable until the night Kirk slumped over in his chair while listening to the Grand Ole Opry on the radio. It was a heart attack, and at seventy, he was gone. The loss devastated Franklin as he once again felt the pain of loneliness and abandonment. Still a young man, with the world in front of him, he felt rudderless. Without Franklin knowing, Kirk had written a will leaving his property to him; but Franklin couldn't accept it. As much as he wanted to stay and build a life in the only place he had ever called home, he was driven to leave, to seek a future away from Cocke County. Something was out there, and he needed to find it.

"Momma, I never heard any of this. It's a wonder Daddy turned out the way he did."

"It's a blessing, RJ," was all Momma said.

After a brief silence, Momma continued her story.

Not knowing where to go, he made his way north, following the Appalachian Mountains until he dropped into Johnson County. By chance, he heard a pig farmer off State Road 91 was looking for a farmhand and, without giving it much thought; he hiked up the highway till he found Papaw's farm at the base of Gizzard's Holler.

The newly arrived worker lied about his skill set, but Papaw wasn't too picky, and they struck a deal. Franklin could sleep in a shed out on the edge of the property and get paid ten dollars a week for his efforts. Franklin was determined to make his first job a success. Despite a lifetime of scraping by, he naturally had a strong work ethic. He didn't mind putting in a long day.

On his first Saturday night on the farm, having eaten supper, Papaw's new farmhand heard the rhythmic sounds of bluegrass and laughter coming from the farmhouse. With a pinch of shyness and apprehension, he changed shirts, brushed his hair and headed over to get closer to the fun. No one asked him to join the session, but no one took special notice when he settled into his chair to listen; no one except Momma.

"I couldn't take my eyes off him; it wasn't every day there was someone new to look at. He was quite the looker. He was incredibly handsome, even striking."

As the hours passed, Momma grew more obvious in her efforts to garner attention from the end of the porch. For his part, Franklin noticed. Momma's glances were unavoidable, leading him to shyly share a slight grin whenever their eyes met. It was the first time Franklin had noticed a girl; he didn't know how he felt, but he liked it. He would later recall, "That night my mind was a jumbled mess; all I could think about was the cute girl who kept smiling at me."

Momma didn't recall when the new farm boy left the jam, nor even anything about the evening, except she couldn't fall asleep.

Two hundred and fifty acres isn't a big farm, but you could go for days and not see someone who was working on the farm and spending their evenings in the shed on the other end of the property; that is unless you were keen to see them. Given the next day was church day and courting wasn't appropriate on Sunday, Momma decided that first thing Monday she was going to "run" into this stranger and introduce herself. Sure enough, the midday sun hadn't found its place in the sky before Momma stumbled into Franklin. "Hi, I'm Nita," she said with a smile.

"I'm Franklin, but you can call me Frankie; everyone does."

Momma was sixteen; Daddy was twenty on that sunny day in July 1947.

Not one to waste time, a trait she learned in a house full of ten siblings, Momma jumped right into a playful conversation and, to hear Daddy tell it, "A thousand questions."

This was an unfamiliar experience for Momma. Not only was Daddy the first person she recalled ever meeting from outside Johnson County, but it was the first time she had felt butterflies fluttering in her stomach; she was smitten from the beginning. Daddy wasn't far behind. "She was as cute as a speckled kitten."

Both Momma and Daddy got lost in the moment and failed to realize they had been talking for most of the afternoon. They were staring at each other and flirting; not worrying about the ticking clock. They might have ignored the passing of time, but Papaw was paying attention to the sun crossing the sky and wondered where Frankie had wandered off to. After an hour of looking over his shoulder to see if Frankie was coming back, he decided he had had enough. Pushing back from the tractor engine he was tending to, he cursed under his breath and set out to find his lost worker. It didn't take long; the giggling from the side of the barn steered him right to the glassy-eyed couple. Momma never forgot the glare Papaw gave her as she looked up at him, tucked her head, and tiptoed back to the house; she also heard what Papaw told Frankie: "Son, you stay away from my daughter."

Papaw's warning did little to slow the burgeoning romance. All the emotions and hormones of adolescent love were not to be denied, no matter what the old man said; and Papaw knew it. She wasn't his first daughter to have fallen silly over a boy, ready to drop everything to marry. Mountain romances had a way of blooming like the rhododendrons in the spring; nothing was going to stop them. Each of his daughters before Nita had married before they were eighteen, and now Nita, at sixteen, seemed hell-bent on following her older sisters. Accepting the inevitable, Papaw made it clear to Frankie, "If you're keen to marry Nita, you wait till she graduates high school, and you wait till you're married to be messin' with her."

"Momma, I can't believe Papaw said that."

"Well, he did." Momma said without further explanation.

Daddy knew he meant it, and whether it was respect for his wish, or fear of his wrath, he followed that admonition and settled into a sweet courting routine, anticipating a wedding within the next eighteen months. And it was a good thing the fledgling couple showed restraint. Mamaw Betty secretly followed them like a hawk. She may have married early, but no matter, she was determined her youngest daughter wasn't going to "do something silly."

Not waiting for a delayed wedding to act, Papaw saw fit to make sure his little Nita and Frankie stayed close to home. As preparations for the wedding began, Papaw started building a small cabin close to the bunkhouse Frankie was staying in. Part of Papaw's agenda was to keep his baby girl by his side, and Daddy working on the farm. He trusted this young man from Cocke County; he even started talking about Nita and Frankie Burnette taking over the farm when he was too old to work it, telling Daddy "Frankie, I'm not getting younger, it sure would make me happy if you would stay on and run the place when it's time."

"I was more than thrilled at the thought of staying on the farm; I had lived nowhere else." Momma recalled.

The familiarity and comfortable warmth she felt walking the paths up and down Gizzard's Holler underscored it was her home; she was excited never to leave it. "I reckon that would be wonderful," Daddy said as he hugged Momma.

The wedding, held at Laurel Bloomery Presbyterian Church with Pastor Willard officiating, came and went only to be followed quickly with news that Momma was pregnant. The appropriate time having passed since the wedding for a new arrival, Momma gave birth to James in the same room she was born in nineteen years earlier. Daddy was there in the early years for Momma, but the demands of the farm were growing. Since the war ended, Papaw had built a larger stock of pigs and cows; that meant times were getting better, but it also meant more work.

It was a good time for Papaw and Mamaw; their kids were all close by, Nita was home, and Frankie was carrying a bigger load around the farm. However, the war left its mark on Papaw. Not only was he alone for the better part of four years, trying to keep his head above water, but he never stopped worrying about his boys fighting overseas; he had spent a year in the trenches in northern France in WWI and understood what war meant and how it could ravage your soul. Papaw didn't talk about his time in France; there were too many emotional scars covering his feelings. Now, years later, four of his boys were in another war. The private emotions he hid wore him down. After each long day of work, Papaw would sit quietly in front of the radio listening to reports about the war from far-flung places in the Pacific and across Europe. It was a frightful time listening to the news. After the report was over, he would go upstairs, get on his knees, and pray for his boys. A simple man seeking divine protection from his Maker.

Naturally quiet, Papaw never let on like he was worried and kept to himself during the war years, staying focused on Mamaw, raising pigs and farming the unforgiving acres. Too proud to ask, he never sought nor received help. He worked for everything he ever had. The farm survived the war years, and it seemed like Papaw's life was turning into a more peaceful existence; but he wasn't the same man after the long war years, and it caught up to him. Tough times had aged him.

"RJ, your Papaw died of a heart attack in 1951 while

tending to the fence at the back of the property; he was 64."

Papaw was the first person buried in the Warren family cemetery, a stone's throw from the house he built.

The death of the man who settled the farm jarred the Warrens; powerful and unflappable, it was hard to accept he was gone. "No one struggled more than your Mamaw. She slowly withdrew from her active life; it was as if she had nothing she cared to live for."

A strong-willed person, who had never been sickly, now seemed to always be down with something and unable to get out of bed. She passed away within months of losing Papaw.

The stories having run their course, Momma smiled, waving her hand dismissively, "Enough of that."

It had been a long day, and Momma was tired. The stories she shared with me filled my heart with love for the family that I was a member of. If only I could figure out how to honor their heritage.

9

You'll Never Leave Harlan Alive

EVEN NOW, OLD-TIME BLUEGRASS JAMS REMAIN A gathering event on Saturday nights in Johnson County. A collection of local musicians who set aside the normal work tools and equipment they held during the week, to play or pick whatever instrument they learned to play. You could expect to hear guitars, banjos, fiddles, mandolins, basses, and even spoons. There was no limit on who could play, nor how many of each instrument could join in; it was an open invitation for all. The group sat in a half-circle and took turns selecting whatever song came to mind; recommendations also came from those crowded on the porch. When it came time for you to pick a song, you were the lead musician, and it was your turn to play a solo, while those around you played the melody.

There was more than just music on those nights. There were lots of stories to be told; rarely was a story grounded in truth. Uncle Alton led the group with wild tellings of events that couldn't be true, but sounded real when he lowered his voice to add to the drama. The bigger the tale, the better. Stories were intended to be funny, and on our front porch, the joke was usually on people from the north, or across the border in Virginia, or even cousins who seemed adept at acting a fool. Tales, music, and mountain beverages kept Saturday night jams going well into Sunday morning or until they ran out of moonshine and muscadine wine.

I spent many childhood nights playfully sitting on the front porch of the farmhouse, listening to generations of Warrens and neighbors who were picking, singing, and laughing to mountain tunes. I loved hearing and playing: *Turkey in the Straw, I Wish I was a Mole in the Ground, Sugar Baby, High on the Mountain, Coal Miners Blues, Cuckoo Bird* and in the fall a recent addition to the East Tennessee playlist, *Rocky Top* was a regular. Eventually, everyone in Gizzard's Holler was expected to contribute to the jam. For me, I picked up the banjo; a favorite of my Uncle Eddie, he took special interest in teaching me how to pick. His patience with me was impressive, as I didn't seem to take to it naturally. But then it all clicked one afternoon, and I became a respectable picker who held my own on Saturday nights.

When I woke up on my first Saturday back in the Holler, it never occurred to me that later that night a gathering would happen on Momma's porch; just like most every Saturday night for decades. My first clue of what Momma had planned for this Saturday night was her placement of my old banjo leaning against the wall in the hallway outside my door. I hadn't been to an old-time jam session in years and had never considered holding a banjo again. Momma's not-so-subtle hint let me know I was going to be on the porch and should expect to play.

With little hope of escaping what was coming, I spent the afternoon on the front porch swing reacquainting myself with my childhood banjo. I was rusty, but in time it came back to me. I had forgotten the joy I felt with my banjo across my lap; the metallic, twangy, high-pitched sounds are piercing; sure to cause toes to tap. Winston's tail even wagged when I rolled tunes.

The fact Momma still hosted the Saturday pickin' session surprised me. I was even more surprised at the turnout. Uncle Eddie was there with his banjo along with his wife, Aunt Dot, and her soft voice. My brother James showed up with his fiddle. His oldest boy, Billie, brought his fiddle as well, like father, like son. Uncle Alton came over for the night with guitar and banjo in tow. Tommy bounced onto the porch like a spry young buck, all smiles, his spoons in the pocket of his overalls. He was famous in the county for keeping a beat with utensils. There were neighbors I hadn't seen since Daddy's funeral, the Davis's showed up with three of Mrs. Davis's apple pies. I made a note the moment I saw her; I needed a slice while it was still warm. After everyone settled in, I counted sixteen people on the porch.

My presence wasn't a surprise to those arriving; there are few things that slip through the rumor mill in Johnson County. I spent the better part of the first hour shaking hands, hugging, and catching up with small talk. It was good to see brother James. He looked well; old enough to be a father figure to me, we still had a distance between us. I hoped I could figure out how to build a relationship. He told me once I was "high-headed," a description not meant to be a compliment. I didn't enjoy hearing it, but I understood what he meant seven years ago when he said that to me, and I understand now why we still have trouble talking.

When I left Gizzard's Holler for college, the folks around

here were happy to see me go, but they naturally assumed I would come back. My surprising decision to move to New York had people saying, "I was livin above my raisin." They were right; I was, but I didn't care; I wanted something else in my life. That didn't sound logical to people who had rarely veered more than fifty miles away from home, never mind travelling up North. My decision to leave left members feeling hurt, built a barrier, and to some, even left them with the sense I was looking down on them. I didn't believe I was, but then again, you couldn't tell me anything when I was in my early twenties. I knew it all.

It wasn't my plan when I came home to see Momma, to mend fences with my brothers and relatives, but that night on the porch solidified my desire to belong. I had left home seeking an escape, a different life, and more than Gizzard's Holler could offer, and I was successful; but I lost so much of what defined me. No longer innocent and lacking the authentic happiness that came with an evening spent laughing at the random times Uncle Tommy got lost with his spoons and took over the song, indifferent to the rest of the group, performing his front porch solo act; my soul felt hollow. Maybe it was the moonshine, maybe it was Uncle Tommy being Uncle Tommy. I don't know what came over me, but I never smiled so freely or laughed so heartily as I did that night.

As was often the case, unrestrained laughter wasn't the only mood. On this night Aunt Dot asked if we could pick a new Darrell Scott song, made famous by Patty Loveless; *You'll Never Leave Harlan Alive*. I didn't know the song, but of course everyone else did. A quiet pall fell over the group as she sang a song that captured the soul of mountain people.

Oh, my grandfather's dad crossed the Cumberland Mountains
Where he took a pretty girl to be his bride
Said, "Won't you walk with me, out of the mouth of the Holler
or we'll never leave Harlan alive?"
Where the sun comes up about ten in the mornin'
And the sun goes down about three in the day
And you'll fill your cup with whatever bitter brew
you're drinkin'
And you spend your life just thinkin' of how to get away
But the times they got hard and tobacco wasn't sellin'
And old granddad knew what he'd do to survive
He went and dug for Harlan coal
And sent the money back to grandma
But he never left Harlan alive
Where the sun comes up about ten in the mornin'
And the sun goes down about three in the day
And you'll fill your cup with whatever bitter brew
you're drinkin'
And you spend your life diggin' coal from the bottom of
your grave

The words pierced me; unable to stop my flood of emotions, tears fell from my face. If anyone noticed, no one said anything. We were all lost in thought. My kin had never expected, nor maybe wanted, to leave the county. The world outside offered them nothing; they had everything they wanted. How could I not have shared that view? No wonder they thought I had turned my back on them. And if they believed I turned on them, why would they trust me? Trust me with their emotions, lives, and secrets.

When it came my turn to choose the song, I chose *The Worried Man Blues.*

> *It takes a worried man to sing a worried song*
> *It takes a worried man to sing a worried song*
> *I'm worried now, but I won't be worried long*

My choice wasn't a natural song for a banjo picker. I didn't care. My goal was to jam with Uncle Eddie and Uncle Alton. I butchered the song, but never let on; toes tapped, and Momma led a group that buck danced their way around the porch. At 70, Momma might have lost a step, but you couldn't tell. She kept pace with the song and never lost her beat. Not a natural song for buck dancers, it didn't matter; the porch was alive, and everyone was eager to do something.

I don't know how long we played, nor how much moonshine I drank, but the clock had rolled over to Sunday by the time we reached the last tune. Befitting the matriarchal role Momma had assumed, she asked if we could end the evening with *Amazing Grace.* A favorite of most everyone in these parts, the laughter and banter receded and with my brother James taking the lead, we played a slow rendition. Every time I heard this traditional church hymn; I thought of Daddy's funeral and the moment before they lowered the casket; *Amazing Grace* was Daddy's favorite song.

> *Amazing Grace, how sweet the sound*
> *That saved a wretch like me*
> *I once was lost, but now I'm found*
> *Was blind, but now I see.*

Tonight's version sounded like it was bouncing off the mountains, returning with a soulful infusion of the trials and tribulations of the people who have toiled in the valley. The song moved me, but I was more captivated watching Momma and her stoic poise. She showed no outward emotion nor any noticeable expression; she looked peaceful and reflective. As I watched the most important person in my life, the foundation of our family, and the giver of so much love, gently mouthing the words to the song, I decided I was staying put. I wasn't going back in a month; this was my home; my future was here, with Momma and my family.

10

Cancer

MOONSHINE HANGOVERS HURT, AND IF YOU ARE OUT of practice, you feel like dying. I was content to curl up in bed, but Momma had other ideas. It was Sunday, and we were off to church. Since Pastor Beauregard Willard began preaching the gospel, the Laurel Bloomery Presbyterian Church, established in 1937, had been a staple in the Warren household. I hadn't been to church in years and didn't share Momma's commitment to the weekly event but was more than happy to drag myself out of bed to join her.

The Laurel Bloomery Presbyterian Church had changed little since its construction. Supported by a brick foundation and oak wood walls donated from the local mill, the church was sturdy. It was everything the two hundred members needed to worship. With a freshly painted white exterior—church members gathered every three years to add a fresh coat of paint—and a stately steeple rising above the roof, the building was a source of pride. The parking lot was gravel, and when there was an overflow crowd, grass. Inside the church, there were floor-to-ceiling columns positioned at the end of every fourth pew on each side of the chapel. The windows were frosted, allowing sunlight to warm the interior. There were ten rows of pews with enough room for every member of the church to have a seat. Last time I was here, the pews were nothing more than hard, wooden benches with a vertical back that were painfully uncomfortable; as a teenager, I don't know what I dreaded more, an hour pinned to those benches or being reminded of all the ways I could go to hell.

Not surprisingly, every person who had enjoyed the previous night's jam was there. Some looked better than others, but all had found their Sunday best and were present; so was most everyone else from Laurel Bloomery. Prior to church, attendees hurried to find their seats. There wasn't enough time to say hello or gossip. That important weekly ritual could wait until after the preaching was done.

I had forgotten the power of fire and brimstone sermons. The booming voice of Pastor Higdon; the successor to Pastor Willard, quickly reminded me. He was in rare form; I sat on the edge of my seat listening to the pastor remind us of the presence of the devil in our lives.

After the congregation had been stirred up and the choir sang us out of church, it was time to say hello to everyone who was there. But before we could gather outside, we needed to pay the obligatory visit with the preacher. As expected, he was strategically positioned at the church's exit; this procession often took a while as everyone had to dutifully thank the minister for saving our souls.

"Good to see you, Pastor Higdon," I said.

"Powerful sermon today."

"Thanks RJ, good to have you home." He said, smiling, as he shook my hand.

As I pulled away from his grip, he held onto my hand. "Say RJ, you be sure and take care of your Momma, you hear? She is a good woman."

As I walked away, I wondered, should I make anything out of the pastor's prolonged grip and seemingly special request. The tone of his voice and the firmness of his handshake showed me that his words had a deeper meaning.

It was a beautiful day, clear and cool. The mountains kept the September heat away. Without delay, Momma walked me around the grounds of the church, reminding me who was who and proudly telling everyone I was home from New York. Momma was a beloved member of the community; it had always been that way. As I watched each churchgoer greet her and give her a loving hug, I noticed a tenderness in each exchange. I don't know how many people we chatted with. We were there for more than an hour; there was no hurry; this was a day of rest; and other than Sunday supper, there wasn't anything that needed tending to. It was a simple reminder of the community's love and the closeness that comes from watching out for your neighbor.

I felt welcome, but not as warm as I might have hoped. Mountain folk had a unique ability to seem sincere while also maintaining a guarded stance. This skill was on full display as everyone I chatted with showed tender sweetness in the most insincere way possible.

On the way home, Momma reminded me of who we spoke to and told me the inside story of what was happening in their lives.

"Didn't you think Mrs. Binghamton looked good? She has had a rough time with her oldest lately; seems he is back in the bottle." She offered.

"I was glad to see Randy Dowd. He hasn't been coming much. Wonder what has been keeping him away. I didn't get a chance to ask him."

"I thought Pastor Higdon's sermon was nice. Not sure why he was so focused on coveting your neighbor. Wonder who he was talking to?"

And so, it went.

As I listened, with a smile on my face, to her share the gossip of the day, a thought hit me; every person who greeted Momma asked her how she felt, not in a passing way, but with more intent. Was Momma sick, and I didn't know it?

I made a career of observing little things and making assumptions about what is really being said and meant. This skill set is valuable, but also can lead to unnecessary worrying. Some say that I borrow things to worry about, and if I am honest, I am prone to chasing rabbits down holes when I would be better off if I let it go. It was in my nature. The combination of my professional background, obsessing over details, and growing up on a farm where things go wrong as much as they go right had created a bit of an obsessive personality. When I focused on something, I would not let it go.

We hadn't made it home before I asked, "Momma, I noticed everyone asking you how you feel. Is there something wrong? Are you sick?"

Surprised, Momma paused and replied, "Not at all, I'm good."

In that moment I knew she wasn't telling me everything; she was holding back. I could tell. When I was young, I couldn't gauge when my parents were keeping something from me. At thirty, I was no longer naïve; I noticed her paused answer, her lack of conviction when she responded.

There wasn't an easy way to challenge her. I had never questioned what Momma said, nor had a cross word with her. I didn't know what to say next. She was fibbing, but I didn't know how to ask her again.

Even though it was only me and Momma, supper was a spread: pot roast with carrots, potatoes, and onions that had cooked most of the afternoon; green beans, cornbread, and peach cobbler. "Momma, do you cook like this all the time?" I asked as I shoved another bite of buttered cornbread into my mouth.

"Most days, I cook something; I like to eat."

We were alone for supper—James and his family were having supper at their place, as were all Momma's brothers—I asked Momma if Ralph ever came by, "occasionally," she said, "but most days he keeps to himself."

It was noticeable how little information she shared about Ralph and the life he lived. Why was Ralph an outlier in our family? No one else took the path he followed. It made no sense, and it made no sense why Momma answered a question about him with a quick response. It was as though he had emotionally hurt her, and she couldn't bear to dwell on what had become of him. Tonight wasn't the night, but sometime soon I needed to learn why Momma reacted the way she did when I brought up Ralph.

It was a quiet evening, but not lonely. Our house never felt empty; there were too many memories, stories, and pictures in the house to feel you were by yourself. Each room had a combination of pictures of my immediate family and Momma's family that first lived in the house. It was a warm feeling and rolling history of the place. A story I needed to take time to immerse myself in, to learn about the lives of those who were born and raised here.

The evening passed at a slow pace, and with our cobbler in hand; we moved to the front porch. It was a cool night for early fall, too early for the leaves to change, but not too early for a hint of mountain chill in the air. I wasn't in a talkative mood as I couldn't slip the annoying thought that Momma had misled me.

Finally, I couldn't hold my need to know any longer. I blurted out, "Momma, I got the feeling today, you weren't being straightforward with me when I asked you about your health. Are you telling me the truth? Are you okay?"

There was an extended pause as Momma stared across the porch towards the meadow; her eyes narrowing and her lips tightening. "RJ, I am sorry, but I fibbed a bit." She replied.

"What is it?"

"RJ, I have cancer."

"Are you okay, what kind?" I said with a high-pitched voice.

"It's pancreatic cancer, and no, I'm not okay." She said, "This is going to get me."

I couldn't process what I had heard; not only did she have cancer, but pancreatic cancer. I knew what that meant, and it wasn't good. This was a bad cancer to have, and it moved fast; it was a death sentence. For a moment, I didn't know what to say. I should have immediately shown compassion, but I had unanswered questions, and they consumed my mind.

"How long have you known about this?" I asked.

"I found out about a ten months ago," she said.

"You have known for almost a year, and you haven't told me?"

I sounded hurt when I said it, and she knew I was. Momma raised her hand to stop the questions and shared with me what I wanted to know.

Momma found out about her cancer after an infrequent visit to her local family doctor. She was feeling pain in her stomach and was bloated; not too worrisome, but the doctor noticed her eyes were yellow. After much cajoling—Momma had little desire to see another doctor, especially someone from another town—she agreed to visit a specialist in Johnson City; James drove her to the appointment. Tests showed she had cancer, so the doctors prescribed a treatment plan.

"They told me I could start radiation and chemotherapy, but it didn't sound like it would change anything except make me sick. Everyone was ready for me to start treatment immediately," Momma explained.

However, despite loud complaints from James, Momma ignored the doctors and chose not to do anything about the cancer. She said, "I am at peace and okay with it being my time to go."

Momma conveyed strength with her words; words supported by her mental and physical toughness and buoyed by her belief in Jesus and his promise. There was nothing I could do; she had decided, and her stubbornness was impregnable.

Before I could object, she continued with her story. "I didn't want a fuss made about this and asked James to keep it to himself."

She knew what I was thinking and said, "Before you ask, I made James promise me not to tell you; you are so busy, and I didn't want to bother you."

She sounded convincing; her face told another story. I pained her not to tell me.

Her words crushed me. Had I become so detached from my family and my home that they couldn't tell me Momma was dying? How could everyone know it but me? It hurt, but I didn't want to show it. Momma had just shared tragic news with me, and I needed to be there for her, even if she had decided she didn't need me to be around.

With tears in my eyes, I asked, "How much time do you have left?"

"Not much," was her answer.

11

We Handle Things

I COULDN'T SLEEP; HOW COULD I? MY WORLD WAS TURNING upside down; the light of my life was dying, and she had kept me in the dark. Life without Momma was unimaginable to me. I had never thought this day would come. But here it was, and I didn't know what to do.

Her choice to hide this from me intensified the fear and sadness I felt when I thought of losing Momma. Was she ever going to tell me? Was I going to get a phone call from James telling me Momma was gone without a chance to be by her side? What were they thinking? Surely, I hadn't been such an ass that they didn't want to deal with me during the last days.

I know she implied she didn't want to bother me, and it was her way of looking after me, but that explanation didn't help. In fact, no scenario I came up with made me feel better. The simple truth was my family had kept this from me. Had I not had a mental crisis at the office, something terrible would have happened, and I would have missed it.

I had seen this before, years ago, while managing an investment roadshow. Someone handed me a note while the CEO of our client company was presenting to a room full of investors. The note said, "Steve needs to call the office immediately. His mother has passed away."

I waited for Steve to finish his presentation and, with an apology, handed him the note. A tough, controlled leader fell apart; guilt for not being there consumed him, and he wept openly in front of strangers as he cursed himself. There was nothing that could console him. Steve finished the week on the road and flew home to offer the eulogy, a broken man. I made a promise to myself that I would never allow that to happen. A promise I almost didn't keep.

The next morning, with little sleep to support me, I attempted to engage Momma in conversation about treatment options, only to be rebuffed.

"Momma, we have options. I can get you seen by the country's best cancer doctors. We can go to Sloan-Kettering or the Mayo Clinic. I have contacts at both places." I pleaded.

"Sweetheart, I don't want to fight this, never did. I'm ready to go home." Was her answer.

"Momma, are you in pain?" I asked. "I'm fine, RJ," she replied as she handed me a stack of pancakes.

The discussion bothered Momma. After a few minutes of my asking questions, she turned around from the sink and said, "Son, I have decided what I want to do. I don't want to talk about it; I just want to enjoy every day and not cause too much trouble."

It was a completely unsatisfactory response, but it was the end of the conversation. Momma had spoken, and nothing I said was going to change that.

As Momma wiped down the countertop, I wondered what I was supposed to do. She wouldn't let me take her to specialists; she wanted nothing from me. How was I to treat her? Could I pretend nothing was happening? How was I going to figure out why they kept this from me? I had no answers.

I'm not good at letting go, and despite Momma's request that I move on, my mind wouldn't let me. I did my best around her not to let on about my fears, sadness, guilt, and hurt; I faked it as best I could. Inside, I was a mess. I came home a lost soul, trying to make sense of my life and my future. I was certain time away would give me clarity; any hope of that was gone. It didn't I was more confused.

Are there other secrets? How much of my life was true? You can let your mind wander, and mine was abuzz with all kinds of crazy theories and ideas. The house I was born in suddenly felt strange to me. Why did Ralph live like a hermit? Why was my relationship with James nonexistent, and my sister's life was cloaked in secrecy? I have never felt more detached from my mooring.

I was getting nowhere with Momma, so I drove out to James's place to see if I could catch him and see what he might tell me. We had talked on Saturday night at the jam, but it was like most of our conversations, small talk, with little substance. Maybe if I sat down with him, he would tell me the truth and help me understand why this happened.

James's place is not too far from the farm, about a mile as the crow flies but five minutes winding through the mountains up Stinking Creek Road. I hadn't been to James's farm in years. No longer a working farm, it was more like a small retreat tucked up against the mountains. James had given up farming years ago and started teaching history at Johnson

County High School; he was also an assistant football coach under Head Coach Brooks Duncan. They fielded a competitive team that was called the Longhorns since 1954—a name that no one around here could explain how they got. A respected member of the community, James, had done well and, best I could tell, was happy with his life.

I found James sitting on the side porch having a cup of coffee, intently reading the local newspaper, The Tomahawk; the weekly publication, founded in 1889, kept locals informed about all the happenings in the county. He smiled over the sports section as he saw me walking up the steps. "Vols look strong this year."

James was always happy to talk about Tennessee football.

"That's what I hear," I pretended like I was up to date.

Small talk on a porch in the mountains is a mixture of gossip, sports, weather, and news from town. Rarely is much time spent on work, business, or politics, or anything beyond the small confines of the valley; we didn't break that tradition. James didn't ask me why I had come home, nor how work was going. Not that he didn't care about me; he just didn't care about what I did. I never took offense, but it made for strained conversations; I had nothing to offer about the goings-on in the mountains, and James wasn't interested in New York.

Our conversation followed the normal path until I broke the seal and asked him, "Momma told me she was sick. Why didn't you tell me?"

James looked out over his lawn for a few seconds, clearly thinking about what he was going to say. "She asked me not to tell you, and I told her I wouldn't," he said.

His statement was a matter of fact; his delivery conveyed a deeper message. Despite our age difference, we were still brothers, and I sensed he wasn't comfortable keeping secrets from me.

"But why didn't she want me to know?" I asked.

"You know, Momma, she didn't want to bother you." He said, trying to show little emotion.

"James, I don't get it. I'm her son. You should have told me." I said with a desperate stare.

"It wouldn't have been a bother; I could have helped."

He didn't respond, and we sat there for a few minutes in silence.

Finally, James said, "RJ, we all love you and we care about you, but you moved on from Gizzard's Holler. That's okay, always was, but life goes on around here at its normal pace. We handle things the way we handle things. It's not that you're not part of the family; it's just that you have moved on with your life and we have moved on with ours."

He considered what he was going to say next. "You know, RJ, Momma didn't want help from outside these mountains. She was born here, lives here, and wants to die here. We know you could have provided other doctors, but bud, that's just not the way things are done. Momma figured she would be just fine here, waiting for her time to come."

Although he didn't mean his comments to be mean or say them with spite, they hurt. It hurt because, on some level, I knew he was right. I had moved on; I was so consumed with getting ahead, with playing the game, with my life, that I forgot my family. For God's sake, I hadn't been home since Daddy died. I am sure I am not the only person who remembered that fact. I lived life in a world that was foreign to my family; they would never consider traveling somewhere to get help from a stranger. It was true. I couldn't offer Momma anything from New York.

I sat motionless on James's porch until my legs fell asleep; I couldn't move with the realization of what I had done. James could tell I was hurting and, even though not big on touchy - feely interactions, reached out and grabbed my shoulder and said, "You know I love you, brother; this will be alright."

It was the nicest thing he had ever said to me.

I needed more. "James, is it that simple? Momma asked you to keep this from me, and that's what you did?"

"Yes, despite all the reasons I gave you and Momma may have, I wanted to tell you, and I would have if Momma hadn't forbidden it. I ain't ever broken a promise to Momma. "

James looked sad. He knew when Momma was gone, he wouldn't have anyone but me and Ralph from his core family.

"RJ, I don't want to go through this alone. I want you to be a part of Momma's remaining days. I am glad you are here."

"Thanks James. I appreciate your saying that. And I understand why you kept this from me. You did it for Momma."

With that, I stood up and hugged James. I don't recall a time when we hugged in the past. As sad as it was, the tragedy of Momma was bringing us together.

The drive back to Momma's wasn't easy, and I pulled over to cry. I felt the weight of years of running away from home pushing down on my shoulders. I was ashamed of myself, but I was also grateful. Something had driven me away from my job and steered me back home, some force stronger than my overactive mind. I thought my departure from New York was about me and my career. It wasn't. It was about my finding my family and remembering my upbringing. If that meant learning secrets that were kept from me, so be it. I was a Burnette and a Warren, and that meant something. Something to be proud of.

12

It's Good Eatin

I T WAS CLEAR; JAMES HAD CONFIRMED IT; MOMMA WAS following the sentiment I had fostered. I had chosen a route that put Johnson County in my past. That conclusion bothered me, but I couldn't fight it; I had to accept it. I also had to accept that Momma was dying.

Despite my tendency to dwell on things, my career had also taught me to focus, to focus on the task at hand; and that meant ignoring how people viewed me, and putting all my attention towards Momma. It wasn't hard to do. She had given so much to me, to so many people, I had to honor her wishes; she deserved that.

Momma didn't want to act sick. She didn't want to let on about anything bothering her, nor any pain she had. Mountain life had been tough, and she could handle whatever came her way. As she wanted, we spent most of the days walking around the farm, hosting neighbors and family members who came by to say hello, talking and laughing on the front porch, and telling stories; some that were family classics and some that were new to me.

I learned Daddy was innovative for a pig farmer; his creativity came out of necessity. Sows have a discouraging habit of giving birth and then killing their piglets. Sometimes they kill them on purpose; other times they give birth and lay on them, thus suffocating the newborn, an unacceptable outcome for a farmer dependent on new arrivals to sell. After cogitating about it, Daddy decided the answer was to separate the sow from her piglets the moment they were born; but he couldn't stand around all day waiting for the moment to occur so he could manually separate them. He had to solve for time and attention; he didn't have time to give the pre-labor pig his full attention, but he needed the piglets to survive. His answer was to build a stall barely large enough to hold the pig; its design was such a pinned sow couldn't move. At the back of the pin, there was a small opening strategically positioned to press against the pig's hind end. Below the hole was a chute for the newborn pigs to fall onto, thus sliding down into a separate protected stall.

A week after a pig's teats grew and prominently showed veins, Daddy would step up his watch of the expecting pig and when he thought labor was imminent, he would herd the pig into the stall with its back end positioned over the opening. Timing was everything, if he waited too long and the sow started the birthing process, he couldn't get the pig up and move it into the stall, if done too early the pig would get anxious, and no one wanted an anxious pig; there was some art to decide when to pen the sow. Daddy was quite proud of his creation and, I gather, frequently talked about it to anyone who would listen. Not your typical conversation piece in the finest restaurants of New York, but perfectly acceptable at a Sunday afternoon picnic with friends in Gizzard's Holler.

If tales of pigs giving birth weren't enough, Momma kept me on the edge of my seat talking about the trials in the Holler. I didn't know about Uncle Tommy and his early years running moonshine. Everyone knew he was wild, but I thought that came from his habit of playing jokes on anyone he could trick. I didn't realize the authorities had caught him selling moonshine in Elizabethton, and he spent six months in jail.

Momma continued, "Not to be deterred by jail time, he came back home and picked up right where he left off; only this time he was craftier and stayed one step ahead of the law."

"What the sheriff couldn't stop, a beautiful young girl from Mountain City did; she grabbed Tommy's full attention and with the charm only a woman can provide, turned him from a lawbreaker to a respectable citizen."

Momma and I talked about everything and everybody; everybody except my brother Ralph. Finally, one day I asked Momma how he was doing and what had been going on in his life. Momma admitted, "Ralph was a handful growing up and always causing trouble. He loved pestering the cows and could scatter them all over the place, forcing your daddy to spend time herding strays back to the farm."

On a bit of a roll, she continued, "He would set off firecrackers around the chickens just to watch them freak out."

"School wasn't a priority, and he was always skipping school to get into trouble. Somehow, he got his diploma; I am guessing because they wanted him gone." Momma laughed again.

Ready to move on, Momma said finally, "I don't see much of Ralph; he's doin fine, I reckon."

"He has always been a loner ever since he moved up the road."

Was I going to let that be the last word? Why was Momma always ready to move on to another topic? I just didn't add up, but it also made little sense to push the point. I didn't want to stir up something with Momma that might cause her anxiety, and clearly the subject of her second son living alone and isolated from the family wasn't her favorite topic.

I hadn't been to Ralph's place too many times; there wasn't much to see. In a one-room cabin deep in the woods, he lived off the grid: well-water, an outhouse, and no electricity. A stone fireplace kept him warm; a dog kept him company; and the mountains kept him fed. Ralph hunted for food, killing and eating anything he could.

Out of curiosity, I asked Momma, "What does Ralph eat?"

"He told me once his favorite was squirrel stew." She offered with a sour look on her face.

He told me, "It's good eatin'."

"I never had Squirrel, but Ralph said, 'Squirrels got a bit of a nutty flavor to it, kinda gamey'."

Momma laughed and said, "Doesn't sound too bad I guess, unless of course Ralph is making it into one of his stews."

Ralph wore ragged overalls that hung loosely on his broad shoulders; he rarely had a shirt underneath. His hair always looked unkempt, and he had a long beard; he wasn't a pretty fella. A committed tobacco chewer, I never recall seeing him when he didn't have a big wad in his jaw; I doubt he had seen a dentist in his adult life and likely hadn't seen a doctor. Time had passed him by, but he didn't seem too concerned, nor bothered. He kept to himself and didn't worry anyone.

Ralph's move up the Holler caused little stir on the farm. No one questioned it or expressed concern. All I recall was

Daddy saying, "Ralph is his own fella, a lot going on with him; he will be alright."

Ralph owned a shortwave radio and would pass the time hunched in front of his only contact with the outside world. Having never left Johnson County, he lacked context for how big the world was, but his radio took him to places his imagination was incapable of seeing. With no interest in talking, Ralph spent hours listening to the world he would never see.

For Daddy's funeral, he wore his best overalls and brushed his hair. Despite his jaw packed with tobacco, he cleaned up nicely. He didn't say much, showed no emotion, but shook my hand and asked me if I was alright. It felt odd not knowing him, nor having any relationship; but he was who he was, and if the family hadn't seen him, nor didn't care to talk about him, I couldn't feel bad about not having a history with my older brother.

My time with Momma opened my heart to a clearer understanding of my heritage. I came from a proud people, who took care of themselves, and if needed, their neighbors. It was a close community that held its feelings inside, uninterested or unwilling to allow the outside world or outsiders into its ranks. Their avoidance of strangers wasn't an embedded trait; nothing had caused distrust; rather, their unwillingness to be open to others was like the mountains' hold on the morning mist. Once the mist settled in the mountains, nothing would allow it to escape; it was permanent. I wasn't an outsider, but to many, I had become one. It wasn't too hard for me to see that I was on the outside looking in. I grew up here but left, and with that choice relinquished my role in the happenings of the Warrens and Burnettes.

As October passed and the days got shorter, Momma

slowed down. Her energy faded, and she didn't want to walk around or stray too far from the front porch. There was a chill in the air; it wouldn't be long before the first snowfall and winter put everything on ice. Momma's conversations and stories became more reflective; she didn't have regrets. She talked about what was coming; she talked often about Daddy and Sue Ann and going to see them. She was ready and just waiting until she was called. It wasn't sad. It was peaceful and beautiful. Momma was in pain, but she wouldn't say anything or take anything. All she wanted was her coffee and biscuits with honey.

Momma's slow decline meant I had to step up. Things she handled before were now my responsibility. There was more to do than I appreciated. Momma made farm life appear simple and easy. I learned it wasn't. Each day I needed to collect the eggs from the coop, feed the chickens, gather firewood for the house, and make sure the farm had all the supplies it needed from town. To top it off, Momma hadn't relinquished the chore of feeding the pigs; a task I despised and dreaded each day. Individually, nothing was too daunting, but the totality of work filled my day.

Besides the chores, the farm manager needed me to answer his questions. He wanted to know what the plan was for the spring planting. What he should do with the excess hay. Did we want to process any of the livestock for the freezer or sell off any pigs? His questions were fair but required me to think about the future, and I didn't know how to answer them. My farming experience was limited, making my answers feel more like guesswork than careful consideration. Worse than that, I didn't know what was going to happen to the farm when Momma died.

Late one day, as we sat by a smoldering fire, Momma asked me, "RJ, when I'm gone, will you stay and take over the house?"

I was stunned. I had never thought about what would happen to the house, nor even considered what I was going to do when Momma passed. Some time ago, I had decided to stay in Johnson County, but I thought I would find a nice place in Mountain City; I didn't know what I was going to do, but I had money saved and time to figure it out. Maybe I belonged at home.

Seeing I was struggling with what to say, Momma changed the subject to a lighter topic. "RJ, did I ever tell you how you got your name?" she asked.

"Come to think of it, I don't think I ever heard that story." I replied.

She laughed. "Well, your middle name, James, is obvious."

"That part I figured out on my own," I said.

"How did you come up with the name Roy? I don't know anyone in our family named Roy."

Momma continued, "I named you after Roy Acuff, the Grand Ole Opry musician, I didn't much care for him, but everyone around here did, and I figured he must be a likable fella and so that was good enough for me."

"Really, that's how I became Roy James?" I asked.

"Yep, that's it." She smiled.

For some reason, her silly little story caused us to laugh out loud — a belly-roll kind of laugh. It was funny; we both needed a good laugh; sometimes laughter was all you had. Momma laughed until tears filled her eyes. I will never forget her lovely face, tears flowing, and her hand rhythmically tapping her knee; she was happy.

"Momma," I said, sounding serious. "If you want me to have the house, then I would be honored," I said.

My response brought the biggest smile I had seen on Momma's face in years. Her little baby was coming home for good; her job was done. With that settled, Momma lifted her head high and stood up. "Come with me, RJ. I have some chicken livers ready to fry for supper, won't you come and keep me company in the kitchen?"

It was an offer I couldn't refuse. Rising from the sofa, I grabbed Momma's hand and held it as we walked into the kitchen.

As the days grew shorter and darkness came earlier, Momma spent her days resting in her favorite chair in front of the fireplace. With nothing to concern me but tending to Momma, I spent my time next to her waiting for her to tell me stories borne from the pictures stacked in the mason-jar box. Pictures that told the story of her life before I arrived.

"He was a handsome man." Momma said as she held a picture of Uncle Bubba.

"I guess I must have taken after him," I said, always looking for a way to laugh.

"Something like that," Momma responded.

I could tell memories of Bubba were powerful. "Momma, what happened to Uncle Bubba?"

"Immediately after the Japanese bombed Pearl Harbour, the Marines drafted Uncle Bubba."

"He was so proud, and I was proud of him. But I was scared. I had never cried so hard as I did the day he left for town and the train station." Momma said, with a tear welling in her eye.

"They shipped him to Paris Island, and then somewhere

in the Pacific. We would get letters from him, and I cherished everyone. After Daddy would read it to us, I would ask him if I could take it to my room so I could read it again. He sounded so close but was so far away."

Momma was emotional, and she looked drained. I walked over to her side and put my hand over hers. She raised her head, the strain of cancer on her face, and forced a smile. Worried, I said, "Momma, we don't need to talk about this anymore. Maybe I can help you to your room for a nap?"

"RJ, don't be silly. I'm old, but I ain't dead yet." Her feisty nature was still in control.

"Bubba spent the better part of three years fighting the Japanese all over the Pacific. He wrote to us after Guadalcanal. The newspapers made it sound awful, but Bubba didn't let on like he was none too bothered."

She grew quiet, and I thought she had had enough.

"I was out by the barn when the military man pulled up to our house asking for Daddy. He looked sad, and fear immediately gripped me. I had brothers fighting everywhere in the world, and we didn't know what this was about."

"It was Bubba. He died on Okinawa in April 1945. He was 28."

The First Marine Cemetery in Okinawa became the last resting place for Uncle Bubba and thousands of other soldiers who gave their lives for world peace. No one in our family has visited Bubba's gravesite; although Momma occasionally talked about making the trip. No one seriously considered that. She had never been west of Nashville; traveling to Okinawa seemed like a stretch. Losing a family member in the service of their country is a point of pride, but it doesn't offset the pain felt by the family. Uncle Bubba's framed picture in his marine service uniform hung on the wall in the study of our house as a constant reminder of his youth and the ultimate sacrifice he paid. Despite his presence in the room, I don't recall the family talking about him nor any mention of his time in the war. Fifty-six years removed from his death, and the pain hadn't diminished. It wasn't until Momma was facing her own death that she opened up to me about the pain she felt losing her older brother.

After a long pause, Momma said, "I miss your Uncle Bubba. But I will see him soon."

Momma's unwillingness to go further with her feelings reflected an attitude rampant in the hills, a mindset I was to learn more about in the coming days. People readily shared stories of fun and good times. They guarded pain and tragedy, burying it to maintain secrecy.

On the Monday morning before Thanksgiving, Momma asked me if I would take her for a walk. It was a brisk day and not much more than freezing outside, and so I asked her if she thought it a good idea. She grabbed her overcoat, frowned at my question, and walked towards the door. Holding Momma's hand, I had the sense she had a purpose and was leading me; unlike the last few days, on this walk I wasn't keeping her steady, she was on a mission. We shuffled across the meadow; going farther than we had in months. There was no small talk, as Momma couldn't spare the energy to talk; her breathing was heavy and deliberate. As we neared the end of the property, I saw the entry to the Ramsey Creek Trail and realized Momma was heading straight for it. Without a word, Momma tugged on my hand to signal she wanted to join the trailhead. Our pace was slow, and progress labored, but Momma was determined to walk this path; I couldn't, for the life of me, understand why.

I was worried about Momma, but I didn't ask her what she had in mind; I held her firmly, supporting every step. After a while we crested a hill, and Momma's pace picked up. And then I saw the rock monument I had found a few months ago. Momma did too. She slowly steered towards the opening, and with a slight smile touching her face, gently lowered herself onto a log next to the rocks. Comfortable and at peace, she closed her eyes and prayed quietly.

I didn't know what to do or say. I sat passively and watched her. She was lost in her thoughts. We stayed for an hour; nothing was said, no emotion shown. I couldn't get that moment out of my head; Momma knew her time had come and wanted to spend her last afternoon in this place. She passed away later that night quietly in bed surrounded by James and me. We didn't speak; there wasn't anything to say. Our momma, who had brought so much joy and life, had gone home.

As the night passed into the next day, I sat alone in the living room, my mind racing between memories of Momma and what she told me up on Ramsey Creek Trail. I couldn't process what she said, nor why she had told me.

"Momma, do you know what these rocks and this painted cross are for?"

"I put them here." She replied, not answering my question.

Her incomplete answer was all I was going to get. She wanted to be alone with her thoughts. Not wanting to be a bother, I stood up and walked back to the trail. Momma would let me know when she needed me.

In time, Momma was ready to go home.

"RJ, can you give me a hand?"

She couldn't stand without me; her body having lost what little strength it had. She couldn't weigh over ninety pounds; she was nothing but skin and bones.

I asked her, as she glanced back one more time at the monument she had erected, "Momma, if you don't mind me asking, why did you want to come up here?"

"I wanted to visit Sue Ann one more time before I see her in heaven," she said.

"Momma, I don't understand what you mean 'visit Sue Ann'?" I responded.

With a hollow glare, Momma looked at me and uttered, "This is where Sue Ann was murdered."

PART II

13

The Answer To Momma's Prayers

I T HAS BEEN TWO DECADES SINCE MOMMA LED ME UP the path to the site of Sue Ann's murder and five years since I found Sue Ann's diary, neatly tucked beneath a loose board in the closet of an upstairs bedroom. Although much time has passed, conversations with James, Momma's family, and the heartfelt writings of my sister gave me an understanding of who Sue Ann was, her impact on Momma, and details surrounding her last months of life.

Sue Ann was an answer to Momma's prayers; a daughter to offset a household dominated by testosterone. After she learned she was pregnant, Momma secretly sewed dresses for months, privately hoping the child she was carrying was a sweet little girl. On a cold, windy winter day, she had her daughter. With Daddy pacing nervously in the parlor, Sue Ann screamed, announcing her presence to the world. Her loud announcement was a precursor of her first year; a feisty baby, colicky, unsettled, and demanding, she was a handful, but Momma never worried, "She will grow out of it," was her standard response to a long night tending to Sue Ann.

In time, Momma was right, and Sue Ann calmed down, with her second-year breaking ranks from the normal terrible twos. She became a delight, her playful smile replacing the prior year's scowl. With curly blonde hair, crystal blue-eyes and a silky white complexion, even for a toddler, Sue Ann was striking looking. Before she was three, she established herself in the community as the prettiest baby these parts had seen in years. The adorable clothes she wore enhanced her natural beauty. Momma, with her needle and thread, kept Sue Ann dressed like a doll; Sue Ann played the part. A natural attention grabber, Sue Ann became the center of whatever room she was in.

James didn't see the point in all the attention Sue Ann got and was therefore more than happy to harass her at every turn. In response, Sue Ann wasn't afraid of her oldest brother and pestered him whenever she could. Normal sibling spats were a daily occurrence; and Sue Ann held her own. She also had cover from Momma, who wouldn't let the boys go too far in their efforts to annoy Sue Ann. For his part, Ralph avoided the harassment aimed at Sue Ann. From an early age, Ralph had a special bond with his sister and an innate desire to protect her. If James went too far, Ralph was there to step in and defend her. The boys fought often; frequently, the spark that drew the first punch had something to do with Sue Ann.

Farm kids are adept at slipping away from adult oversight to find trouble. Six months after Sue Ann's third birthday, she followed, without Momma noticing, her older brothers out the door as they headed on an expedition to find a frog they could adopt. James, the leader of the pack at seven, walked at a fast pace hoping to lose Sue Ann, but to no avail. After they walked half a mile or so up Laurel Creek, they found the place James was seeking, a small eddy that held the potential for the perfect pet frog to be hiding. The boys in their overalls, and Sue Ann in her polka dot dress, plunged into the water in search of the "best" frog. This wasn't the boys' first adventure seeking pets. The boys had previously captured turtles, salamanders, crawdads, a garter snake, crickets, and hundreds of bees, only to see them each die an untimely death. But there was always hope for something bigger. Each day they checked their elaborate trap they had built specifically to catch an unsuspecting squirrel; someday it would work. On this day, what began as a mission to find a pet, devolved into splashing about in the water, throwing rocks into the air to see who could make the biggest splash, and wading into the deep end to see who could go the farthest. Sue Ann didn't know how to swim, but it didn't faze her; she was fearless. Besides, she had Ralph there to rescue her.

The Burnette youngins, like most mountain kids, relied on imagination and ingenuity to fill their days. If they didn't know how to do something or have the tools for their project, they made do until a better idea came along. Their search for frogs abandoned, the Burnette kids turned their attention elsewhere, a wild splashing contest in the cool mountain waters. They were having a great time; Momma, however, was panicking. She couldn't find Sue Ann, and when she looked around, noticed the boys were gone too. None of their favorite hiding places yielded evidence they had been there. To make matters worse, Daddy hadn't seen them, and none of the farmhands were helpful. She looked in the attic, around their pretend fort, along the small brook that flowed across the property; she didn't find what she was looking for. Momma was beside herself and demanded everyone drop what they were doing to find her kids. Daddy wasn't happy about this, but he knew there was no arguing with Momma when it came to the children.

"Nita, I don't have time for this. I am sure they are fine. Likely just playing in a new place." Daddy weakly offered.

"Frankie, I don't care how busy you are, help me find these kids."

It was futile to resist, and Daddy knew it.

The hastily organized search group split up and began looking for clues, or better yet, for the three kids. It was Momma who stumbled onto her little ones playing in the creek's pool. She heard them off in the distance and began calling out for them; they either didn't hear her or were ignoring her as no matter how loud she yelled, they didn't respond. The closer Momma got to the sounds of her kids, the madder she became.

"I have half a mind to switch these kids," Momma mumbled to herself.

It didn't take long for Momma to walk up to the eddy and see what her kids were up to. Anger and relief flooded her heart, and for a moment she was ready to grab a switch and teach them a lesson, and then, she laughed. The kids were startled because they hadn't noticed Momma and immediately believed they were in trouble. That is until they heard her laugh and saw her broad smile; her laughter was unrestrained, giving permission for the kids to follow suit. Slowly they followed with their own giggles. Years later Momma joked, "I think I shocked em, they didn't know I could be so much fun."

Before the laughing stopped, Momma ran towards the kids and with childlike enthusiasm plunged into the cold, clear mountain water. If they were playing, she wanted to as well. Life on the farm was hard, but it could be lighthearted. Momma had swum in this same spot as a child and knew the freedom of afternoon shenanigans; watching her kids share in that unrestricted play was all she needed to remind her of her childhood and why she loved her home.

Their fun seemed to have no end, that is until Daddy rounded the bend in the trail and saw his family. He was none too happy. Sure, fooling around is great, but he had dropped what he was doing, and stopped his workers, to search for these missing kids, only to discover what they were up to; and to think his wife saw fit to join in the mischief. Daddy didn't join them. He had too much to do. After making eye contact with Momma, he turned around and walked away, cursing under his breath. "Damn kids, there's work to be done, and I have to deal with this."

This story became a legend on our Gizzard Holler farm. For years, anytime Daddy got stressed or too serious, Momma and the kids would threaten to run off and hide at the swimming hole. Daddy claimed he didn't like the teasing, but everyone knew he secretly enjoyed the memory of his family's unabashed playfulness.

Part tomboy and part little lady, Sue Ann readily slipped in and out of whatever situation she faced. A disciplined young girl at church, always proper and respectful, she could just as easily help Daddy slop the pigs; labels couldn't define or constrain her, nor could her parents. By her fourth year at Laurel Bloomery School, Sue Ann had found a passion: reading. She read everything she could get her hands on and was constantly asking Momma to take her to the Johnson County Library. Her natural love of reading translated into her schoolwork, and before long she was the best student in her class. Her favorite subject was English; poetry captured her imagination, as did William Faulkner.

She also pursued her wild side and could get into trouble with the best of them. Her tendency to joke wasn't because she was bored and looking for something to stimulate her mind. Her mind was always involved in something, and school didn't have to be all she thought about. Some said she had a bit of Uncle Tommy in her — smart as could be, and never too far from trouble. People knew she put crickets she caught in the teacher's desk, and many believed she was part of the group that captured an opossum and released it in the school building. Her teacher never suspected she was involved. Sue Ann was too sweet — a proper mountain girl who wanted to please everyone. She could never find trouble; her school never suspected the devious side of her nature.

Truth is, Sue Ann was her momma's daughter; and Momma knew that. From the beginning, she possessed the same free-spirited attitude Momma had learned growing up in the mountains. Fiercely independent, Sue Ann sought to push the boundaries of her sheltered life; sometimes that was through mischief, and sometimes her rebellious nature was to blame. Sue Ann knew there was a bigger world beyond Gizzard's Holler and her expanded family. Momma may never have left Johnson County, but Sue Ann was certain her future would lead her away. For her part, Momma wanted to ensure Sue Ann had no limitations; she wanted her to find whatever the world held for her; she gave her the freedom to explore, and Sue Ann took it.

Sue Ann's precocious childhood endeared her to Daddy. He wasn't ashamed to admit he had a special place in his heart for his little girl. By the time Sue Ann was five, she was riding on the tractor with Daddy as he cut the hay or plowed a field, teaching her all the interesting things you learn on a farm. They chased crickets exposed from the hay cutting until they collected enough to take fishing—it is also where Sue Ann got her supply for the teacher's desk.

Daddy and Sue Ann would go on long walks. It was during these times that she witnessed a side of him her brothers rarely saw. He seemed to relax when he was with Sue Ann, allowing his natural ability as a storyteller to flow freely. He told her about the time he got lost on White Mountain tracking a bear. Focused on keeping pace, he failed to notice where he was going. Unable to find his way out, he had to bed down amid a haphazard collection of branches. He wasn't prepared for an overnight stay, but he survived and adapted. "I wasn't worried about the bear, just snakes looking for a warm body to curl up against."

The next morning, having slept a bit, and with a clearer mind, he found his way to the truck.

"I never told your momma I got lost," Daddy confided. "No need to listen to her teasing me."

These cute stories made Sue Ann feel special; she was learning things about her Daddy that no one else knew.

After countless stories, Sue Ann realized Daddy had never talked about being scared; most of his adventures would have caused alarm for most folks, so why not Daddy? Because she wasn't shy, she asked, "Daddy, have you ever been scared?"

"Naw, not really," he replied.

Unconvinced, "Come on, you have never been scared?" she responded doubtfully.

"Well, there was this one time," Daddy said with a grin.

"We used to have a boar hog that was meaner than a

trapped rattlesnake. He couldn't be around anything without destroying it, or, if close to other livestock, trying to kill it. He was ornery."

"I hated dealing with him and meant to ship him off but always seemed to find a reason to keep him. One day, I was trying to move him from one pen to another, and he was having none of it. I was getting annoyed at his stubbornness, and I got too close."

Daddy got quiet as he whispered. "He charged me, his eyes fixed on me, meaning to kill."

"What did you do?" Sue Ann asked.

"I did the only thing I could do; I shot him in the forehead."

The story hung in the air for a moment as Sue Ann thought about her daddy defending himself from a raging boar hog. Daddy's chuckle broke the silence. Sensing his daughter's confusion at his laughter, Daddy said, "You want to hear the funny part? He wasn't worth eating; too tough. I fed him to the other pigs. Seemed fair."

As Sue Ann got older, Daddy shifted from treating his girl as a little farm buddy who joined him on his chores, to feeling the need to protect her; dads can be that way. Dads notice when others look at their daughters differently, when a smile seems to linger too long. After all, they have been there and remember their teenage days; staring at beautiful young girls and the thoughts they created. Like most dads, Daddy was slow to see Sue Ann growing into a young woman. There is a natural blocking mechanism that prevents dads from noticing what the rest of the world sees. However, in time, something happens that clicks and wakes them up. Daddy had his moment when Sue Ann was twelve.

Having just rounded up the cows he had left out in the

field, Daddy was standing at the gate waiting for Sue Ann to join him for a walk up to Laurel Creek. He was excited to see her and relaxed knowing he had just finished a boring task. With his mind at ease, he saw Sue Ann walking his way; he also saw his three new farmhands off to the left cleaning up the barnyard. As if on cue, the two oldest boys noticed Sue Ann walking by, stopped what they were doing, straightened up their stances, offered an awkward hello and watched her until they noticed Daddy was glaring at them.

The world changed that day for Daddy. He decided right then and there that he needed to make sure Sue Ann stayed away from those boys. Sue Ann enjoyed the attention; she knew she was pretty. With her naturally curly blonde hair that looked like a Shirley Temple cut, she now resembled a model in one of the fancy magazines you could buy at the town grocery. Her body filled out in all the expected places. She was tall, trim with the stature of an eighteen-year-old girl. Her awkward teenage puberty years were in her past. She looked like a young woman, but she wasn't yet thinking that way. Her innocence was pure, and her desires still unknown to her. Her body was mature, but in her heart and mind, she was still Daddy's little girl. Daddy knew Sue Ann hadn't made the leap to thinking of boys that way, but he knew it was only a matter of time; and it scared him to death.

14

Hell to Pay

WHAT STARTED OUT AS A PROLONGED GLANCE BECAME a game the farmhands seemed more than willing to play as Sue Ann knowingly sought their attention. The McGinnis brothers — Grant, Dan, and Dillon, were backwoods boys from Greene County, Tennessee, who had found their way to the Burnette farm. Grant and Dan, identical twins who recently celebrated their twenty-first birthday, shared the same rugged mountain stock and looked haggard for their age; long black hair and an unkempt beard dominated their faces. Grant's eyes held a cavernous distance, seeming never quite to connect with the person he was talking to. Dan's demeanor was more engaging, but a closer look at his pained expressions showed deep secrets controlled his mind. Growing up poor was normal for people along the western slope of the Appalachian Mountains; so were dysfunctional families. The McGinnis boy's father terrorized them and their mom. He regularly beat them, driven by rage and alcohol. His drinking habit contributed to a recurring problem; there wasn't much money around to feed the family, forcing all the members of the household to scrounge for whatever they could get. The natural result of their haphazard childhood was the boys' failure to gain an education; neither of the twins made it past sixth grade. Naturally, both Grant and Dan had an inherited mean streak in them. Any efforts they made to evolve past their dad's tendencies had failed, and they were always a moment away from getting hostile. They could be just as mean as he was. Aware of this weakness, they worked to hide their emotions and became good at concealing who they were. They could lie, and not just a little white lie here and there, but more like a sociopath lies, without a conscience or care about who it hurts.

When the McGinnis twins responded to Daddy's posting of openings for farmhands, they knew how to act and what to say to convince Daddy to give them a chance, and Daddy was inclined to believe in them because of that. Their past looked an awful lot like his upbringing — tough, and without love and support. He couldn't help but remember what old man Kirk had done for him. If he could offer hope to boys who had had little to hope for, he was going to do it. He hired the twins, paying them a fair wage, and offered Dillon a job for half the twin's rate.

When his brothers were around, Dillon, the quiet and unassuming black sheep of the clan, received little attention. With the face and stature of a fourteen-year-old, Dillon was seventeen. His chin looked cleanly shaven, but upon closer inspection, it was obvious he hadn't yet grown facial hair. His brown hair flowed freely and, although he had paid little attention to it, looked groomed and well kept. Dillon's brown eyes were soft, never settled. They shifted from one direction to the next with a melodic ease suggesting he was in no hurry. Soft-spoken, with a squeaky voice that explained why he didn't like to talk, Dillon rarely said anything. There was nothing to say; his older brothers took care of that for him. Dillion was more educated than the twins; a result of them protecting him from their dad, thus ensuring he went to school and learned what he could. He completed tenth grade before his brothers announced they were leaving home and told him he was coming with them.

"Dillon, get your stuff; we are movin on," Grant announced.

"Where we goin?" Dillon wondered.

"Don't know and it don't matter, we're leavin in the mornin."

Dillon never knew what the plan was for the three brothers and didn't want to find out. Grant and Dan were tough, and he suspected they were running from or looking for trouble. He was okay with that. He had followed their lead his entire life and, in his thinking, if they had found a way to a better life, who was he to question? Dillon hadn't expected his brothers to seek employment as farmhands; he'd expected wild excitement and adventure. It didn't seem to fit their style; after all, they weren't keen on being told what to do. They were used to taking what they wanted and looking after only themselves and no one else.

Despite this unnatural fit, the McGinnis boys quickly proved themselves to be everything Daddy needed. They did what he asked, didn't cause trouble, and were earning his trust. Grant and Dan worked to keep their cover intact. No need for farmer Burnette to know what they had in mind, nor what they were capable of; as long as he believed they valued farm life, hard work, and steady pay; all was well.

Sue Ann's physical development and growing desire to show off energized the twins and added stress to the burgeoning relationship between the farmhands and Daddy. They noticed Daddy was watching them as they stared at his little girl. Though Daddy paid attention to the boys, the boys did not give up. The boys would not slow their enthusiasm for Sue Ann. Where they came from, courting didn't have age limitations; heck, all their relatives had married off before they were seventeen. That Sue Ann was twelve was of little concern. She was beautiful, and she looked fifteen.

With the extra attention the boys gave Sue Ann and their recent tendency to lose focus while working, Daddy had a talk with the boys to make sure they understood his expectations.

"Boys, I've noticed lately you seem interested in getting my daughter's attention." He started.

"I want that to stop. Stay away from her."

And then he dropped the hammer. "I better not find out you've been talking to my little girl; it'll be hell to pay if I do."

A man of few words, he delivered what he wanted to say.

But threats did little to slow the efforts of Dan and Grant. For the first time since joining the farm, their past habit of ignoring authority reared its head. They had no intention of listening to Daddy. They just needed to do a better job of avoiding his watchful eye.

Daddy wasn't the only one to notice the twins' growing obsession with Sue Ann; her brothers learned what was happening and were worried about it.

From their arrival, James didn't trust Dan and Grant. He sensed there was a dark side to them that held secrets that could open a window to suppress evil. It wasn't the way they looked; most people from these parts looked rough; it was the way they moved about, like wolves methodically encircling unsuspecting prey. He couldn't put his finger on it; but he noticed they acted differently when they weren't around Daddy. They seemed to speak to each other in a stunted, unrecognizable language, always while holding a crooked smile. It was as if they lived in their own world and occasionally stepped out of it to interact, when needed, with the outside world. It scared James, and he wanted nothing to do with them. He never worked by their side on farm projects and kept his distance. As such, he didn't initially notice they were focusing attention on his sister. When Daddy told James about his conversation with the boys, James was relieved to hear Daddy speak up but doubtful it would matter; the McGinnis' weren't to be trusted. No, he needed to look out for Sue Ann. He knew she wasn't ready for the kinds of things the boys trafficked in.

Protective of his little sister, Ralph immediately noticed what was happening. He was ready to intervene. In his way of thinking, Dan and Grant were creepy, scary, and dangerous; he could think of nothing worse than them trying to garner the attention of Sue Ann. He decided he was going to talk to her and make sure she knew what was happening.

Ralph and Sue were close — closer than she was to James.

"I am sure in Sue Ann's way of thinking, I felt like an extension of Daddy and not a brother." James reflected. "Ralph and Sue Ann shared an adventurous side; if mischief was to be had on the farm, history showed they were in the middle of it. They shared a bond; a relationship that made it easy for them to talk."

James recalled the time Ralph tried to talk to Sue Ann.

"Sue Ann," Ralph started.

"You need to be wary of those twins; they seem to have their eye on you, and they can't be trusted."

"Come on, Ralph, ain't no harm in a little flirting." Sue Ann countered.

"But there is sis, these guys aren't like us. They have a dark side, and you never know what they are thinking. Promise me you'll stop giving them attention."

He stared at her, waiting for a response. All he got was a nod.

"Also, promise me you'll pay attention and not get caught alone with one of them. You hear me?" he asked.

Again, she nodded and smiled.

It was a completely unsatisfying response and brought Ralph little comfort. He didn't think Sue Ann was in immediate danger, but his instincts told him the twins were trouble.

15

Black-Eyed Susan

S UE ANN WAS WISE BEYOND HER YEARS, AT LEAST THAT was her opinion; she didn't want or need counsel from Ralph. It was nice he cared, and she feigned interest in his words, culminating with a manipulative smile, but any attempt to deter her from the fun she was having was futile. She was feeling something — butterflies in her stomach and fanciful dreams about one of the McGinnis boys; he had caught her eye, and she was determined to make sure he knew she noticed him.

Like her mother and her grandmother's upbringing, Sue Ann wasn't to have a girl becoming a woman mother-daughter conversation; proper women didn't talk that way, at least not till the night before the wedding. Anything learned in this county, about the opposite sex by a young girl was through giggling chatter with schoolmates, and trial and error. Sue Ann was no different; she knew nothing of love, except for the Beverly Cleary novel, *Fifteen*—the first installment of Cleary's First Love Series — she found stacked away at the Mountain City, town library. The main character, Jane's story spoke to her:

*Jane, said Mrs. Purdy, "it seems to me that you are seeing
a lot of this Stan Crandall."
Here we go. This Stan Crandall again.
"But Mom, you said yourself he was a nice boy."
There. She had known she could get that in some place.
"But you are only fifteen," protested Mrs. Purdy.
Only fifteen! That old argument.
Well, she wasn't going to be fifteen all her life.*

Through Jane's adventures, and Sue Ann's imagination, she pieced together how to capture Dillon's attention.

Free-minded and ambitious, Sue Ann acted fully developed. This only added to the appeal she brought to the twins. Beautiful, with bouncing blonde hair she let flow freely below a hat, a rapidly maturing body, and a smile that suggested nothing but fun, Sue Ann was the picture of what every young farmhand dreamed about. And yet, Dillon didn't seem to pay her any mind.

If Sue Ann was mature for her age, Dillion went the other way. Unsure in his steps, often with his head tilted down as to avoid looking ahead, Dillon was more than shy; he was painfully apprehensive. The first time he noticed Sue Ann had her gaze fixed in his direction, he felt embarrassed, quickly diverting his glance away to avoid making eye contact; a reaction that pleased Sue Ann. His shyness provided the perfect stimulus to encourage Sue Ann's pursuit. Not only was he cute, but, unlike the twins, he was a challenge. And Sue Ann was driven by challenges.

As chance would have it, late one afternoon Dillon cleaned up downed tree limbs on the mountainside of the house at precisely the moment Sue Ann conveniently rounded the corner. Caught unawares, Dillion turned away from Sue Ann, hurrying in the other direction with no obvious sense of why.

Undeterred, Sue Ann called out, "Hey where ya goin'?"

Unable to ignore what he heard, Dillon turned and mumbled, "Headed around the back of the house to the barn."

And so, it began. The seal now broken with the first words uttered between two kids, one an immature seventeen-year-old and the other a maturing twelve-year-old.

Dillon wasn't clueless. He had noticed Sue Ann, but he also had watched his older twin brothers vie for her attention; joke about what they wanted to do to her; and quibble among themselves about who was going to have their chance. Dillon knew to rely on experience and his instincts, and they were telling him to avoid any confrontation with his brothers. If they liked Sue Ann and had their minds set on fighting for her, he wasn't about to insert himself. He intended to stay away from Sue Ann and ignore her. It shouldn't be too hard; he knew how to disappear in any crowd.

What he didn't know how to do was control the feelings he was having. He couldn't get Sue Ann off his mind. Thinking of her introduced emotions he had never felt before. It wasn't puppy love; he had never loved anything or anybody. It was an open door to a vault of feelings and emotions; a strange, unknown box that garbled his mind. Dillon's newfound ability to feel or long for something scared him and sparked a fire within his body he didn't know was possible; he wondered, what was it about her that made him hope for a different life?

A growing conflict consumed Dillon. Sue Ann made him feel something — warmth and excitement about the future. It was the first time he had felt hope. He no longer saw himself as the tag-along to his older brothers. And yet, every time his mind wandered away from Sue Ann's charm, his past, and what he had seen his brothers do, pulled him back. He wasn't by nature an evil person. Any evil he possessed was a learned trait. Too young to process the contradiction between what he wanted and who he was, he moved ahead like he had always done without thinking. His newly felt emotions told him he didn't have to emulate his brother's psychotic behavior, his experience telling him he should.

Unable to control his growing urge for Sue Ann and a new future, he wandered about the farm, hoping for another chance encounter. He didn't have to wait very long. Sue Ann was determined to stumble into Dillon, and there wasn't much that could stop her. Headstrong, energetic, and focused, to the point of obsession, Sue Ann got what she wanted.

Oddly, before the week was up, it was Dillon who got the courage to act. Figuring it was time to say hello out beyond the backyard, he saw her walking aimlessly through the field, casually picking wildflowers, seemingly oblivious he was there. But she knew he was watching, and when she saw him turn his gait in her direction, she couldn't help but smile; Dillon was on his way to her. Uncertain and nervous, with his awkwardness on full display, he forged ahead.

"Hello," Dillon called out with a crackling voice implying he had missed puberty. "Hey there," Sue Ann said confidently.

Unprepared for a quick response, Dillon froze. Fear gripped him, and he came within a whisker of turning and running away; but he didn't; he stood his ground, staring at Sue Ann with a country-boy grin painted across his face. A protracted silence followed as both kids looked at each other, searching for what to say or do; as much as they wanted to open the path to courting, neither knew what came next. Paralyzed by the extended quiet, Dillon did what came naturally. He bent over and gently picked the yellow and black flower of a Black-Eyed Susan and, with a smile on his face, handed it to Sue Ann.

The simple act of chivalry was all it took for Sue Ann. Dillon liked her, and she liked him, and there was so much to talk about. Sue Ann's enthusiasm on full display made Dillon smile, and he laughed at her playfulness. He couldn't keep up, though. Before long, Sue Ann and her questions overwhelmed Dillon. All he could offer were short answers.

"Where're your brothers?" asked Sue Anne

"Behind the pigpen."

"What's it like where you're from?" She wanted to know.

"It's okay." He offered.

"Ever had a girlfriend?" She wanted to know.

"No." He giggled innocently.

"When's your birthday?" She continued.

"June."

"What day?" she wondered.

"I don't know; no one ever told me."

For what seemed like an hour, Sue Ann playfully asked Dillon questions, all the while flashing a welcoming look. They lost themselves in the moment. Consumed by a strange attraction and innocent desires, they couldn't understand or explain. Dillon started thinking about holding her hand and was fully engaged in how to accomplish that task when his brother Dan yelled across the yard, "Hey Dillon, get your butt over here."

The spell temporarily broken, Dillon jerked his head

towards his brother and immediately saw both brothers weren't pleased to see him talking to their target. He knew he had to answer to them, but something drew him back to Sue Ann, and without thinking he reached out, grabbed her hand, and smiled into her eyes. It was the first time he had ever looked someone in the eye; it was the first time he had touched a girl. His face flushed, he released her hand and ran over to his brothers.

"Don't be talkin to that girl," Grant said sternly.

"You heard what her paw said. Besides, she ain't interested in no boy," he laughed ominously with an icy stare.

For the first time in Dillon's life, his brother's threatening posture didn't scare him, but he didn't let on; he looked back at Grant submissively like he always had. No need to cause a fight he couldn't win. There was no need to listen to what he said. He was going to pursue Sue Ann, and he didn't care what his brothers or her paw said about it.

Driven by raging emotions, Sue Ann and Dillon were determined to see each other. What started as random moments when they crossed paths became organized efforts to spend time together. Sue Ann placed markers around the farm, intending to grab Dillon's attention and direct him where to go. The brief hints were unnoticeable to anyone not clued into the scheme, or the coded meanings of the placed items. A flower left by the fence post marking the entrance to the hay meadow meant they were to meet behind the house on the mountainside, the site they first spoke to each other. If the brick on the front porch shifted from the right side of the steps to the left, Dillon needed to head to Laurel Creek and the bend where the water gains pace and, at least for a moment, turns into rapids. Three rocks stacked together at the bottom of the back steps was the sign to meet at the Ramsey's Creek trailhead. This game of deception added intrigue to their growing fun; they were kids playing hide-and-seek in search of adult pursuits.

Their time together was always brief, but each longed for the fleeting moments when they could sneak away. As mischievous as their hideaways suggested, they remained pure. It was more than a week of rendezvous before Dillon found the courage to hold Sue Ann's hand for more than a few seconds. In time, holding hands progressed to hugs and Dillon putting his arm around Sue Ann's shoulders. They had been slipping away for more than a month when Sue Ann finally lunged forward and kissed Dillon on the cheek. Stunned, Dillon offered no resistance nor response. He satisfied himself by pulling Sue Ann closer with a hug and a smile.

Life was perfect for the fledgling lovebirds. They were feeling and doing things they had never done, and despite the age difference, despite having nothing in common, despite being completely unique personalities, and despite an unsure future, they were learning what love felt like.

But they weren't alone; Grant was watching. He was always watching. A life of mischief and violence had taught him to observe what was going on around him; he rarely missed anything. He noticed the way Sue Ann and Dillon looked at each other when they were around a larger group. He watched Sue Ann and saw her place her clues, only to then see Dillon seek the messages. When Dillon slipped away to meet Sue Ann, he tracked Dillon and never let him out of sight. He had seen everything, and he would not let this continue. Sue Ann wasn't to be with Dillon; she was his, even if she didn't know it.

This wasn't the first time Grant had spied on young lovers, back in Greene County, at the age of Twelve he had stumbled across his distant cousin Mary and her beau canoodling on the ridgeline where her paw had run his still; now abandoned it was a perfect place for a love nest. Grant had never seen a woman naked, nor had any idea what happened during sex. He was innocent no more. Seeing Mary's naked body transfixed him with sadistic thoughts of power and control. The erotic nature of the scene only added to his perverse urge to see Mary hurt. His thoughts didn't scare him or cause him to recoil. He was drawn in, and he wanted more. Grant's obsession with hurting girls grew as he watched Mary's frequent encounters. At no time did he have the urge to approach them or act on his impulse. No, he was enjoying fantasies in his head fed by what he witnessed; it would be some time before he acted on his evil desires.

For the first time in his life, Grant kept a secret from Dan. He didn't want to share what he had seen and was thinking, not even with his twin brother. This was his and his alone.

Grant may have started the brother's sociopathic behavior, but it wasn't to be his alone, nor a rare event. In time, the McGinnis twins became known throughout Greene County as crazy, not to be messed with. They had been rotten from an early age, and no attempt to control them would gain ground; better to avoid them than to show any sign of caring about their lot in life. No one had ever confirmed they were killers, but people turned up missing in Greene County all the time, and it was as believable as anything else that the responsibility for the doomed souls rested with the twins.

Greene County, known as the birthplace of Davy Crocket and Andrew Johnson, tried to present itself as a sophisticated mountain town. It had a movie hall, and a theatre where traveling music shows performed, and a train station that provided quick access to Knoxville and all its modern amenities; but it had a dark past. Years of hard living, economic failures, and battles over moonshining rights had scarred its people and taught them that fighting was the best way to resolve any dispute. Murders occurred frequently, and people feared offending or challenging families who built their power on hate and violence. You didn't want to cross the wrong people. Below the surface of the well-to-do lawbreakers, there was a more sinister band of criminals who lived by their own code. Because they couldn't join the more respected criminal enterprises, these misfits had to fight among themselves and take advantage of anyone vulnerable. If no one would notice they were gone, they were a prime target for abuse. Given the law was too busy partnering with the refined, gun-toting families, they didn't have time to be bothered with the dredges of the community. They had full rein because people left them alone. All they had to do was stay away from harming someone that mattered. The McGinnis twins had mastered the art of harassing the unwanted.

When they left Greene County with Dillon in tow, it was a relief to folks who knew them; good riddance was the accepted view. When they got to Johnson County, they weren't shy about telling anyone who would listen about their brutal upbringing and their desire to escape a cycle of tragedy; they projected themselves as boys seeking a new life and an honest living. The twins fanned the flames of deception; no need to change people's minds. If they were now known as trusted boys, who had escaped a dark past, all the better. It was a show. They weren't looking for a place to start over and settle into a respectable life; they wanted virgin, fertile ground that was unaware of their true intent and unlikely to notice their behavior. In time, when they had taken all they could from the underbelly of Johnson County, they would move on.

16

Indian Summer

THE RHYTHM OF THE BURNETTE FARM SHIFTED AS THE sun set lower in the sky. In these parts, days rapidly got shorter when the calendar turned to October; the mountains blocked the southern sun, and shadows covered the farm much of the day. It hadn't snowed yet, but you could feel it in the air. Daddy was busy getting the farm ready for frozen days and snow; hunkered-down days when taking care of the livestock was the focus. Repairing the roof of the barn was at the top of his list. A tree clipped the barn as it fell in August during a violent thunderstorm, and the opening it caused needed to be covered.

James, Ralph and Sue Ann were in school most days, and Momma was caring for her brother Alton, who lived alone and was down with liver problems; it was likely caused by too much bad whiskey. It was a busy time, with little opportunity for fun or secret meetings. As a result, Dillon and Sue Ann hadn't kept up the frequency of their private time, and they were growing frustrated. They needed more than a passing moment or a quick kiss; their bodies were telling them that.

With Momma going to Alton's place most days, Daddy feeling the calendar weighing on him, and James and Ralph with Daddy, it should be easy for Sue Ann and Dillon to get their desired time. They needed Dan and Grant to be focused on some bigger tasks with Daddy, while Dillon handled the menial task of slopping the pigs.

Their big break came on one of the remaining warm days in late October—Indian summer in these parts--, when Daddy and the twins headed to town to pick up supplies to work on the barn repair. As usual, Dillon stayed behind. The opportunity came with Sue Ann's early arrival home from school; the teacher, having fallen sick with some horrible stomach flu that no one wanted, the principal had seen fit to send the kids home. Without a school bus, a neighbor had to give Sue Ann a ride. At Sue Ann's request, the neighbor dropped her off at the turnoff onto Stinking Creek Road. She walked the rest of the way to the house. As she approached, she noticed Daddy's truck was gone, and it was quiet. Could everyone be gone? Or even better, was everyone gone but Dillon?

A rush of excitement filled Sue Ann's body.

Momma got home in time to whip up supper. It had been a tough day. Alton wasn't well, and she worried he had little time left; so sad to see family pass. The house was empty, nothing too odd about that. It was early for Daddy to come in, and the boys were almost certainly helping him with the barn. She didn't see Sue Ann but thought nothing of it; a pretty day had likely drawn her to a peaceful place where she was reading or doing homework.

The boys gave the barn repair their full attention and nearly completed it. It was an all-hands-on-deck effort, and Daddy liked the result. "This should work just fine," he told them as they cleaned up the tools before calling it a day.

Over at the house, Momma was putting the final touches on supper and heading upstairs to freshen when it hit her — Sue Ann should be home by now. I guess she is out front and will come in when supper is on the table; she thought to herself. That wasn't to be.

As she welcomed Daddy and the boys from the barn, she made eye contact with Daddy and with a hint of worry said, "Where's Sue Ann? I haven't seen her all afternoon?"

Everyone stopped dead in their tracks, as the boys and Daddy realized they hadn't seen her either. "We have been around the barn all afternoon and haven't seen her, figured she was here at the house."

"I hadn't seen her since this morning," James said. "Me too," was all Ralph said.

Now nervous, Momma grabbed the phone and called Mrs. Mable Sheffield, Sue Ann's teacher. What she learned from Mrs. Sheffield sent chills down her spine. "Sue Ann rode home with Sophie's mom, Daisy, I was sick, and we let the class out before lunchtime," she explained. "Is she not home?"

Daisy confirmed during another quick call that she dropped off Sue Ann at lunchtime at the bottom of Stinking Creek Road. "Dear God," Momma said.

"Where could she be?"

Panic set in as Momma and Daddy immediately looked at each other. They needed to find Sue Ann and now. They quickly drew up a plan and split up to search for her. Daddy yelled out to the McGinnis boys to come over to the front porch; everybody needed to help. Daddy said he would walk the path to the bottom of Stinking Creek Road to see if he could find anything. Ralph headed to the far reaches of the property across the hay meadow, James volunteered to search the bottom half of Laurel Creek, Dan said he would climb the mountain trail, Grant quickly offered that he and Dillon would search the upper reach of Laurel Creek, Momma said she would walk up Ramsey's Creel trail. They agreed to meet back here when they found her or, worse case, in an hour.

Daddy walked at a brisk pace, wanting to cover a lot of ground; he was worried. This didn't seem right. His mind wouldn't let go of a nagging thought: "What did I miss? Was something going on and I didn't see it?" It was his job to take care of his family, especially his little girl, and now they couldn't find her; the more he walked, the faster his pace increased. Fear gripped him; he had a bad feeling. At the bottom of the road, he turned and retraced his steps; this time his pace slowed. He wanted to make sure he looked at everything, didn't miss a sign of Sue Ann or overlook something that mattered. Despite his slower pace, he was the first to return to the front porch.

Dan was in no hurry to walk the mountain trail. He wasn't all that worried or interested in the kid having wandered off; "the things I have to do," he mused to himself. They would find her; learn she was off on some half-cocked adventure and not paying attention to time. He wanted to be resting and eating; it had been a long day, and now this silliness.

Grant and Dillon walked slowly along Laurel Creek; they didn't talk. There was an unfamiliar edge between them, more than the normal tension that existed. This was more; something had happened, and they both wondered what the other person was thinking. As they moved along the creek, neither seemed interested in searching. It was as though they knew they wouldn't see Sue Ann; she was somewhere else.

Having half-heartedly searched their assigned segment; they made their way back to the porch to report to Daddy they had seen no sign of her.

James set out for his stretch of the river confident everything would be alright; it didn't occur to him that something was wrong. His mood suddenly changed. He saw a flash in his head of the look on Momma and Daddy's faces. They were scared, and fear was not something they experienced often. The image of their fear chilled him; could Sue Ann be in danger? Who would hurt her? At seventeen, James was yet to experience danger or the thought of something terrible happening to someone he loved; he was naïve. That was about to change. As he completed his leg of the river, he was relieved he had found nothing. His growing confidence that he would return to find everyone laughing on the front porch and Momma pulling supper out of the oven supported a new sense of relief.

Ralph struggled to open the gate to the meadow. He felt scared, and his shaking hands couldn't grab the lever. Frustrated, he cried. It was not altogether surprising reaction; he was only fourteen years old. It took a moment, but his cries subsided, and he pried open the gate. They had cut the meadow before him in early September so he would not have to walk through high wheat. It was still a garbled mess and could easily hide someone who didn't want to be seen or serve as a place to stash someone or something. Ralph walked with measured and slow steps. He didn't want to miss anything. His pace being slow, he didn't finish as the others expected. He should have been back at the house first; he wasn't. He was still in the field when he heard Momma scream.

17

She Was Gone

RALPH WASN'T THE ONLY ONE TO HEAR MOMMA CRY out. Daddy, standing on the porch with James, heard Momma scream and immediately stopped pacing. His head whipped around trying to interpret Momma's voice. Confident this was a cry for help, Daddy jumped down the stairs and began running to the trail and the sound of his wife. Daddy didn't interpret Momma's cries as a sound of fear or danger; rather, her wailing foretold tragedy and despair. It was more than he could stomach. Had something happened to Sue Ann? Were Momma's screams leading him to something he couldn't bear to see?

Ramsey's Creek Trail is steep, with numerous switchbacks used to ease the ascent. Papaw Thomas had used the trail in the early years of his still operation. The top of the trail crossed Ramsey's Creek and flattened a bit as it wrapped around Jenkins Mountain; it was here that the still operated.

Momma cried softly most of the way up the trail; calling out for Sue Ann. She couldn't shake the feeling that something had happened to her baby. A mother's sense is powerful, and Momma could feel Sue Ann's presence from the moment she stepped on the trail; she knew she was on the right path. With a mother's intensity, she kept a strong pace, fighting back tears and the urge to break down. Memories of Sue Ann as a baby, her first dress, her laughter, smile, and ability to brighten every room flowed through Momma's mind. Momma admired Sue Ann's energy and capacity to love, and even though she could be a handful, loved her independence; Momma cursed herself for not watching over Sue Ann more. "How could I have let this happen?"

In late October, the fall leaves were well on their way to settling on the ground, creating a crunching sound of dried foliage with every step Momma took. It was the only sound that broke the silence; it was eerily quiet. Breathing heavily as she climbed and with fear consuming her body, Momma grew tired. Her body shaking uncontrollably, she trudged ahead. It was a mommas love that drove her. She could have easily collapsed, exhausted, and unable to take another step, but love for her baby girl wouldn't allow it.

A few hundred yards below Papaw Thomas' old still camp, Momma pulled up, standing upright and stiff; she heard something.

It was Sue Ann whispering to her, "Momma, I am okay; don't worry about me."

"Sue Ann, where are you?" Momma cried. There was no answer.

A strange peace came over Momma. Her little sweetheart had told her she was okay, everything was going to be fine; but was it? Momma regained her balance and trekked farther up the trail; she needed to find Sue Ann. As she advanced, her tears now slowing, Momma took notice of the beauty that surrounded her; the rhododendron, ivy, wild ferns, hemlock trees, and moss covering the exposed rocks; all part of her life, farm, and these mountains. What a lovely place, she thought.

A few hundred yards past the still camp, Momma glimpsed light blue fabric blowing in the wind. Calling out for Sue Ann, she leaped forward to get a better view; there she was, leaning comfortably against the base of a maple tree. Relief filled Momma's body as from her angle, it looked like Sue Ann was reading a book and had fallen asleep resting snuggled next to the tree. Relief instantly turned to anguish as Momma realized something was wrong.

Sue Ann sat on the ground, legs extended, arms resting at her waist, her chin against her chest; she wasn't asleep. Her skin was grey, her body cold, and stiff. Sue Ann was gone. It was more than Momma could process, and she screamed at the top of her lungs, raging against her life, her loss, and her anger at whoever did this to Sue Ann. Brushing Sue Ann's hair to the side, Momma kissed her on the forehead and hugged her tight, tighter than she had ever held anything.

It didn't take long for Daddy, James, and Ralph to find Momma lying prostrate on the ground; they had run as fast as they could across the meadow and up the trail. When they found Momma, she was rocking back and forth, clutching Sue Ann. Daddy fell to his knees, unable to take another step; the boys stood passively crying, trying to process what they were seeing.

It looked like someone had purposely placed Sue Ann's limp body in this natural position. There was no sign of a struggle. The area was undisturbed. There wasn't anything lying on the ground. It was as though Sue Ann simply sat down for a rest and died while taking a nap.

Daddy asked James to run to the house and call the sheriff; something didn't seem right, and he wanted the law to see this. Unable to get Momma to go home, Daddy sat next to her and held her as they waited for Sheriff Cogburn to arrive. An hour after dark, the sheriff and two of his deputies crested the trail and walked over to greet the despondent Burnette family.

"Frankie, are you alright?" Cogburn asked. All Daddy could do was nod, his eyes transfixed on Sue Ann.

"Frankie, can you tell me what happened?"

"Not really, Sheriff, Sue Ann was missing. Nita found her bout two hours ago." Daddy mumbled.

"Okay, Frankie" was all the sheriff could say.

After a long pause, Sheriff Cogburn gently asked Momma and Daddy to go back to the house so he could look around; Deputy Waters offered a hand and slowly led Momma, Daddy and the two boys down the mountain. The sheriff had dealt with unexplained deaths and murder before. Johnson County was small but still had its share of violence. Mountain folk often chose guns to settle things; disputes that weren't hard to figure out; it was always clear who had done the killin. Death wasn't a new thing. The unexplained death of a child, however, was different and grabbed his attention; he had a bad feeling about what he saw, and didn't want Momma and Daddy to see what he was going to do.

As the family slowly made their way down the mountain, Sheriff Cogburn stood quietly above Sue Ann and prayed.

"Lord, give me guidance to figure this out. Give me wisdom to know what to do, and the strength to support Frankie and Nita."

After a brief moment of silence, Sheriff Cogburn went

down on one knee on the left side of Sue Ann's body. It didn't take long for the sheriff to confirm what he feared. As he gently lifted the side of Sue Ann's dress and looked underneath her body, he saw blood, blood on her dress below her waist.

Confident Sue Ann had been murdered, the sheriff scanned her clothed body with his flashlight. Above the neckline of her dress, he noticed bruise marks around her neck; that was all he needed to see. Someone raped and strangled Sue Ann.

The sheriff and his deputies stayed on the mountain the rest of the night looking for clues — anything that could tell them what happened; they found nothing. In the morning, they wrapped Sue Ann's body in a quilt they got from the farm, carried her down Ramsey's Creek Trail, put it in the back of the hearse, and took her to town for a deeper evaluation.

The county kept Sue Ann for a few days before sending her to the funeral home for burial preparation. Within a week she was back on the farm, in a casket, lying in the farmhouse parlor; it had all happened so fast.

Sue Ann's funeral attracted a crowd. Everyone respected the Burnettes, and all who knew her loved their girl. Paying respects and being there to see the heartbroken family was an expectation that everyone in the county could meet. Momma and Daddy were in a daze, barely able to greet people; they couldn't process what had happened. They weren't alone; everyone wondered how this could have happened here, in Johnson County. The sheriff told Momma and Daddy that he was certain someone had murdered her, but he omitted details he thought were too much for parents to hear. With promises to the family that he would find the killer, Sheriff Cogburn privately committed to himself that he would figure this out and he would make it right. There was no other way. His focus was clear. This is what he was here for — to deliver justice.

On the morning of the funeral, Momma and Daddy slipped into the parlor and opened the casket for the last time. Uncontrollable emotions consumed them; she was beautiful, peaceful looking. They held hands and prayed for Sue Ann's soul; with tears rolling down their faces, they leaned forward and gave her one last kiss. She was gone, and their world would never be the same. In the hallway were James and Ralph; too young to know what to do or say, they sat muted, holding in their feelings and anger.

They buried Sue Ann under the tulip poplar next to Papaw Thomas and Mamaw Betty. She was two months shy of her thirteenth birthday.

PART III

18

A Cold Friday Night

TIME WITH MY KIDS SHARING MEMORIES OF SUE ANN'S life and murder resurfaced the emptiness I felt in the days immediately following Momma's death. The house was quiet, too quiet; Momma's passing had sucked all the energy and life from the farmhouse, a place I now called home, and I was struggling to figure out what to do next. I didn't have a job, hadn't reconnected with old friends, no longer watched TV, and didn't feel a passion towards anything; so much had happened in a short period. I abandoned my career, took a leap and committed to staying in Johnson County, discovered Momma was dying, and watched her pass quickly, realized my family skillfully kept secrets, and learned my sister was murdered. That is a lot to process, and I became stuck in my head; caught in the same cerebral trap that had caused me to quit my job and flee New York.

I felt overwhelmed. For the first time in my life, I had just watched someone I love die. Combine that with the pain and fear that goes with not knowing how to go forward; darkness was descending upon me. When Daddy died, I was sad and felt the surge of mourning that comes with losing a parent, but it was brief. After the funeral, I spent a few days with Momma, but I wasn't there emotionally. I was already back in New York, my mind consumed with a transaction and my need to get back on the job. It was a built-in distraction. Nothing, not even Daddy's death, deterred me; I was obsessed with work. My rapid return to the city masked any internal feelings I had about losing the primary male influence in my life. I didn't allow myself to mourn; I didn't know how.

My avoidance of any emotion after Daddy's death deadened my ability to share compassion with Momma. I left her in the mountains without her life partner, alone in a house that suddenly seemed big. It was a personal failure, like so many times in the past. I wasn't there. Momma never shared how she was feeling; it wasn't her way. "You need to go back to New York," was all she said.

She showed strength and the fortitude to send me back to New York with a loving smile and powerful hug; but I now understand how she must have felt. Like her before me, I now sat alone in this house, left with memories of the past, and guilt for my failures as a son.

I needed to talk to someone, but who? I had had no friends for the last twelve years, and I wondered about how the people around here would react to me. Searching for something to do, I went to the annual Christmas parade. With a small parade with trucks for floats, old man Heny dressed as Santa, and the high school band playing, it would be a chance to see people.

It was a cold Friday night, but the whole county appeared to have shown up. I was comforted because I knew almost everybody, but it bothered me that most people didn't want to talk beyond quick greetings. Feeling isolated among a throng of people you know fosters a deep level of loneliness.

As I was about to leave, I noticed a group of my old high school friends gathered in front of the post office. They appeared to be joking about a fun subject.

I walked over to join them, and they immediately greeted me with subdued hellos. They weren't rude. But my reception wasn't a warm welcome. I sensed I had walked into a conversation they didn't want to have around me. I don't know what it was about, but I wasn't part of the group.

After they exchanged forced pleasantries and brief condolences about Momma, silence ensued. I said, "Well, I need to be getting back to the house. Lots to do."

"Sounds great, RJ. Good to see you." That was all I got in return.

It wasn't my first time feeling alone. Even though I lived in a city with over eleven million people and worked in an office with over three hundred colleagues, I lived the last eight years of my life alone, with only my thoughts to keep me company: how I could advance my career, and what the next transaction was. That's not to say I was a recluse, walled off from humanity and personal interactions. I interacted with people all day long; spent most of my day talking, but it was superficial. A dance we all played, angling to gain an advantage, or better yet, more power — power in the firm, power in the transactions. Competitive forces dominated each day. The company paid us to win, and they paid us well. I made more than I ever thought possible. But money wasn't the primary stimulant; it was pelts on our wall. Deals were how we showed our prowess. The more deals we had, the more swagger we carried and the more we fed our internal hunger for more. Success became my own personal scorekeeper and validation that I had overcome my past.

At the firm, they taught us we were part of a team. That was a joke, and everyone knew it. We were out for ourselves, and if that meant working alongside colleagues, or using others for our own agenda, it was a small price to pay; or was it? The relentless fierceness with which we chased success naturally led to seclusion; an isolation I was more than happy to accept; but why? At no time during my days in New York did I question my motives, nor the ease with which I followed the culture. Sitting alone in Momma's house, I am haunted by a thought I can't escape. What led me to become cold and detached, focused only on me and my outsized goals?

I didn't know it but looking back, I now see, I immediately sensed a break with my family and their ways, the moment I decided not to return home after college; a decision that wasn't done to hurt anyone or in spite, I thought it was what I wanted. A chance to be something other than RJ from Gizzard's Holler; a chance to prove I was better than where I came from. A simple life choice quickly evolved into something more impactful. My once gregarious desire to connect with people, to laugh with them, and to be fun-loving died. I didn't have time nor the inclination to open myself to others. I no longer sought friends. Subconsciously, I knew that the new people in my life were nothing like the mountain folk I grew up with. I closed myself off, put my head down, and focused on my job; I had something to prove. It's easy to see how I became so disconnected from my true core country being. I didn't know how to fit in; I didn't want to fit in. I wasn't with people I understood and didn't want to be with those who saw the world differently than me.

I completely opposed entering the dating scene. It's not that I was insecure; I wasn't. I couldn't picture myself meeting a girl who would be like the women I grew up with. Truth be told, I still had feelings for my old girlfriend, Alice. She was all I ever wanted, and I had run from her; just like I ran from everyone else. I knew I had hurt her. It pained me to think I could be so cold to someone who meant so much to me. My departure was a personal rejection, even if I didn't mean it that way. I doubted Alice would ever forgive me. I wondered if I would ever forgive myself.

In New York, I had opportunities to meet women. A coworker, Joy, once suggested I meet a friend of hers for drinks.

"RJ, you need to get out more. I think you will like my friend."

Without thinking, I laughingly responded, "No thanks, I'm good. I bet she doesn't even know how to make biscuits."

Joy and I had a good laugh about this, partly because she thought I was joking, and I was, but I was also expressing a deep-seated feeling I had. I realized I wouldn't meet anyone in New York who I would ever consider spending the rest of my life with. No matter how hard I tried, I couldn't shake who I was, or the memory of Alice. I was a country boy who felt best when I was around people whom I understood.

Free from organized activities, my mind wandered; I began to think about Momma's faith. Religion had never been my calling card, and that void in my life was now noticeable to me as I processed Momma's death and my isolation. When I lived in Gizzard's Holler, everyone expected me to attend church. Since leaving home, I hadn't graced the steps of a church. I saw no reason, and I couldn't spare the time, nor could I imagine the city churches held the warmth I knew at the Laurel Bloomery Presbyterian Church. I believed New York churches couldn't be a community. The city smothered togetherness.

Momma's death didn't suddenly create an urge to worship in church, but it opened my mind to consider spirituality, faith, and death. The more I thought about life, the more questions I had about faith; alone in this house and with no one to talk to, I turned to Momma. I spent countless hours sitting quietly next to her grave, engaged in an unspoken conversation with her, seeking to understand what had become a new mystery to me. I couldn't grasp the concept that death was permanent, that we spent this intense time on earth, growing, learning, striving for goals, only to have it end abruptly, without a choice. And then what? The Bible taught us about heaven, but I struggled to understand what that meant. I wasn't having a crisis of faith. I was exploring what faith was; what it meant to my family, to those in this small mountain town; to those who had never experienced certainty in their lives.

My exploration led me to Pastor Larry Higdon's office. A staple of the community, Pastor Higdon had led the congregation for years. He was a perfect fit since he had been raised within five miles of the church. Larry was a childhood classmate; the last person you would have predicted would stand up, holding the Bible, and proclaim the road to the promised land; I guess we can all change.

Pastor Higdon looked surprised when he opened the door and saw my face. "RJ, hello. What can I do for you?"

"I was hoping I could speak with you for a minute?"

"Sure, have a seat. What's up?"

I didn't know where to start or what to say. "Pastor, I am

struggling to figure things out. Momma is gone, and that has been difficult for me."

"I understand losing a loved one is hard. That's why we rely on the good word to comfort us." He had said that line before.

"I know, but I feel alone. Not just because of Momma's death, but because I am learning things about my family I didn't know before. I am wondering if I belong."

Pastor Higdon's already stiff demeanor hardened further when he heard my reference to secrets. Suddenly, he seemed nervous; eager to end our time together. Hesitantly, he asked, "What do you mean by learning things you didn't know?"

"I found out Sue Ann was murdered."

"Well, RJ, I know nothing about that." His response was quick and decisive.

"RJ, I understand you are struggling. I will pray for you. I hope you will take up praying as well. It will be good for you."

Standing up, he leaned forward and said, "RJ, I am sorry, but I have a matter I need to attend to. Hope to see you Sunday at church." With that, he was gone.

My last hope for spiritual refuge and guidance walked out the moment I brought up my family's past. Despondent, I hurried back to my truck and sped home.

If I were going to get through this, I was going to have to do it alone. With nowhere to turn, I returned to Momma's grave.

My time at Momma's grave was draining. I became intensely driven to work things out in my head. I also gradually found a measure of peace in not knowing everything. This was new to me. The firm taught us never to admit you don't know everything. Confidence, even when it wasn't warranted, was a prerequisite. That was in my past, the spirit of Momma and Daddy consumed me, and I slowly allowed myself the freedom to accept I didn't have to have all the answers. I learned it was okay to work at maturing my spiritual self, to allocate time, the most precious commodity, to grow my understanding of the role God played in the lives of those I loved. I knew I could do this; I knew how to grind, how to work through problems.

The bitter days spent under the tulip poplar became a few weeks; I can't recall doing anything else. And then one day, I felt a peaceful sensation wash over me: a previously unknown bridge to my family, and to God. There wasn't an aha moment, rather a progression of simple thoughts leading to a simple conclusion; faith wasn't a statement of certainty but an admission of the unknown, intermingled with belief; belief in something powerful and hopeful. Momma and Daddy didn't profess to know everything about God; they just believed. It was okay if I followed the same path, maybe my journey wasn't as far along as there's had been, but I was walking the path. For the first time since I left home more than a decade ago, I didn't feel emotionally lonely. Ironic because I was more alone than I had ever been.

With a newfound spiritual peace and healing after Momma's death, my mind was free to wander about other things that were negatively impacting me, and a wandering mind can end up in unfortunate places. Wild thoughts dominated my thinking. I was attempting to relearn what I believed to be true about my past; what was real, what wasn't? Every brief story I remembered from my childhood seemed doubtful. Truth, and who knew what, consumed me; the first hint of my doubts coming during Momma's funeral. Throughout that last day, I couldn't help but look at James and Ralph and imagine what other secrets they held. What about my aunts and uncles? They obviously knew about Momma being sick and Sue Ann's murder; what else had they kept from me? Losing Momma left me alone again. Looking at my family and extended relatives on the day of Momma's funeral made me feel isolated; isolation compresses your soul.

Nearly a decade living in New York and away from the flow of home had hardened me, creating a border that allowed me to function independently of my history—it made it okay for me to ignore my family and their mountain ways, and I had become detached, even cold. My distant feelings weren't only mine. Years ago, my family had emotionally said good-bye to me as I departed their world in search of another. I understood how they felt and did little to deter their attitude; we were blood relatives, but no longer in each other's lives. And now I was home; but not because I was attempting to reestablish my place in the family. When I left New York, I was running from what I had become. I wasn't running to them. At least, that is what I thought. Maybe I was wrong; maybe subconsciously I came home seeking to recapture my identity as a Burnette.

That I had been an outsider in the family long before I moved away complicated my search to identify my heritage and identity. They purposely misled me about Sue Ann. That reality left me cold, and angry and hurt. How could I understand who I was and what my foundation was based on, when doubts about the validity of my past dominated my thoughts?

I wanted to lash out, confront family members and put them on the spot for lying to me; I wanted them to feel the sting I was feeling. I roleplayed in my mind countless interactions where I would corner James and ask him hard questions about Sue Ann, my life, Momma and Daddy. Each time I imagined the confrontation, it ended poorly, and I felt more distraught. I thought about driving up to Ralph's place unannounced with a list of things to discuss. Not big on surprises, every time I envisioned walking onto Ralph's property, he greeted me cautiously and eventually asked me to leave. Each scenario I created in my head had the same outcome. I was over the top, obnoxious, and unfair. James and Ralph were annoyed, offended, and did not want to be part of my pity party.

Days of drinking coffee, rocking on the front porch swing with Winston, and stewing about my scrambled emotions had gotten me nowhere. Finally, after a few days of pouting, I became disgusted with myself. I stood up, spat out the last swig of coffee, and screamed at the top of my lungs; "Dammit!" My outburst startled Winston from his morning nap, causing him to roll off the swing and land on his side. I couldn't help it; I laughed out loud. Taking my laughter as a sign that I am okay, Winston's tail wagged vigorously, and he trotted my way. The freeing burst of pent-up anger, and a loyal dog were the tonic I needed; my mind felt stimulated with fresh thoughts filled with hope and optimism. I knew then I was going to get through this.

My shift in mood was long overdue, and I was ready to move forward. It was time. My very being was under a self-imposed microscope, and I didn't like what I saw; was it possible I could change the picture? Could I understand the attraction of this place to the people who lived here? Would the loss of Momma and the secrets that have unfolded be a source for my renewal, or was I destined to be a stranger in my home?

I had to accept that I had been sheltered from the truth, and it was systematic. Everyone took part in the concealment. It served no purpose for me to hold bitterness or anger towards those who lied to me; they all did it, and I suspect all thought it was in my best interest. You can justify a lot of unpleasant truths if everyone thinks it best and all conspire to execute the deception. I am sure there was never any harm intended.

However, my powerful self-reflection and analysis failed to soothe me. Accepting that others kept me in the dark wasn't enough. I needed to explore what I had missed, understand our family secrets, and unpack how long I had been separated from my kin's reality. I needed answers.

I quickly looked through Momma's belongings. Specifically, the cedar chest she kept at the foot of her bed. I assumed that looking at the things she collected would surface new secrets I hadn't known about. Perhaps I would learn about fun times and humorous anecdotes, or about interesting things that had slipped away, never shared with me, and Sue Ann's fate was all the darkness in our family's past. I might find out who killed Sue Ann and how she died. It was an open question that was gnawing at me. I had to know more than what Momma had told me on her last day. Maybe the chest will open a door to my better understanding of my family, Johnson County, and why people act the way they do; or maybe none of this will happen.

Momma's cedar chest lived against her oak four-poster bed Daddy had crafted when they were first married. Resting comfortably on top of the chest was a hand-stitched, green and blue quilt blanket. Momma's grandmother made the quilt and passed down to her; still colorful, the blanket looked like it had another hundred years of use left in it. The cedar chest was a gift from Daddy to Momma on their first anniversary. Daddy had spent weeks crafting the piece; his skills showed in the inlay features he displayed on the top. With a beautiful finish that featured the red tone of the cedar, the chest was Momma's most prized possession.

I had never looked inside the chest, nor been around when Momma had it open. I did not know what lay inside. The mystery of its contents didn't create excitement. No longer was I a seven-year-old sneaking behind Momma's back to look in a closet she had told me to stay away from. I was an adult processing my momma's passing, a life without her, and an uncertainty about my identity. I was, however, apprehensive, and a little scared. What if there were things within the confines of Momma's beloved chest that contained memories I didn't want to know, or couldn't handle?

I stared blankly at Momma's stowed-away secrets, doubting whether I wanted to open them, trying to talk myself into taking the first step to uncovering the past. With a slightly shaking hand, I picked up the blanket and sat it on the Queen Anne chair positioned next to the chest, pried open the latch, and gently raised the lid. Resting at the bottom of the box were three items: a faded powder-blue dress, a stained envelope, and a shoebox full of papers bound by a pink ribbon.

19

An Albino Squirrel

A FTER WEEKS OF SULKING ALONE AT HOME, IT WAS TIME for me to reacquaint myself with my reclaimed hometown; I needed to get out of the house. It was a new year, and the desire to renew my connection to Mountain City motivated me. On previous trips home, I experienced a strange feeling. I felt out of place, like I didn't belong. It was my fault. Being aware I wouldn't stay in Gizzard's Holler for long made it easy to feign interest in the goings-on, thus resisting any meaningful engagements. The fact is, I didn't want to invest in the lives of those I knew and grew up with; I was passing through on my way back to my important job, dealing with important people. What I now realize is my attitude was apparent to all I big-timed. How could it not be? Appalachian people know fake. They have seen carpetbaggers roll through town with promises and hope for more than a hundred years. They knew me when I was one of them; now I stand out like an albino squirrel.

Mountain City had changed little in the last several decades; the county seat of Johnson County and home to

2,300 residents, it was the big city for me and my family. A little over eight miles from the turnoff to our farm, Mountain City was all I knew until I left for college.

My first stop in town was Porter's Hardware. I didn't have a specific purpose; I just wanted to check on Mr. Porter. A long-time friend of the family, he turned up whenever we needed help, ready to work, with a broad tobacco-chewing smile. If there was a real problem that needed tending to, Mrs. Porter came along with a box full of casseroles. "You gotta eat" is all she would say as she unpacked enough food for a high school reunion.

"Hey RJ," Mr. Porter belted out as soon as he saw me enter. "How you doin my friend?"

He called everyone his friend, probably because everyone was his friend. The owner of the town's only hardware store, Mr. Porter, had seen this town through every need and crisis for over thirty-five years.

"I'm great, Mr. Porter, just stopped by to say hello." I responded.

"Listen, RJ, I'm so sorry about your momma. She was the best, a real angel, that lady." Mr. Porter smiled softly while paying his respects.

I nodded in reply, acknowledging his kind words. "How's the family?" I asked.

Mr. Porter's daughter, Becky, and I went to high school together; she later married Bud, my senior year Saturday night cruising partner.

"Becky is great, has two youngins, they are a mess and always into something. Billy works at the mill and still ain't settled down. There seems to be no way to manage his wild side."

Mr. Porter smiled as he described life for his two kids. He was proud, and why not? Granted, they lived a modest life, but most everyone around here did; nothing wrong with finding happiness in daily life.

We talked for the next hour, interrupted occasionally by the infrequent customers who walked through the front door; it was good to catch up. My sense of belonging found a solid footing. Mr. Porter made me feel less like an outsider and more like a native — a good sign I might figure out how to reform my "high-headedness."

"Mr. Porter, is Alice still in town?" I wondered.

Pleased with my question, Mr. Porter said, "You betcha, I'll tell her you asked about her."

"That would be good," I responded, unable to hide my smile at the thought of seeing Alice again.

I was eager to hear about my high-school sweetheart. It would be nice to see her, if she weren't too sore with me. My unexplained departure and dismissive behavior were hurtful and rude. I hadn't left town in the best way.

As peaceful as my time with Mr. Porter was, an anxious need to ask questions about the past dominated my mind. There was so much to explore; I held off. I meekly concluded, no need to jump into a bunch of questions when we were practicing the slow catching up that happens with people who aren't in a hurry, and perfectly happy to skim the surface on every topic.

Mr. Porter's style was the epitome of how life in the county could proceed while burying unpleasant truths, as though nothing had happened. He shared the widely accepted view that whatever happened is best left in the shadows. That was frustrating for me. I was from here, but obviously I didn't have that mindset. I wanted everything out in the open. The more I stewed on the reality that Mr. Porter knew exactly what happened to Sue Ann, who killed her, and what happened to the murderer, the madder I got. And then it hit me. The townspeople weren't keeping a secret from each other; they were keeping it from me; the New York outsider.

Stuck, and with nothing to say, it was time for me to move on.

"Take care, Mr. Porter, best to your family," I said as I shook his hand and walked to the door to leave.

My next stop was Jesse's Barbecue for lunch. A simple red brick building with a smoker on one side of the building and picnic tables under an enormous oak tree on the other side; a great outdoor spot most any day, except on a frigid day like today. I headed into the dark indoor dining area to grab a table. This place looked as it always did. There was a framed picture on the wall of Jesse and the big buck he killed his senior year in high school. Above the jukebox machine was a picture of the 1965 Johnson County High School football team, which won the district championship. Displayed prominently above the bar was a signed picture from Coach Fulmer, the head football coach of the Tennessee Volunteers, and the Ten Commandments framed for all to see.

I recognized most everyone in the place, and based on their staring at me, most people knew who I was, but no one came over to say hello. It is a strange form of isolation to be among people you grew up with, who are choosing to avoid you like you're the carrier of some obscure, contagious disease. My arrival converted a joyous gathering into awkward silence. I was thirty years old, and yet, felt the insecurity of a seven-year-old walking into a classroom of strangers. In this moment, I felt more alone than I thought possible.

It wasn't until Jesse walked over, with a messy kitchen towel draped over his shoulder, and a welcoming smile that the ice broke.

"RJ, good to see you, bud. I hear ya, you here for a while?"

"That's the plan. It is good to be back."

"Great, get yourself some ribs; they're as good as ever."

Thanks to Jesse and his warm welcome, the mood in the restaurant changed. He broke a seal and gave locals permission to say hello.

Regardless of my strained past and fractured relationships with the people I grew up with, by the end of lunch, I had talked with everyone in the building and promised to find time to have dinner with most of them. These people were warm, but they were guarded. They hadn't decided if I had become an outsider not to be trusted.

As I was leaving Jesse's, I bumped into my best friend from high school, Mark Wheeling. We hadn't seen each other in years; we hadn't ended on an unpleasant note, we just failed to stay in touch. For as long as I could remember, Mark and I were always in trouble — nothing bad, just country boys being country boys. As I think back on every misadventure during my teens, Mark was always there. We were inseparable and always in the thick of some mischief.

We put the cows in the principal's backyard the day he left town for a weeklong trip to Myrtle Beach. Cows can leave countless large, unwanted deposits in a confined space if given a week. And that is exactly what they did. They fulfilled their minimal task and soiled the yard. When the principal returned home, he was disturbed to see the yard full of cow dung. At least we had removed the cows before he got home.

It was also us who let the air out of the tires of those attending a PTA meeting to discuss male students and their long hair. It was funny, but our resistance failed, as a mandate that boys trim their hair soon followed. I didn't mind the haircut; I just didn't like being told what to do.

Our most famous prank involved us being the ringleaders in organizing the effort to move the desks in school from their classrooms to the roof of the basketball gym; an impressive feat accomplished by our senior class the last week of classes. It took us all night to accomplish this childish activity and included most of the forty members of the graduating class. I doubt there was a senior prank that was better executed, more hilarious, or more despised by the faculty at Johnson County High School.

Before Mark sat down for a plate of pulled pork barbecue, I mentioned he should come out to the farm so we could catch up. "I would like that," he said.

We shook hands and smiled at each other, hoping we both meant it. Sitting in my car outside Jesse's, I thought back to my time in Johnson County, and the fun I shared with Mark. Seeing Mark reminded me that this place made me who I am. I'm glad I remembered that.

Having nothing to do was a foreign concept when I lived in New York. In the short few months I had been home, that had all changed. I was enjoying no schedule, no cell phone, no overbearing boss, and no noise; I liked my new routine. Instead of heading back to the farm after lunch, I drove aimlessly around town with no clear agenda other than to take it all in. I tuned the radio to 102.9, *The Mountain*, a classic country station, and sang along to Merle, Waylon, Willie, and George songs without a care in the world.

Merle Haggard's "*That's the Way Love Goes*" blared through my speakers; it was a perfect song.

> *I've been throwing horseshoes*
> *Over my left shoulder*
> *I've spent most all my life*
> *Searching for that four-leaf clover*
> *Yet you ran with me*
> *Chasing rainbows*
> *Honey, I love you too*
> *That's the way love goes*

It was one of the best afternoons I had spent in a long time.

The day gave me strength. Enough strength to get the courage up to stop by Alice's house in town to see if I could talk to her. Alice lived in a small cottage on North Church Street, close to the center of Mountain City. I hadn't been to her house but had driven by there a few times, hoping by chance I would see her in the yard and could act like I stumbled upon her. I wasn't stalking her; I missed her.

Pulling up to the cute little wood-framed cottage, I noticed Alice's car parked in the driveway. If there ever was a time to explain my actions to Alice, it was now.

Before I could get the nerve to knock on her door, a rush of emotion overcame me. Years of running from home, from Alice, from everyone filled my mind. For the first time, I could see the stakes this meeting represented. The apprehension the rest of the community had about me and my return bothered me, but I could work through that. A rejection by

Alice would be a blow that would last my entire life. I had to reconnect with her.

After two knocks, Alice opened the door. I startled her, and she didn't know what to do or say. I broke the ice. "Hey Alice, it is nice to see you."

It was a weak opening line, but graciously Alice regained her composure and replied, "Nice to see you, RJ."

I wanted an invitation to come inside, but Alice didn't seem willing to offer that next step. Stuck in the moment's awkwardness, I said, "Can we sit on your front porch for a moment?"

Begrudgingly, she agreed.

I was wondering whether Alice still cared for me. Her demeanor offered little hope. She was furious. The memory of my leaving her twelve years ago, without explanation, was fresh in her mind.

Small talk being the norm on a southern porch didn't fit the mood. Neither of us wanted a friendly chat.

Breaking the silence, Alice said, "RJ, why are you here?"

She didn't mean in town; she meant on her front porch.

With a breaking voice, reflecting my emotional state, I said, "Alice, I owe you an apology. More than that, I owe you an explanation."

Alice said nothing; her expression confirmed my statement but offered no concession. She was right; this was on me, and I had to do the talking. Something I hadn't done when I ignored her and failed to respond to her pleas years before.

"What I did was terrible. I was so eager to escape this place I forgot what I was leaving. I loved you, but I didn't act like it; I don't know what I was doing. Leaving you was the biggest mistake in my life."

I still loved Alice; but now wasn't the time to say that. Words were hollow, at least my words were hollow to Alice. I created that lack of trust, and it would be up to me to regain it, if I could.

My initial salvo to explain was lacking; she needed more.

"When I was at UT, I experienced the world beyond these mountains, and it was exciting. I got caught up in what was out there and forgot myself. It was like a drug, and I was an addict. When you allow yourself to get consumed by outside forces, it is hard to break away and regain your balance. Leaving for New York, in my mind, wasn't about leaving you. It was about my selfish need to make the world about me."

Alice stared at me. My words would not eliminate her pain, but maybe my heartfelt explanation would soften her view.

Finally, Alice spoke up. "Why didn't you take me with you to New York? You never asked if I wanted to go."

Her question stung me to my core. She was getting at my worst secret.

"Alice, I am sorry about this, but I had grown to believe I was better than my past. I didn't ask you to join me because I thought you couldn't handle the big city."

I knew those words hurt, but I had to be honest. A small tear fell from Alice's left eye. I felt crushed. My being here was making it worse.

"Alice, I now know I was wrong. Not that you didn't belong in New York. My mistake was that I didn't belong in New York. I belonged here, with you."

"Please forgive me."

There wasn't much left to say. I had said all I could, and Alice had listened without yelling at me. We sat silently for a few minutes wondering what was next. It was Alice who broke the silence.

"Thanks for coming by. I appreciate it. I am glad you are back in town," she said with a faint smile on her face.

"Alice, I can't express how much I appreciate you saying that. This is where I belong."

Standing up to leave the normal southern habit of hugging seemed like too much. Instead, I smiled at her and said, "I hope to see you again soon."

She nodded affirmation and turned to walk back into her house.

I did it. The truth, which had been unspoken for years, finally came out. The simple act of telling Alice the truth lifted my spirits. It also gave me hope that there could be a future with her. My drive home reflected my hopeful enthusiasm. I rekindled my life with Alice. I couldn't ask for more.

Back at the farm, Winston greeted me with his customary enthusiasm; having slept most of the day on the front porch, he was ready to go for a walk. Open space, and life without a collar had transformed Winston into a curious, playful friend who embarked on every walk with energy and gusto. If he were lucky, he would stumble across a critter and give it a vigorous forty-five second chase.

Our walks were a daily occurrence, with no limit to where we would go; we loved to walk along Laurel Creek. The creek was cold. The water temperature was always in the fifties, but Winston didn't mind. He still found the gumption to stand in small eddies for a drink while he gazed down into the water, hoping to see a fish darting about.

Despite our tendency to meander to the creek, today Winston led me across the hayfield toward Ramsey's Creek

Trail. I hadn't been on the trail since I followed Momma up on her last day. The memory of our last walk together and what she told me had been too fresh to revisit the day. Winston seemed eager to travel a fresh path, and I willingly followed him.

My day in town had left me comforted and in good spirits. There was no sense of dread or anxiety in climbing the path up the mountain. I soon realized that I had temporarily sealed away the complex feelings of what I had learned about Sue Ann. However, I did not lose them, and my heart raced as I got closer to the site where Momma had built a small monument to Sue Ann's last moments. I am not sure what I thought I would feel when I saw the stacked stones with a cross painted on one of them, but I didn't expect the flood of tears and emotion that followed. I was still despondent over: the loss of Momma, my loneliness, my guilt and confusion over the mystery that was Sue Ann's murder. Years of pent-up feelings I had suppressed as I faded farther from my past came bursting out. I needed a good cry, and that day on the mountain, I let it all out. Unsure how to react, Winston did what every good dog would do. He cuddled up next to my legs and licked my hand.

20

The First Snow

T HE ROOSTER'S POWER WAS GONE, NO LONGER DID HIS early morning wake-up call get me moving nor encourage Winston to rise from his slumber at the foot of the bed; he was quickly becoming an old farm dog, and I was getting used to slow starts to the day. However, the first snow of the new year made me want to get up this morning. I love snow and seeing it fall softly out my window. I was eager to move, hurrying to get dressed, scampering downstairs to get my coffee brewing, and a coat on; I wanted to spend the morning in my front porch rocking chair.

Snow in these parts brings a pronounced silence to the mountains, as though every living creature takes wonder at the beauty. The only noticeable sound is the gentle landing of each snowflake, first on the leaves on the ground and then as the snowpack builds on top of the growing snow-covered landscape. Low-hanging clouds block the view of the mountaintops, but the bare trees, void of their leaves, open the eye-level horizon, and you can see points of the farm and surrounding woods normally hidden from view.

As I sipped my JFG Coffee, I quietly took in the scene before me. The sky was dropping snowflakes on this tiny farm; the world around me was changing, turning into its own postcard, one flake at a time. Time stood still. For a minute this morning felt like the most peaceful moment in my life; I was alone, with my thoughts, my dog, in the house I grew up in, consumed by the beauty of the morning and nothing else. As I watched the evolving snowpack, I had a brief flashback to my first snowfall in New York. I was so excited. Before my first Manhattan snow, I had imagined how fun it would be for a winter storm to blanket the city, with thousands of people escaping their studio apartments to play in nature. It was my childlike personality driving my enthusiasm for a day frolicking in the snow; of course, that wasn't the case. New Yorkers saw snow as a hassle, an annoyance that infringed on their busy lives and never-ending need for movement; snow didn't create peace, it created anxiety, and noise. Horns blared more frequently; snowplows roared down every street. The city had declared war on one of my favorite childhood joys and delivered a reminder that I wasn't in Johnson County.

With memories of New York behind me, this morning leisurely passed with little excitement; even a nearby chipmunk bounding in front of the porch couldn't interest Winston enough to cause him to pursue; Winston having decided the view from the porch was better, and dryer. The transition from morning to lunchtime went unnoticed, and with the snow showing little signs of slowing, I was content. My stomach had other ideas and forced me to move inside to grab a quick bite; I had a pot of pinto beans from the day before that were waiting to be warmed. Pinto beans were perfect on a day like this, and one thing I could cook that's close to the quality of Momma's cooking; all I needed was beans, an onion, some bacon, black pepper and salt, and I had a meal. My mastery of pinto beans aside, Momma didn't leave handwritten recipes, nor had she taught me to cook, but I was trying, and could now cook beyond barely edible, to good enough. Maybe someday I will figure out how to make cornbread and chow chow to go with my hearty beans.

I didn't know this until I moved up north, but chow chow is a uniquely Southern staple. Made with vegetables from the garden, farmers made chow chow to preserve summer vegetables for year-round enjoyment. Momma made a slightly spicy chow chow, and it always topped her pinto beans. Maybe I thought, James will know how she made her chow chow and can teach me.

A full stomach and a roaring fire in the fireplace led me to the first-floor study and my favorite high-back leather chair. I settled into the receptive chair without a care in the world or a desire to find one. And then a passing thought reminded me of my walk the day before up the Ramsey Creek Trail, which turned my attention to Sue Ann. Suddenly I had to know more about what happened to Sue Ann. If I were honest, no matter how hard I tried, I couldn't cast aside my curiosity; it was always lurking in my head. That meant I had to go back to Momma's cedar chest and look closer.

Standing up from my chair, I glanced over to see if Winston intended to follow me; unmoved; he opened his eyes to acknowledge he saw me, but didn't so much as raise his head. I was on my own. The sense of anticipation and apprehension I felt the first time I opened the chest was gone. I knew what was inside. This was more of a mission than an exploration; my demeanor reflected my intent.

It was immediately obvious to me the significance of the neatly folded dress placed at the bottom of the chest. There could be no other explanation; it had to be Sue Ann's. Not a Sunday-fancy dress with lace and a high collar, this dress was more every day; and yet, it was still beautiful. Along with its beauty, the garment before me looked practical, something a proper girl would wear to school, or while doing chores on the farm. Farm living compelled practicality. Sunday clothes were for Sunday. The rest of the time, you could look nice, but there was no time for idle hands. The dress conveyed that mindset, and why wouldn't it? Momma obviously gave it to Sue Ann, and she was well known for practicing measured practicality.

As I leaned inside the chest and stared at the dress, I noticed a tear in the fabric across the left shoulder, and a sharp burst of energy shot through my temple. For the first time, I realized I was looking at the dress Sue Ann wore when she was murdered. Overcome with sadness, I pushed away from the opening of the cedar chest and glanced across the room. Did I really need to uncover hidden truths about Sue Ann's murder?

Predictably, the answer was yes. I wanted to know what had happened. No, I needed to know what happened. She was the sister I never knew, and her life, and murder had impacted my family in ways I hadn't explored; it was now impacting me. If I were to truly understand my past and family, I would have to know what happened; there was no going back.

I carefully reached in and pulled out the open shoebox and its stack of neatly bound papers and set it aside on the floor. I then picked up the envelope and set it to the side of the box. Next, I reached in and pulled out the dress with both hands, one on each shoulder, and held up the dress in front of me, holding it high enough to see its full length. Within a split second, I saw a large stain on the dress just below the waistline; it looked like dried blood. "Dear God, no."

I had never considered before how someone had murdered her or what had happened to her. It was all I could do to process that she had died by someone else's hands. A new secret was now exposed. If I were to go further, I would have to know about her last moments; the blood stain told me something very dark was within that secret. There were no tears, no emotions. I sat motionless for a long time, processing what I was holding.

In time, I neatly folded the dress and placed it back inside the chest. I was likely never to look at it again. I wasn't trained to consider clues, nor was there anything more for me to learn from the dress; it had told me all I needed to know and didn't need to know. My stomach felt ill, I was lightheaded and overwhelmed with disgust; it took time for me to recover. I am sure Momma and Daddy never did.

Moving on from Sue Ann's dress, I wanted to see what was inside the envelope. Picking it up off the floor, I unfolded the flap and opened the top of the envelope, reaching inside to pull out a handwritten letter. Sheriff Willis Cogburn signed the letter, which was dated October 28, 1964. It read:

> *Nita,*
>
> *I am troubled by your loss and sorry that you and your family are enduring this pain. No one should have lost a child like this. And what a special child she was. Sue Ann was loved by all. She brought a smile to every room she was in. We are all worse off having lost her beautiful spirit.*
>
> *As I told you last night, I will find the person who did*

*this and make sure justice is served. You can count on me
not to rest until we make this right.*
I am praying for you.
Sincerely,
Willis Cogburn III

Sheriff Coburn's rise to his position as chief law enforcement officer in Johnson County was an ordained ascension. His father and grandfather had both worn the sheriff's badge, having served the county since before the turn of the century. It was only natural that the people would elect Willis Cogburn III after his father retired. Sheriff Willis Cogburn III — his friends called him Willie — an army veteran having served in Europe, was twenty-five the day he took over in the Spring of 1949 following a landslide vote—the only votes for the challenger were from known moonshiners, who were seeking someone else to run from other than a Cogburn.

When it came time to elect the third Cogburn, the citizens of the county had no reason to depart from the Cogburn family, since 1888 a Cogburn had been in charge. The elder Cogburns had managed reconstruction, a growth spell in the county's population after the turn of the century, the depression, and the war years, when most every young man was gone. For the first two Cogburn, their tenure was unremarkable; nothing much happened that would interest a sheriff or its townsfolk. That is except for the murder of Lilly Shaw on October 22, 1903.

Lilly was twenty-two, well known to most folks in the county, and the mother of two small kids: a result of a marriage to a man three times her age.

Lilly disappeared while walking to Mountain City after

having spent the evening with farmer McQueen. Retracing the steps Lilly took to town, Sherrif Cogburn discovered her lifeless body.

Acting on a hunch and with no evidence, the sheriff focused his attention on Finley Preston. The boy he never trusted and worried was capable of heinous acts. An unannounced visit to the Preston homestead discovered Lilly's bloody dress hidden in the attic.

The sheriff scheduled a speedy trial for the guilty party. Time was wasting, and people wanted justice. The jury found Finley guilty of killing Lilly, and the judge sentenced him to hang on November 7th, 1905. It was a big event for such a small town. The state sent a professional hangman from Knoxville, and builders constructed temporary seating areas for the crowd that gathered to watch the doomed man die. It felt like most of the county turned out along with people who traveled from parts outside the area to witness the execution. Annoyed by all the attention, Sheriff Cogburn said, "We should have quickly handled this ourselves quickly."

Despite the circus-like atmosphere, the day's events progressed in an orderly fashion. As was the practice, they allowed the condemned a chance to say one last thing, and history records that he said, "A great crowd is now gathered around the jail today to see my execution, and hear what I have to say. I must die on this scaffold for murdering poor Lilly Shaw. That others might see me die and learn respect for the law. Take warning, thoughtless people. Remember what I say: if you sin against your maker, you're sure to rue the day. I've begged him for forgiveness, upon my bended knees. And I am going home to heaven, forgiven and at ease." The crowd listened silently with rapt attention and seriousness to Finley's last words. When he was done, and without more fanfare, the hangman pulled the lever and Finley was no more. The hanging of Finley Preston was the last state-sanctioned hanging; the electric chair became the preferred option for the State of Tennessee.

Since the hanging in 1905, keeping peace in this mountain county rarely generated much excitement, and the first Cogburn retired as a respected member of the community. For Willis Cogburn II, there was an occasional fight out at Bobby's tavern, and every once in a while someone would pass through town with nefarious intentions, but mostly the county was quiet. It was just the way he and the townsfolk liked it. Sheriff Cogburn III saw the wisdom of keeping things calm, and he was determined to follow in the footsteps of his father and grandfather. He had heard all about the murder of Lilly Shaw; hearing his father tell the story of how his daddy had found the killer and delivered justice. Not big on performance, Willie Cogburn was determined never to let a tragedy, like the killing of Lilly Shaw, become a spectacle in his town. God forbid anything like that ever occur. When there was policing activity, the sheriff preferred to handle things internally, hoping to keep the judge bored and the matter discrete; he grew up knowing right and wrong. He possessed an uncommon amount of common sense. Sheriff Cogburn understood the people in the county and respected their trials and struggles. He believed people shouldn't overthink or complicate problems that could be handled easily in the traditional way. He was a believer in swift justice. With a family legacy, an understanding of the county's history, and a tendency to solve things himself, Sheriff Cogburn was the perfect person to solve Sue Ann's crime and deliver Johnson County justice.

As ringleaders of local pranks and foolhardy attempts to be funny, my buddy Mark and I had our fair share of run-ins with Sheriff Willie Cogburn. Most notably, the sheriff didn't care for our failed master plan to divert traffic around town to allow us to throw an impromptu high school party. It was the late eighties, and we were bored. Having gained access to a keg, we were feeling bold. Looking back, it was a flawed plan from the start; combine teenagers with too much beer, and you get stupid, and we were that. We had barely begun passing out the solo cups to the gathering group of Johnson County High School students when Sheriff Cogburn walked up and quietly asked if he could have a word with me. Never one to shy away from a buzz-induced conversation, I gladly shuffled his way. He didn't arrest me or any of my co-conspirators, true to his style, he gathered us together and secured rides home for each of us with his small number of deputies. To his thinking, having us arrive home in the backseat of a police car and escorted to the door by a man with a badge would deliver the message and ensure our parents had the ammunition necessary to get their point across. As Sheriff Cogburn guided me to the front door, Daddy and Momma were sitting in their favorite rocking chairs passing the night away. Noticing my parents off to the right, Sheriff Cogburn redirected his path and led me straight to Daddy. With a gentle push of my shoulder, the Sheriff handed me off to Daddy and said, "Frankie, if he gives you any trouble, let me know. I'll see you Sunday at church, ya'll have a nice evening."

I would have preferred to be arrested.

I appreciate the sheriff's style. He rooted his belief in our ability to take care of ourselves and our own. He knew we might all have moments that weren't too impressive, no need to overdo everything. If you did something wrong, you paid for it and, if you could, moved on from it.

I hadn't seen the sheriff in years, but heard he was still kicking at the tender age of seventy-six, living quietly at home with his eldest, widowed daughter, Debbie. The passage of Cogburn sheriffs to the next generation ended with the third Willis Cogburn. A father of five, he had the numbers to find a suitable replacement, regretfully; they were all girls, and after having tried for a decade to have a boy join the brood, his wife's wisdom prevailed, when she decided enough was enough. They would have girls, and the sheriff had no choice but to accept it.

Since Cogburn became sheriff, his wife gently convinced him the rundown cabin they lived in was no longer adequate. Determined to please his wife, the newly minted sheriff purchased the home and moved his growing family into the two thousand square feet, two-story home. A nondescript white farmhouse with a proud front porch, green windowpanes, and a red front door. They immediately planted roots and added three more daughters to the household.

On most nights, you could pass the Cogburn home and see the sheriff and his wife sitting on the front porch swing, intently talking, as he slowly smoked his daily cigar. "Evening, Sheriff," everyone who walked by his house gladly greeted him, to which he always replied, "Evening, ain't it a beautiful day?"

It was a predictable scene, as certain as the sun setting in the western sky; and it brought routine joy to the people of Mountain City; so much so that most people would make sure their evening walk included a stroll by Cogburn's place.

Soon after his retirement from the sheriff's office, Sheriff Cogburn's wife passed away from a stroke. It was a blow to

Willie. Having been married for over fifty years, and having raised five daughters, he was used to having a woman's touch in his life, and now he was desperately alone. It wasn't long before life became dark for Sheriff Cogburn, and the towns-folk became worried about him. Just when it looked like the sheriff was fading away, his oldest daughter's husband died in an accident at the steam plant. Grieving the loss of her husband and feeling unexpectedly lonely, Debbie turned her attention to her daddy and moved back into the house where she was raised. That was ten years ago.

21

A Feeble Old Man

"Hello, is Sheriff Cogburn available?" I asked. "Who is this?" was the sweet response.

"Oh, I'm sorry, this is RJ Burnette, Frankie and Nita's youngest boy."

"Hey RJ, this is Debbie. Didn't recognize your voice." Debbie responded like we had been close friends for years.

"Daddy's resting right now and can't talk."

"I understand, say I was wondering, could I come by and say hello to your dad sometime? It would be great to see him." I asked.

"Sure, RJ, any afternoon between one and three works great. I am sure he would love to see you. He loves visitors."

I hung up the phone with dread and anxiety. I wondered out loud, "Is this a good idea?" drumming up old memories and asking people to fill in the gaps my family had left me. Maybe nobody wanted to talk about the murder of Sue Ann; maybe the entire community was in on the organized deception, and I would never know; maybe there was a good reason the truth should stay buried. Regardless, I was forging ahead, undeterred and committed to filling in the blanks. I was being selfish, practicing a skill I learned to compete for big dollars and pride.

It made sense to seek the sheriff's version of what happened. After all, in his letter, he promised Momma he would rest only after he made this right. Did he deliver justice? What did he do? Surely, he will answer my questions.

It was a cold, dreary day when I pulled into the sheriff's driveway. Not cold enough to snow, but close. It was a day befitting my mood. I hadn't slept the night before; the house and my soul felt empty. Every time I conjured up a memory of my childhood intended to bring me joyful thoughts, doubts and fears of what had really gone on drowned it out. What secrets did they keep from me? I was so young compared to my siblings that I wasn't a part of the core nuclear family, and I was just now figuring it out? I had returned to Johnson County feeling like an outsider running from the life I had been living. Maybe I had always been an outsider.

Unable to move, I sat in the Cogburn driveway shaking, not from the cold, but from fear; my body was trembling, and I couldn't stop it. I wanted to flee, to run from what I might learn. I wanted to leave, but I couldn't; there was no turning back. Eventually, I gathered myself, opened my car door, shuffled my way up the front steps, and gently knocked on the door. In a flash, the door swung open, and Debbie greeted me, smiling from ear to ear.

"Come in, RJ; you must be freezing to death." I was cold, and I am sure she assumed that is why I was shaking, but it wasn't the temperature that had me rattled.

"Can I get you a cup of coffee, or maybe some hot chocolate? You need something to warm you." Debbie offered.

"Coffee would be great," I said.

As I hung my coat on the hallway hanger, I glanced up to see an inviting fire in the room off to the right; seated comfortably next to the fire was the sheriff. He had a quilt draped over his legs, worn-out brown slippers covering his feet, peeking out of the bottom of the blanket. He was wearing a hand-stitched sweater, a 4H hat covering his white hair. While gazing at the flames, he neatly crossed his hands on his lap. He hadn't heard me enter the house, or was so comforted by the fire, he didn't feel the need to look in my direction. He appeared older than his age, older than I expected. His face was drawn in, and he stared at the fire with the expression that is typical of elderly men. A frozen face stuck in a painful expression. Not knowing what to do, I stood motionless in the hall waiting for Debbie and the coffee.

I briefly lost myself in thought while staring at the sheriff. He didn't necessarily physically remind me of Momma or Daddy but seeing him propped in the chair and wrapped up to stay warm; caused me to reflect on the passage of time; how my parents had aged and how diminished a person became as the days moved from one to the next. I felt a tinge of sadness, and in that moment, wanted to hug Momma and Daddy.

I didn't notice Debbie standing next to me until she handed me my cup and said, "Come on in. I will tell him you are here."

"Daddy, you have a guest. This is RJ, Frankie and Nita's boy. You remember him, don't ya Daddy?"

As if snapped out of a trance, the sheriff looked up, eyes turning to my face, his skin brightening, and his previously stone-faced expression gone; with enthusiasm, Cogburn said, "RJ, how are you? So good to see you. Come sit here next to me and let's talk."

He instantly looked ten years younger.

"Sorry to hear about your momma, RJ; she was a fine lady," the sheriff offered.

"Thanks, Sheriff, I really miss her."

"How are you feeling, Sheriff?"

"I'm fine, just slower than I used to be, but my mind is as sharp as ever. Just don't use it as much as I used to."

We talked for thirty minutes about everything and nothing at all, all at the same time. We followed a simple ritual of southern communication; some gossip, a dab of storytelling, a little exaggeration, and lots of talk about family, food, church and sports, and oh yes, some down-home jokes.

"RJ, did your daddy ever tell you about his fear of standing on a stage to speak?"

"No, he never did."

"Yea, bout twenty years ago, he was supposed to introduce me from the stage in the gym. Prior to people showing up, we were standing on the stage, and he said the scene reminded him of the platform his uncle was standing on back home when tragedy struck."

"Not yet finished with his story, your Daddy looked me in the eye and said."

"Willie, he was standing upright on a stage just like this when all the sudden the floor below him gave way. It was a terrible sight. We all believed he'd broken his legs had it not been for that rope around his neck."

This old story caused uncontrollable laughter for the sheriff; he laughed from his toes. It was good for him, and it was good for me. Home-spun tales are a part of mountain heritage; laughter feeds the soul; I missed laughing at silly tales.

I learned that Daddy and the sheriff went on an annual

three-day hunt for feral hogs using hound dogs from the sheriff's cousin.

"We'd leave out of your place and work our way up to the top of the mountain range and then head north till we hit the state line; we covered a lot of ground in three days."

"Feral hogs are a problem, and the only way to manage the problem is to hunt them down. Hound dogs can track them, but they had to be careful not to get too close; feral hogs are mean, and they are dangerous."

"Your daddy was accurate with his rifle, and he was relentless chasing them damn hogs. We were always successful and had fun doing it." Cogburn said with a pleasant smile.

"Meat on em wasn't too bad. Made for a good stew."

"Those were some of my favorite days here in these mountains. That and our special snipe hunt."

I knew what this meant, but didn't know it was a frequent event.

"Every so often we would welcome a new neighbor to our town by taking them out for a snipe hunt. It wasn't nice, but no harm was done. It sure was fun." The Sheriff winked when he said it.

A snipe hunt involves taking an unsuspecting victim out to the middle of nowhere and strategically positioning them to grab the fleeing snipe when it goes stumbling by. The snipe is running from the band of locals who have spent the evening out hunting and driving the terrified two-legged creature to the waiting net of the new resident. Described as about eight inches tall, a snipe reportedly most closely resembles a roadrunner.

After hours of waiting, the lonely net holder hears yelling and screaming approaching his location. Not wanting to disappoint his new friends, the outsider always gets anxious and energized for the chance to grab the bugger. He has a lot at stake; he doesn't want to fail and be ridiculed. Eventually the band of locals shows up, all excited to see the snipe the victim of the prank has caught. They go on yapping for a while about how the snipe ran right past him and how come he didn't see it. The prank having been successfully executed; the locals joyfully reenact the scene at the expense of the failed snipe hunter.

As they slowly make their way back to the truck, the pranksters let the new guy in on the story. There is no such thing as a snipe. They weren't chasing anything; they were drinking beer at the truck. The whole affair was all in good clean fun. And it is. I have done a few of those dangerous snipe hunts myself, and they are always a good time. Unless you spend all night waiting for something that doesn't exist.

Even though I didn't have a close relationship with the sheriff, it felt like I was spending time with family. The moments shared with friends like this in my little mountain community always felt like they were family. I guess we were extended family because we shared a lifestyle, way of thinking, and history, which closely bonded us.

The engaged banter with the sheriff relaxed me, overriding the initial fear I had to ask about Sue Ann, but that is why I came and after a while, I decided it was time to see if the sheriff would tell me what happened.

"Sheriff, the day Momma died, she took me to the location where Sue Ann was murdered." I said in a low tone.

I noticed his face stiffen, and the prior smile fade.

"She didn't tell me what happened, and I hadn't known this was how Sue Ann died." I continued.

"The other day, I found a note in Momma's cedar chest from you. You told her you would make it right and find who killed Sue Ann."

"Were you able to solve the case? Did my family get justice?" I asked in a harsher tone than I had intended.

The sheriff turned his stare away from me and back to the fire.

Unsure how to react to his mood shift, I asked him directly, "Do you remember Sue Ann's murder and the note to Momma?"

A long pause filled the room. The sheriff was calculating in his mind what to say, and he wasn't in a hurry to figure it out. After what seemed like five minutes, he returned his face to me and said, "RJ, that was a long time ago, and I don't really remember any of it. I am sorry."

That couldn't be true. He had spent the last thirty minutes proving that his mind was sharp. He had regaled me with reflections of memorable moments we shared and of times he had with my family before I arrived. How could he now claim not to remember the single biggest police activity during his entire tenure? It wasn't believable. I could tell he knew I was on to him; his attempt to suggest the events had slipped his mind hadn't worked.

Finally, owning up to his effort to deceive, the sheriff said, "RJ, we all buried what happened decades ago, and the county has moved on. I know it must be hard for you, but you should let it go. It would be best for you, and all involved. I am sorry, but that's all I'm going to say about it."

Stunned, I looked at him and wondered what to say. He had effectively silenced me and told me I would be better off remaining in the dark, despite him knowing the truth.

The sheriff looked shaken by my inquiries. I felt bad because I had disrupted his peaceful afternoon. But his response wasn't good enough. "Sheriff, I am sorry to bother you about this, but why are you keeping this from me?"

He bristled at my pushing him. "RJ." His voice rose as he spoke.

"When I was a young man, I pledged an oath to protect this community, and I might be a feeble old man, but I intend to protect it until the day I die. Now, if you don't mind, I need to rest for a bit."

My composure shaken, I stood and reached out to shake the sheriff's hand; however, that didn't seem adequate. Leaning forward, I wrapped my arms around his shoulders and gave him a hug. It was an odd thing to do, and yet a natural response. Even though he avoided my question, and despite my disappointment with his lack of forthrightness, he looked like he could use a hug, and in these parts we always hug.

"Sheriff, thanks for your time and for all the times you set me straight," I said as I pulled away from him.

"You bet; don't be a stranger."

As I turned to leave, I saw Debbie standing at the hall entrance; she had a broken smile on her face and tears running down her cheeks; she needed a hug too. As I reached forward, she said, "thanks RJ. I know this doesn't seem fair, but it is best."

My sadness and confusion turned to rage as I turned the key to start my car. Why the hell does everyone seem to think it best if the past stays hidden? Maybe this isn't about me and keeping me in the dark; maybe it's about never revisiting what happened in Johnson County in the fall of 1964. Whatever happened all those years ago, it seems maintaining my ignorance isn't the only driving force behind the secret. The people in my hometown have a secret, and they are determined to keep it locked away.

22

Not From Around Here

THE FIRST THAW AFTER A LONG WINTER PROVIDED energy to find answers, an obsessive, all-consuming focus that never left my mind. It was like an annoying song that repeated itself in my head on perpetual replay; nothing could distract me. Something happened, more than Sue Ann being murdered, and whatever it was, it united everyone in this town around a common cause. Thirty-six years later, no one was wavering or talking.

"This is bullshit," I said, slamming my hand against the railing on the front porch.

"Who were they trying to protect? Me?"

I could handle it, or at least I thought I could.

By the time the sun rose above the ridgeline, my heart rate had slowed, and I considered rationally what I should do. Foremost in my mind was the nagging question that I was missing something obvious. I had learned over my brief career that sometimes; hard answers are right in front of you and not that difficult to find. It is easy to overreact, to confuse yourself, to fall into a hopeless circle with no way out. Maybe I did that now. It was possible the answer of why people were resistant to telling the truth was clear, and I was too close to see it. Or maybe this is the way it is in Johnson County; secrets, like people, have a way of disappearing in these parts, never to be heard of again. Many things have happened in these hills that those on the other side of these mountains will never learn about. It is a protective measure; what happens here stays here.

With little direction or idea of how to proceed, I called an old friend I met at college; I heard he was in law enforcement in Knoxville, maybe he would have advice.

"Hello Stack, is that you?" I didn't know his actual name when I met him; everyone called him by that nickname, and I never heard him called anything else. I was told it had to do with his impressive ability to stack spent beer cans against the wall as a monument to his drunken frivolity; that story was as good as any.

"Uh, yeah, I guess. Who is this?" he replied, taken aback to be called a name he hadn't heard in a while and was trying to forget.

"Sorry, man, this is RJ." How you doin?

"Hey bud," Stack shot back, relaxed to hear his old nickname was from his past and not some recent friend giving him grief.

I jumped right into my problem, but I shared few details with Stack. I wasn't trying to be coy; without thinking, I was practicing the same mindset I was fighting — a strong aversion to opening up. He didn't mind, nor even act like he noticed.

Finally, I said, "Stack, if you were trying to learn about a murder from over thirty years ago, where would look?"

"That's tough bud, you might find details in old newspapers, but those might be hard to get your hands on," he said.

"The best source of information would have to come from the local police department files. If they have kept their records for that long, they would certainly have a file with everything they knew about the case."

"Well, that makes sense," I said.

"Say, RJ, is there anything I can help you with?" he offered with a note of concern.

"No Stack, I'm good, thanks though."

"I hear ya RJ, just let me know."

"Will do, Stack. By the way, I've moved back to Tennessee. I am living outside Mountain City. If you are ever up this way, let me know and we can go fly-fishing. The Watauga and South Holston both hold some great trout."

"Thanks, bud, appreciate it. Welcome home."

I found it hard to believe the sheriff's office would keep records of an event that no one would talk about; but it was the best idea I had.

Fresh off another lousy night of sleep and with nothing to do at home, I drove over to the Johnson County sheriff's office. It hadn't changed; it looked the same as it always had. The only difference being the entry sign on the front door didn't have a Cogburn listed as sheriff. That honor went to Sheriff Blountville Crawford, a transplant from Elizabethton, about thirty miles southwest of here.

A friendly face greeted me when I opened the front door. It was my old buddy Boone Dixon standing behind the counter dressed in an oversized deputy uniform that belonged on an XL man; Boone was decidedly diminutive. Ten years apart hadn't dimmed our jovial connection, and we immediately started smiling.

"I heard you were in town and planning on staying," Boone said.

"That is awesome news. Really glad you're back."

"Thanks, it is good to be home. I don't think I am going anywhere soon."

I shot back, surprised to hear myself openly and publicly repeating that I was home for the long haul.

"RJ, what do I owe for the pleasure of your stopping by today? You havin a problem out at your place?" Boone inquired.

"No, nothing like that. I was just hoping to meet the new sheriff and ask him a quick question."

"Sure thing, let me get him."

He said as he hurried down the hall. Not two minutes later, Boone and Sheriff Crawford walked down the hall to the lobby.

"Sheriff Crawford, this is RJ Burnette. We went to high school together. He says he wanted to say hello. He also promised me he wouldn't share any secrets from our reckless youth."

Boone laughed loudly as he stepped aside so I could shake the sheriff's hand.

"Nice to meet you sheriff, I recently moved back home and have taken over my old family place since Momma died; I wanted to make sure I said hello." I started.

"Nice to meet you RJ, I thought the world of your momma and daddy. Good people." He responded.

Sheriff Crawford struck me as someone who carried himself differently than Willie Cogburn. He was built sturdy, like the Cogburns, and stood a little under six feet tall with a flat-top haircut. His handshake was firm but didn't have the toughness of the men I grew up with. Originally from Roanoke, Virginia, he attended Virginia Tech before moving to Elizabethton; certainly, no Yankee, but also not from around here.

With little interest in small talk, and not much to connect me to the Sheriff's experience in Mountain City, I blurted out, "Sheriff, I have learned my sister Sue Ann was murdered in the fall of 1964. As you might imagine, I am trying to find out everything I can about the case. I don't know what happened, or who did it, or what became of them. I am wondering whether your office still has a file on this and, if so, can I see it? "

The subdued look on the sheriff's face was immediately replaced with a scowl. He didn't like the question or my attempt to insert myself into a police matter, even if it was three decades old. Boone noticed the change in his boss's stance and glanced at me with a strange gaze, wondering what I was up to.

"RJ, I wish I could help; I really wish I could, but we don't have records from that far back, and I know nothing about the case."

It was his last few words and loss of eye contact that gave him away. He was lying to me; it was obvious. He knew more about what happened than he was pretending.

I was stuck. I knew he wasn't being honest, but I also didn't think I could reasonably accuse him of what I suspected. Not sure what to do and with no ill intent, I stared at him for longer than I should have. Sensing things were off the tracks, Boone jumped in and said, "Hey RJ, I am sure this is hard, but as the sheriff said, if he could help you, he would."

I appreciated Boone and his being there, but something about what he said and the way he said it seemed odd to me; again, I was probably imagining things. Or maybe Boone was on my side and couldn't let on in front of his boss. I could use a break; maybe Boone would be the source of something positive. If he were going to help, it was obvious it wouldn't be today, in this setting.

It was also clear that the current sheriff didn't appreciate my inquiry. He appeared to take offense. His reaction was odd. Why would he have an emotional connection to a story that predated him? He had taken the same oath as Sheriff Cogburn. Was this murder part of that oath? How could the covering up of the details of this murder survive from one sheriff to the next? Whatever the secret was, it was still relevant to the community all these years later.

I had struck out with Cogburn. Now Sheriff Crawford, who was likely not born when Sue Ann was murdered, continued the deception. It was feeling hopeless; the grip of secrecy that can settle in these mountains, like the early morning fog, was firmly in control; it was unrelenting. Without someone trusting me and my remaining core values, I was likely never to learn about my family's past.

I went to bed that evening wondering why my kinfolk and neighbors found comfort in sheltering themselves from painful events and influence from the outside world. What is it they are trying to avoid? Is it a deep insecurity preventing them from exposing their realities to others, or maybe a mistrust of what will happen if they let outsiders have a say about how they live? Was this a remnant of the spectacle that became the hanging of Finley Preston someone hundred years before; a sample of how outside influence can delay judgement, and permit others to observe life in the county?

My obsessive habit of mental gymnastics and what-ifs kept me staring at the ceiling instead of sleeping. Finally, deep in the night, when the birds had fallen asleep, I let go and decided I would move on. I had been fine for the first thirty years of my life, not knowing any of the secrets of the past. I would be fine. It was time to get on with my new life, time to decide what was next for me. I still had work to do to reconnect with family and friends, to show them they could count on me; to reinforce that I was one of them. I was ready to do that. The simple act of waving an imaginary white flag soothed me; it was time for sleep and a new beginning.

23

Breaking and Entering

BOONE HAD OTHER IDEAS. IT DIDN'T SIT WELL WITH HIM the way the sheriff dismissed me. In Boone's way of thinking, I was part of the Johnson County clan and, although the sheriff was a good guy, he was an outsider. Boone knew he could get into trouble if he helped me, but once he got something stuck in his head, he couldn't shake it. Boss be damned. He was going to do something.

Well after dark, Boone drove out to Gizzard's Holler. Not wanting to alert me, he turned off his lights and snuck onto the porch. He had a note he wanted me to see, but the careful side of him thought it better if he didn't hand it to me directly. Once on my porch, he placed the note on the right side of the porch under a big rock he carried from the yard. Satisfied I would find it, he hurried back to his car and drove off into the darkness.

I didn't notice it at first. A normal morning routine meant coffee and a swing on the front porch. It wasn't until Winston walked back from his morning constitution and started sniffing a rock at the other end of the porch that I realized it was there. Immediately curious, I walked over, pushed Winston away, and looked down at what appeared to be a folded legal-size piece of paper. I opened the paper and immediately saw a key taped to the page. Below the key was a handwritten note. Peeling the key away from the paper, I read the note.

"RJ, keep this between us. Hope it helps, Boone."

The note continued, "Down at the sheriff's office there is a basement that used to house inmates. It is nothing but old jail cells. Years ago we stopped using these cells and decided they would be a perfect place to store old case files."

Boone's note had my full attention.

"On the back side of the building, there are stairs that go down to a door, which opens into the basement. No one has opened it in years, but it likely still works."

Boone was taking an enormous risk in giving me this key. And he suggested I take one too. To get the information I wanted, I was going to have to break into the sheriff's office and dig around empty jail cells. There was irony in breaking into a jail cell.

"RJ, please be careful. If you get caught, remember we have never met." Boone's dark humor ended his note.

My instinct was right; Boone wanted to help. Finally, a chance to learn the truth, but my process was not that simple. Just five hours ago, I was giving up on pursuing the truth. Now, anxiety about the unknown thrust me back into an unsettled place. Once again confused about what to do, I tucked the key into my pocket and shuffled back to my swing and still-warm coffee; whatever was inside the box in the sheriff's office could wait. I needed time to collect my thoughts.

Most of the morning passed as I stared at the cemetery across the yard. Looking back, I don't know why I was hesitant; I had been trying to find the truth for a while now, but as I wondered what secrets were in front of me, I wasn't sure I wanted to find the case files and introduce feelings I didn't know existed. I was at peace when I woke up and accepted my reality, if only for a few hours. Now everything was upside again.

I accomplished nothing that day. My mind was in a circular loop, unsure what to do. By late afternoon, without a conscious decision point, I imagined how I was going to pull off this heist.

Not being a seasoned criminal or a thrill seeker, this operation was far outside my comfort zone. My occasional encounters with the local police were high school shenanigans. This was a criminal act, and although I couldn't imagine being charged with a crime, I didn't know. This sheriff wasn't a local. His perspective could have differed from how the Cogburns did things.

My first order of business was to decide when I was going to execute my crime. I concluded I would do it next Sunday night, after midnight. Nothing much happened in Mountain City, but if it did, it wouldn't be on a Sunday night. I suspected there might not even be anyone at the station.

The days passed quickly, and the appointed day arrived whether or not I was ready. I ate a small supper; I had no appetite. Besides, I figured I needed to be nimble in case someone chased me.

Around 1 a.m. I drove into town. There was nothing stirring. Still doubting my idea, I parked a block away from the back lot bordering the sheriff's building. Casually, I walked to the property and jumped the chain-link fence that prevented people from wandering onto the lot. Immediately after scaling the fence, I glanced to my left and saw a gate to the yard. Some criminal I was, I could have opened the gate and walked in.

I ran to the back of the building and quickly descended the stairs to the closed door. My descent wasn't without a challenge. Years of spiderwebs wrapped around me. Without thinking, I cursed out loud.

With a growing sense of fear and anxiety, I put the key in the lock and turned the knob. It worked. The door slid open, and I was inside.

I turned on my flashlight hoping to gain my bearings. What I saw caused me to want to flee. The basement had all the hallmarks of a dungeon. I couldn't imagine anyone had been down here for years. It was also full of boxes, hundreds of boxes. It was overwhelming.

Despite feeling intimidated by the daunting task in front of me, I drew on my gained skills as a New York banker and became laser focused.

I don't know how long I was down there. It is impossible to gauge. But it was longer than I wanted to be. After canvassing two cells with no luck, I was about to flee when I tried one more.

As soon as I pushed open the metal door, I knew I had hit pay dirt. Sitting on the floor to the left, but in front of the other boxes, was a white box. Written on the lid with a black marker was, "Burnette, Sue Ann, October 1964."

I grabbed the box and bolted for the door. Closing the door behind me, I looked in both directions to see if I saw anyone. Certain my path out the back gate was clear, I sprinted to the fence, flung open the gate and hightailed it to my truck.

I could barely catch my breath; I was out of shape. I was

also struggling to process what I had just done and what secrets existed in the box next to me. Without delay, I started the truck and headed for home.

Before I got home, I threw the key out the window. I had heard of killers throwing out the murder weapon, so why not get rid of the evidence of my crime?

Home didn't slow my adrenaline. I was jumpy and nervous. Unable to sleep, I started a fire and tried to ignore the box sitting in front of me.

When the sun finally rose, I was ready. It was time to learn what had happened in 1964. Confident in my resolve, I opened the box.

Inside the box was everything Sheriff Cogburn had collected related to Sue Ann and her murder. It included transcripts of interviews with Grant, Dan, Dillon, James and Ralph. Notes and letters from anyone who knew Sue Ann, and a hand-written confession, found weeks after the murder, from the killer with details of the day; it was a step-by-step description, with supporting documents of what happened. Catching my eye immediately was a thin folder that was yellow and shaped differently than the other folders; inside was a comprehensive summary report written by Sheriff Cogburn. The flowing manuscript of the summary was more suitable for a novel than a police report.

The sheriff's report and the information I gathered over the years enabled me to gain a clear picture of what happened. Where a gap in knowledge existed, some details are based on educated guesses derived from Sue Ann's diary entries leading up to the fateful day. A lot of sources combined to paint the picture as best as possible, but, as I tell my kids the story, I am confident in the portrayal's accuracy.

PART IV

24

Ramsey Creek Trail

Tuesday, October 27th, was a warm day — warm enough for Sue Ann to wear a dress without an overcoat to school. The day started, like all the rest, on the farm; everyone had chores to do. Sue Ann collected the eggs from the coop and made the beds in the house. A relatively light load and one Momma designed for Sue Ann; Momma wanted her to be busy and helpful but focused on school.

At the schoolhouse, Sue Ann and her class noticed their teacher wasn't in the classroom. It was a full thirty minutes after the beginning of the day before she entered the room, clearly not feeling well. Mrs. Sheffield tried to carry on, manage the students, and manage the day, but stomach pain and frequent bathroom visits kept her from continuing. After an hour passed, it was Principal Morgan who decided there was no point in Mrs. Sheffield staying at school, and there being no substitute teacher available, he announced everyone in Sue Ann's class could go home for the day and help with family farm needs. It was naïve of the principal to assume the newly released students would use the day for productive activities, but he decided he was being thoughtful.

For Sue Ann, she immediately thought of Dillon and how to see him. She knew Momma was away at Uncle Alton's; and hoped, with luck, Daddy would be so busy he wouldn't notice she was home and plotting time with her boyfriend. Sue Ann's first order of business was to get home, and her classmate Sophie gave her the ticket.

"Mam, can you give me a lift home?" She asked Sophie's momma.

"Of course, dear," was the response she got as she jumped into the car.

As Sophie talked endlessly about what she was going to do when she got home, Sue Ann was quiet. Her attention was elsewhere; imagining her freedom and how she could best make time with Dillon. A few miles up State Road 91, as the car approached the turnoff to Stinking Creek Road, Sue Ann blurted out, "Just drop me off here; I can walk home."

Sue Ann knew it would be easier to slip home without being noticed on foot as opposed to in a loud station wagon.

"Sure, dear, have a great day. Tell your Momma and Daddy hey from me."

Skipping and smiling her way up Stinking Creek Road, Sue Ann allowed herself to have thoughts that were new to her. She wanted to touch Dillon and have him touch her in ways that she had only read about; thoughts that had never entered her mind were consuming her. She didn't exactly know how to think about her "dirty" thoughts, or even how it might happen, but she was twelve and, at least to her way of thinking, this was normal; it was time she grew up.

Just before the last curve in the road before her house,

Sue Ann stepped off Stinking Creek Road and entered the woods; her sneaking home was adding to the mystery and excitement of her day. She noticed immediately that the farm was quiet. There wasn't a sound; could it be that no one was home? What if everyone were gone? She smiled to herself.

Confirming no one was around and seeing no sign of Daddy's truck, she relaxed her covert approach and walked into the house through the front door. Opening the door, Sue Ann called out to see if anyone would answer; the house was silent.

Quickly, she went to her room and deposited her schoolbooks and lunchbox on her bed. Without hesitation, she scampered down the steps and bolted out the door, heading for the barn in search of Dillon. Despite her rapid pace, crossing the short distance from the house to the barn seemed like an eternity for Sue Ann; she had to find him. As she neared the barn door, Sue Ann slowed her gait, deciding it would be fun to sneak up on Dillon. Peering around the barn door, she saw him there, slowly whittling on a piece of wood, without a care in the world.

Sue Ann watched him unnoticed for as long as she could stand it before crying out, "Hey Dillon, watch ya doin?"

Startled, Dillon dropped his carving knife and looked towards the barn entrance; and an immediate grin filled his face. Sue Ann looked beautiful, and butterflies filled his stomach; he had never seen a prettier sight.

"Sue Ann, what are you doin here?" He asked.

"They let us out of school," she responded in a flirty voice she hadn't used before.

"That's great," was all Dillon could muster back.

"Where are Daddy and your brothers?" Sue Ann asked.

"In town picking up supplies, hadn't been gone long. I expect they will be away for an hour or more." Dillon heard himself say.

A long silence ensued as the two young fledgling lovebirds stared at each other, each trying to process what they were feeling, what it meant, and what came next. Dillon was older and had seen more, but it was Sue Ann whose maturity exceeded his. Dillon didn't know what to say; he sat motionless. Sue Ann broke the silence. "Let's go for a walk."

With relief and excitement, Dillon stood up and walked towards Sue Ann; if she was going to lead the day, Dillon was okay with that.

In no hurry, the teenage couple walked casually across the field towards the entrance to the Ramsey Creek Trail. Sue Ann had her mind made up, and she knew the perfect spot for her and Dillon to stop. As they entered the trail, Sue Ann's hand reached down to grab Dillon's, and he readily accepted. Making their way up the mountain, they nervously flirted, suggesting nothing more than innocence was in their future.

Despite whatever cultural trends that existed in the country, life in the mountains still moved much like it had since the first Scottish settlers crossed the Appalachians and called this home almost two hundred years before. Mountain folk grew up fast; they had to; they married early and started families in their teens. Momma had married young; her momma even earlier. Despite that fact, she didn't want that life for Sue Ann; she wanted more and was raising her to be a more modern mountain woman. All the best intentions aside, Sue Ann was a product of her surroundings; sheltered from the outside world and ill-informed about the feelings she was having. Having had no talk with anyone about sex,

Sue Ann was winging it, thinking about the books she read in secret. Sue Ann believed her feelings were normal. It never occurred to her that she was too young. Age didn't matter to Sue Ann; it was just a number. Her emotions had control of her; she was hell-bent on being a woman.

Sue Ann had previously scouted out the spot she wanted to be with Dillon; in recent weeks she had climbed the trail, settled under a gigantic oak tree and read her Beverly Clearly novels; it was a perfect location.

Dillon wasn't on the same wavelength; although he was excited and his body was leading him to a place he hadn't been before with a girl, he was scared and not sure what was happening. He was following the whims of Sue Ann.

After what seemed like forever, Sue Ann stopped, stepped off the trail, and sat down in a leaf-covered, open patch of ground; with a wave she summoned Dillon to sit next to her. Hesitantly, he lowered himself slowly. He put his arm around Sue Ann.

Silence filled the air, and both were nervous; Sue Ann yearning to have Dillon kiss her, and Dillon terrified about what he was thinking. In time, Sue Ann kissed Dillon.

Anticipation of what was to come was longer than the actual hurried moment Dillon and Sue Ann broke the barrier from childhood to adult behavior; in an instant it was over. Immediately Sue Ann sat upright, pulled her legs together, and her feet close to her bottom. Dillon turned away from Sue Ann, a look of fear on his face.

A soft whimper coming from Sue Ann broke the extended silence. She wasn't crying because she didn't want to do what they had done. She cried because the emotions were overwhelming; what happened no longer seemed innocent, and she didn't know what to do. Minutes passed as Sue Ann continued to cry quietly. Nobody spoke.

Dillon's mind was spinning. He remembered watching Grant do this back in Greene County, and although it was the same act, his time with Sue Ann seemed different. Sue Ann's tears were confusing him; he hadn't forced her. He thought she wanted him to do what they had done. How could she be upset? Every time he watched Grant with girls, they cried throughout, afraid, fighting his actions; they hadn't wanted Grant to touch them; he had done it anyway.

An unexpected rage built in Dillon's body; this wasn't supposed to be how this happened. He didn't want to be like Grant, but now Sue Ann's crying was telling him he was no different; he was just like his brother. Dillon rocked back and forth, mumbling to himself; what was he going to do? He knew what Grant did each time he had been with a girl; is that what he was about to do? Is this what Grant would expect of him?

With a quick thrust towards Sue Ann, Dillon lost control; terror and evil on his face, he grabbed Sue Ann's waist, pushed her back onto the leaves, sat on her chest, and wrapped both his hands around her throat with intensity and force. For the first time, Sue Ann realized she was in trouble and struggled for her life; to no avail. Dillon's strength and rage made him unstoppable. Slowly, life fell from Sue Ann's eyes as she watched the boy she thought she loved take her future.

Dillon held onto Sue Ann's neck long after life had left her body; years of anger at a life with a demonic brother had come forth, and he was no longer the quiet boy who sat passively and watched. He was a killer; his brother was a killer. In a last, delusional show of kindness, Dillon softened his touch and sweetly laid Sue Ann against the tree a few feet behind where he killed her. He used his hands to close her eyes and gave her a kiss on the forehead; he had to get back to the farm.

Dillon wasn't sure what to do next. He had just killed the only person he had ever loved. He had touched her in ways they both wanted, and then years of watching Grant hurt girls had taken over, and he had followed his brother's ways. His mind raced with conflicting thoughts. He was ashamed of his actions. Although he did not want to hurt Sue Ann, he also felt energized. There was a rush of adrenaline that filled his body; he felt alive; he felt powerful for the first time in his life. His eyes flittered about, his breathing grew rapidly, and he muttered to himself as he bounded down the mountain, "Sue Ann wanted this; it's not my fault," he repeated, again and again.

Dillon needed to find Grant; he had to talk to him. Grant would know what to do next. Grant had experience with this sort of thing. Dillon didn't know how many times Grant had killed; all he knew of was the handful of times he witnessed the act. Eager to find his brother, he picked up his pace and ran down the mountain. He wasn't running from what he did; he was running to what he had become.

Dillon found the farm as quiet as when he had wandered off with Sue Ann; no one was there. Alone with his thoughts, all he could do was wait, wait for them to come home, wait for Grant to tell him what to do next. Mindlessly, he picked up his whittling stick and knife and went back to carving the same wood block he was when Sue Ann snuck up on him.

In time, Daddy returned home with the twins. Dillon was eager to greet them and help unload the truck; but helping wasn't his agenda. No one talked as they worked. It was a normal day, and there wasn't anything to talk about; other than Dillon, no one knew anything about what had happened.

After emptying and organizing the parts, Daddy gave the brothers their marching orders for the rest of the day. He had work to do that didn't require any help; the loner in Daddy yearned for time away from his farmhands. Almost as soon as Daddy left the brothers, Dillon spoke up. "Grant, can I talk to you, got something I need to ask you about."

Uninterested in much of what Dillon had to say, Dan grabbed his hammer, a pinch of tobacco for his cheek, and a bag of nails; having all he needed, he walked out of the barn towards the left side of the shed to begin his work.

"What's going on, Dillon?" Grant asked, annoyed to deal with anything his brother had to say.

Without hesitation or shame, Dillon answered, "I killed Sue Ann."

"What?"

Grant shouted, his eyes cutting through Dillon.

"After ya'll left, she showed up early from school. We went up the Ramsey Creek Trail and sat down for a moment. She kissed me, and then we did it." Dillon said with no emotion. Grant's face became a stone, replacing his angry demeanor.

"After we were done, she started crying, and I snapped. I did what I know you have done before. I don't know why, but I did."

Dillon explained, hoping he would get approval.

"Where is she now?" Grant asked.

"She is still up there where we were, right off the trail, leaning against a tree," Dillon said in a meek voice.

Grant said nothing for a long time. This was trouble, and

he knew it. The girls he had killed before weren't important to anyone. No one even knew they were gone; this was different; it would only be a few hours till the entire farm was looking for her. There wasn't time to hide her body. She would remain where she lay. If there were any evidence Dillon had been there, it wouldn't take long to point a finger at him.

"Dillon, listen to me; you can't say anything to anyone. When they ask questions, you need to tell them you never saw her, didn't know she was home." Grant said firmly.

"You got that?"

Dillon shook his head; for the first time, he realized Grant wasn't proud of him, and he might be in trouble. His body shook violently; he was panicking.

"Get a hold of yourself, dammit." Grant scolded Dillon as he quickly stormed out the barn door.

After he regained his composure, Dillon joined the brothers and spent the rest of the day hammering away. It was what he did. He was back to mindless, repetitive behavior, submissively following Grant; he was incapable of considering his actions or the repercussions. After a while, Grant spoke up and said, "boys the time has come for us to move on. We will stay for three or four days and then head west."

Confused, Dan looked at Grant, wondering what he was thinking. Before he could say anything, Grant said, "It won't be long now till you understand why we have to go. Trust me."

Dan knew that look on Grant's face, and he welcomed it. He liked trouble, and Grant's message foretold something was brewing.

Grant was right. Before their work was done, word spread that Sue Ann was missing. Needing to find her, everyone was given their assigned path to search. It was a chaotic scene, followed by a subdued pal that fell over the Burnette homestead. As news spread that they had found Sue Ann spread down the mountain, the McGinnis boys faded into the darkness. They figured they would be suspects. It would only be natural to assume they had something to do with it, and it didn't take long for the sheriff to seek them out for questioning. To the Sheriff's disappointment, the twins had alibis; they had been with Frankie when Sue Ann returned home. Daddy vouched for them and pointed out Dillon was sitting exactly where they left him when they pulled up from town. In Daddy's way of thinking, the sheriff needed to look elsewhere.

Sheriff Cogburn wasn't so sure. Something didn't feel right; he didn't trust those boys. But he had nothing to work with, and a dead young girl; he needed to catch a break.

The day after Sue Ann was buried, the break happened. The sheriff got a call from Daddy. "Sheriff, you need to get out here."

That was all Daddy said.

When the sheriff pulled up to the farm, he immediately saw why he had been called. On the front porch, he could see Momma, Daddy, James, and Ralph. They all looked stunned and overwhelmed with grief. However, their pained looks couldn't hold the sheriff's gaze. The sheriff looked at the body hanging from the tree next to the barn.

Before exiting his patrol car, the sheriff grabbed his radio and called for his deputies to join him at the farm. "Guys, this is Willie. Get out to the Burnette farm. Something has happened."

After taking a moment to gather himself, Sheriff Cogburn climbed the steps of the porch and shook Daddy's hand.

"Frankie, is there anything you can tell me about this?"

He had to ask.

"Sheriff, none of us knows anything about this. I saw him hanging when I walked outside this morning and called you right then. I haven't even gone over there. Nobody else in the family saw anything either. We all went to bed early, and this is what we woke up to."

"Thanks, Frankie, I am sorry to suggest anything."

The sheriff apologized. Daddy nodded his head in acknowledgement as his and the sheriff's eyes met.

After thirty minutes of wandering around the tree's base, the sheriff greeted his deputies. It was time to release the body from the noose around its neck. No one present had ever seen a hanging; they hoped they never would again. As the deputies slowly lowered the body, Sheriff Cogburn asked Frankie, "Is this who I think it is?"

"Yes, that's Dillon, the young boy that came along with the twins." Daddy responded.

With his antenna going up, the sheriff asked, "Where are the twins?"

"We haven't seen them this morning, and I don't see their truck." Daddy offered.

After sunset and before the sun rose, the twins had left the Burnette farm. They were gone and left nothing behind except their little brother.

—

It took me several days to process the case files. There were a lot of facts and details that suggested Dillon was the killer;

the evidence pointed directly at him. A note in Dillon's pocket that read 'justice' and the fact that he was hanged in our yard created more questions than answers.

Tucked neatly below all the other files was one final skinny folder; I opened it up and saw a formal-looking document, which outlined the conclusion of the sheriff's work. At the bottom of the last page, it simply read, "After a thorough investigation, the murder of Sue Ann Burnette is closed. May God bless her soul."

25

The Good Name of the Burnette Family

THE WORD CLOSED WAS DEFINITIVE, WITH NO ROOM for interpretation. Sheriff Willie Cogburn with certainty had determined Dillon killed my older sister. He had fulfilled his promise to make it right, even if someone other than the local judge administered the punishment. It was a tidy ending to a horrible four days in Gizzard Holler; it was too tidy.

With all the evidence confirming Dillon was the killer, I felt compelled to accept that conclusion. The sheriff had, and best I could tell, my family had as well. However, the rapid and unexplained departure of the twins left some unanswered questions; namely, who hung Dillon? Maybe the sheriff wasn't interested in pursuing it any further. Surely, he must have considered, at least for a moment, that the twins had hanged their brother to cover their guilt. He must have wondered if Dan and Grant had killed Sue Ann and, to get away, blamed their weak brother. It was an interesting thread but fruitless. Daddy had vouched for the twin's time on that day and provided them with an alibi. They couldn't have killed Sue Ann; but maybe they hung Dillon.

Was it possible they hung Dillon out of anger? Dillon's actions didn't sit well with the twins and their need to control everything. It is not unreasonable to think they decided they didn't want to deal with him and threw him away like they had everyone else in their life. Or maybe after learning Dillon was the killer, they inflicted justice on behalf of Sue Ann. That theory seemed unlikely. Why would they have inserted themselves into the police matter? Taking this route would not have been consistent with mountain practices. They were nothing but trouble, but adept at avoiding getting trapped and held accountable. They would have wanted no part of the case nor what was possible in Johnson County.

After a fruitless waste of time considering possible versions of what happened, I decided I needed to find the twins and talk to them. Maybe one of them was still alive — they would be in their fifties — and they could give me a picture of what happened. It was a stretch, but I decided I was going to try.

With more information than I could process, I stored the box away for safekeeping. The sheriff would not notice it was gone, and if he did and he asked me about it, I could lie to him like he lied to me. Descending from the attic, I adjusted my evening plans. Instead of going downstairs to build a fire and read, I went to bed. I could figure out my search strategy in the morning.

After a hearty breakfast of eggs and bacon, and a slow walk around the farm with Winston, I drove to town to find a place where I could dial into the internet. A relatively new resource, the web was the logical place to search for where the twins might be. I knew figuring out where the transient boys had gone would be hard; they lived by their own rules. Maybe I could get lucky.

I didn't. There wasn't anything online about the McGinnis boys. On a whim, I drove over to see if Boone could get a cup of coffee. I was not let down. As one of Mountain City's finest, he was all too eager for a cup of joe and a muffin at Jen's West Main Cafe.

Boone had proven to empathize with my need to uncover the truth. I knew it was hard for him and suspected he could get into trouble, but maybe he could give me advice.

Everyone at the cafe knew Boone. A regular visitor to Jen's, he had to shake hands with the staff behind the counter and in the cafe seating area. That took a few minutes. Waiting patiently at our table, I watched with envy as I witnessed townsfolk practicing the ritual of exchanging pleasantries and small talk. To the uninitiated, you might think they hadn't seen each other in a while. I knew better. The towns-folk performed this routine day after day. They had time to catch up, even if it had only been twenty-four hours since they last saw each other.

Finally, with his rounds finished, Boone walked over and sat down, a contented grin on his face.

"Thanks for asking me for a cup of coffee." Boone raised his mug in appreciation.

"My pleasure, bud. Hey thanks for thinking of me." I offered.

It was my veiled attempt at acknowledging what we both knew. He had helped me despite the risk to his job.

"Sure, RJ, no problem."

"Listen," I began. "I was wondering if you knew anything about what happened to Grant and Dan McGinnis. They worked on the farm for my daddy. I was hoping to track them down. I am trying to reconnect with as much of the farm's history as I can."

He knew the framing of my question was a cover. An attempt to learn more about the events of Sue Ann's death while not being explicit.

I hoped that if I asked for information the right way, it would free Boone to offer insight. If he knew anything. My hopes paid off.

Boone looked at me and smiled. He was onto my game.

"You know, I know nothing about where those brothers are. Heard nothing about them. But I tell you who might know." He said with a big smile.

"My Uncle Rufus lives over in Bristol. He's been there for nearly fifty years. He knows everything about what goes on over the mountain. Maybe he remembers something about those boys. If you want, I can call him and tell him you're going to be coming by to see him."

"Oh, by the way, if you go see him, bring a can of snuff. He'll appreciate that."

"Will do." I said as I stood up to leave.

"Thanks, Boone, you are a good man."

Boone acknowledged my comment and extended his hand. "Good luck."

The one-hour drive from Mountain City to Bristol follows a winding road that feels designed to make you sick. It didn't elicit that reaction from me, but had I been in the passenger seat, it would have been a different story. The uncomfortable roller coaster state road wasn't all bad; it rewarded drivers with a stunning view of South Holston Lake on the descent down the mountain into Sullivan County. The Tennessee Valley Authority created the South Holston River dam in 1950 for flood control and hydroelectric power, which created the deep-water lake. A tailwater dam resulted in a trophy-class trout fishery below it. The scene instantly reminded me of the region's natural beauty. Despite their hardships, the residents of these mountains are blessed with a landscape that always grabs your attention.

Bristol is a small Tennessee town on the border with Virginia—half the town is in Virginia and half is in Tennessee — known as the birthplace of country music and home of the Bristol Motor Speedway. With a population of a little over twenty thousand residents, it was a big city for the folks who traveled from Mountain City.

It had been a while since I had been to Bristol, but I quickly found Rufus King's house. He lived on Windsor Avenue in a small two-story craftsman home. He had lived in this house for most of his life.

As soon as I pulled in front of the house, I saw Rufus sitting on the front porch. He looked like he spent most days there, quietly observing the cars pass. I grabbed my can of tobacco. I was going to need to break the ice, and opened the gate to his front yard.

Not wasting time, I called out, "Mr. King, this is RJ Burnette from over in Johnson County. Boone said he was going to let you know I was coming by."

He smiled and waved me onto the porch. "Call me Rufus."

Before sitting down, I shook his hand and delivered my goody package. The smile on his face said it all; he was running low on his favorite habit.

"Welcome to Bristol, RJ. Boone tells me you are trying to find some boys who used to work for your daddy."

"That's right. Boone said you might help."

Without delay, Rufus started doing what he did best — telling a story.

"I remember those fellas. They were a bad lot," he said with a deliberate voice.

"I was just a young man back then. Into all kinds of things Momma told me not to do. Always down at the bars on State Street. No good ever came of it, but I saw some things."

"Anyway, those boys hightailed it into town in a hurry to get somewhere. Took up at a little place down on the corner of State and Sixth Street hoping to go unnoticed and to get some rest before they headed out."

"That was their first mistake. No one slipped into Bristol in those days without drawing attention." He said matter-of-factly.

"Their second mistake was getting thirsty." He laughed.

"By the time they walked into the bar, everyone in there knew they were in town, and knew their story." He stopped to replenish the depleted tobacco in his lips.

"Anyhow, they weren't sitting on their stools five minutes before Ray Thompson and his buddies decided it was time to say hello."

"Ray was the sheriff's oldest boy, and he was a downright dangerous fella. It was smart to stay on his good side."

"I remember it as if it were yesterday." Rufus said with a bit of nostalgia on his face.

Ray says, "Hey bartender, let me buy these guys a drink before they leave. It will be their last one."

One of those twins stood up and said, "What do you mean we just got here? Besides, you are not big enough to make any difference to me."

"That was all it took. Ray and his band of buddies jumped those two boys and began beating them to death. It was a God-awful fight. I admit I jumped into the fight for shits and giggles. By the time it was over, the twins were dead."

Rufus stopped his story and stared out from his porch, not sure what to say next.

"Rufus, why did Ray jump the twins?"

"They had it coming."

The dots still weren't connecting for me until Rufus's last words.

"The bar was a mess, and of course the sheriff was called in. He walked around and looked for anyone who was injured. He wasn't in any rush."

"Satisfied with what he saw, the sheriff went over to the bartender and asked for a shot of whiskey. Grabbing his whiskey, he turned around, faced us, and said, 'To the good name of the Burnette family.'"

Stunned by what I had just heard, I shook my head and said, "Are you serious?"

"Yep, that's the way things were done around here."

The twins hadn't lived for two days after their departure from Gizzard's Holler. Mountain justice had grabbed them and stopped them from any future terror they might inflict.

I didn't know what to think. It sounded like something out of a western movie that was untrue. How could this town full of churchgoing people allow this?

I was glad to know what happened but not able to understand why people would do this. Maybe I'm not cut from the same cloth. It sounded like the McGinnis boys were horrible thugs. But was that the way to handle it?

Leaving Rufus's house, I drove down State Street. As I looked at the people walking up and down the street, I couldn't picture a time when a town would let this happen. I couldn't picture it, but it was true.

On the way home, I felt unsettled. My goal in coming to Bristol was to see if I could confirm who hanged Dillon. All I learned was how the people in this part of the country handle things. I struggled to understand how to process vigilante justice. And then it hit me. I had to refocus on my core question: who hanged Dillon?

My initial idea that the brothers took Dillon's life was misguided. It was easy to label them as the guilty parties, but that narrative didn't fit my recent experience. If Sheriff Cogburn thought his brothers lynched Dillon, or he had hung himself, thus closing the books on the tawdry incident, there would be no need for secrecy. The sheriff and the residents of Johnson County shouldn't have any problem with retelling the story, as tragic as it was. The story would have been complete. Instead, the permanent residents of Johnson County wanted the secret kept. They kept the mystery a secret to ensure no one knew who had hung Dillon. If no one ever spoke of it, nothing would come of it.

There it was. Local folks weren't keeping me in the dark to protect me. They were staying quiet to protect the person who delivered justice the old-fashioned way. Dillon paid an immediate price for his evil; that was enough. We shouldn't judge the hangman.

For the first time, I wondered if a member of my family had exacted vigilante justice. Could Daddy, in a rage, have avenged his daughters' death? What about James? He was now a pillar of the community; if he had hung Dillon, there would be ample reason to keep that quiet. Then there was Ralph; he was close to Sue Ann. When he could, he fled the closed inner circle of Johnson County and resorted to living as a nineteenth-century mountain man. What was that about, really?

You could also imagine the sheriff hanged Dillon. The more I thought about it, the more believable the idea became. Admittedly, it would be strange for him to have hung Dillon in Daddy's front yard, but it was easy to imagine he concluded Dillon was guilty and did what his grandfather had wanted to do a hundred years ago. It would also explain why he was unwilling to talk about the fall of 1964, or why the current sheriff clammed up when I asked for help.

Suddenly, this felt more personal. Sue Ann was family, but I never knew her. She was a ghostlike figure to me, someone I had heard about from stories; many of which were only recently told to me. If someone other than the twins killed Dillon, I likely knew the responsible person. That introduced a new set of emotions. I was suddenly uneasy.

26

Aren't Sure They Can Trust You

"Hello," I answered as I cradled the phone.

"RJ, this is Mark. How ya doin bud?"

"Great Mark, what's going on?" I asked.

It was good to hear Mark's voice. We hadn't spoken since running into each other at Jesse's; I had been meaning to call him.

"Not much, say we are having friends over tonight for a jam session, was wondering if you wanted to help us with a little banjo pickin?" Mark said.

"Absolutely," I replied, "would love to."

"Awesome, say, why don't you come over early and we can catch up a bit?" Mark suggested.

"Sounds good, see you soon."

I was excited. It would be good to get out and reconnect with friends; other than a few moments at Jesse's Barbecue, I hadn't spent time with many people, and although Winston was a splendid companion; I was feeling a bit withdrawn. The time I spent grieving the loss of Momma and pursuing answers about Sue Ann's murder had consumed me. My focus didn't allow for anything else, certainly nothing productive or fun. I didn't want to repeat the life I had in New York. I was a boring person with little to offer except for my obsessive drive. In New York, it had been my work; for the last several months, it had been insecure self-pity.

As I approached Mark's house, I felt no need to discuss with him or anyone else my recent pursuit of information about the past. I needed to let that rest; I needed to have fun. Mark's house was a comfortable two-story brick house with a generous front porch; plenty of room for a family of four. Mark had done well; an insurance agent for State Farm, he had a simple life, absent stress and worry. His biggest concern was coaching his oldest boy's youth football team; it wasn't easy to call plays for eight-year-olds.

Mark's wife, Tammy, greeted me at the door. She was his high-school sweetheart. They had been dating since sophomore year and the homecoming dance that followed the upset win against Erwin. A big win, combined with a small flask of whiskey, offered all the courage Mark needed to ask Tammy for a kiss; they have been inseparable since.

"Evening, RJ, so good to see you."

Tammy smiled as she opened the door. Still as cute as ever, it was good to see she still had her strong southern accent.

"Hey Tammy, how you been?" I asked as I gave her a hug.

"I'm great. Mark is in the den. Can I get you a beer, or maybe a bourbon?" she offered.

"Well now, I see our tastes have improved over the years," I said, laughing at the thought of my buddy drinking bourbon.

"I'll take a bourbon neat, if you don't mind."

"No problem, RJ." She winked as she walked away.

I found Mark fully reclined, sitting in a leather Lazy-

Boy recliner, watching basketball on the tube and holding a half-full glass of brown water that could only have been his favorite bourbon. Mark didn't get up to greet me; that would have been too formal. We were buds from way back, and formality wasn't in the cards.

Mark had changed little. Sure, he was older, and carried himself a little more responsibly, but his personality and demeanor were still that of the country boy I ran with throughout school. It was good to witness his happiness. He had figured it out, no need for him to change. Life in the country hadn't changed and wasn't going to; no need for him to become a different person.

"RJ, what are you going to do with the farm?"

"Damn if I know, been thinking about kicking it back up and seeing if I can make a go of it. But honestly, I don't know what to do." RJ admitted.

"Did you know anything about banking when you ran off to New York?" Mark responded, a jabbing grin on his face.

"Hell no, Mark. I didn't know anything about anything."

I shot back with a laugh. It was a good point. Sometimes not knowing what you're getting into is a good thing.

"How's your business?" I asked.

"It's insurance; not much changes. I have my clients, and when they need something, I help them. Not enough new people coming into the county to grow my business. That's alright though, I like what I have."

And he did, you could tell his aspirations revolved around his family, friends and neighbors, not a career.

As we talked, I knew we had experienced the last eight years differently. My time was a hectic, never-ending push for what was next; pursuing any edge I could find. Every day full of activity and intensity; a hectic existence that had flown by. Mark spent his time living each day as it came. There was depth in his days. Without a need to worry about tomorrow, Mark settled into a routine that he, Tammy, and now the two kids easily followed and valued. He and Tammy had built a shared life; it was special, and as I relaxed on Mark's sofa, I felt envious.

It was an ironic feeling, to feel jealous of my best friend. Not too long ago, I lived in the most dynamic city in the world, convinced that when my old friends and family thought of me, they felt a twinge of envy. Sipping my bourbon, I realized I was wrong. The people I left behind weren't longing for my life; they had the life they wanted. A life much like their parents had lived, and if they were lucky, the life their kids would enjoy.

As we spent time alone, Mark shared with me his joy in coaching his son's team; his pride in his daughter's art drawings; and the fun times he was having with his dad, fishing the Watauga.

"I love coaching Junior's football team. The personal joy I get from watching him compete and work to get better is indescribable. I never thought I would feel this way." He beamed.

"Then there's Missy. She is so artistic; she didn't get her creativity from Tammy, and you know she didn't get her talent from me. I am so amazed at her imagination and ability to create a picture."

As I listened to him, I realized that not one deal I closed brought me as much joy as Mark experienced with his family; it left me feeling empty. I couldn't remember the last time I had waded in the Watauga River, nor any time spent with Daddy after I left for college.

Two bourbons into the night, friends from the past started arriving to play some music. Everyone who showed up held some part of my past; there were no strangers in this small mountain enclave. Boone was there with his girlfriend Peggy, and Jesse brought his guitar and barbecue potato skins. A respectable crowd; there were ten Saturday night musicians ready to contribute. With drinks freeing my personality, I quickly became the old RJ, full of jokes, laughter, and silliness. It felt so good to recapture who had been before heading off to the big city.

When Boone walked into the room, we made eye contact, and I gently raised my glass to thank him; beyond that, we avoided any hint of what he had done. I was grateful he had taken a chance to help me out; it was a kind thing to do. He was that kind of guy; it matched his role as a deputy, the need to help others. He wasn't in law enforcement to chase people; he wanted to be of service to the community he grew up in; a place that had been home to his relatives for over one hundred fifty years.

Alice was there. She was cute as ever. A middle school history teacher and member of the church choir. Her voice was beautiful, and it captivated me all night as the group played songs for her to sing. Our time chatting was brief. We did not mention our talk on her front porch. It appeared she wanted to move forward; I know I did. What a relief. I had, after all, been a jerk, and she deserved better. Maybe when she looked at me, she would see the young boy who asked her to prom, took her out to the lake and to that special spot for a special night. Maybe she will forget I told her I would never leave her. And instead, we will remember the dreams we shared about building a family together.

Watching Alice laugh, her hair bouncing off her shoulders, and her eyes glancing my way, I realized I would never find the happiness I sought if I couldn't share my life with Alice. She had never married; I hoped that meant she felt the same way about me.

Since returning home, this was the first opportunity I had to internalize the magnitude and depth of what I had lost and the sacrifice I made pursuing a dream I didn't believe in. Lost were the laughter, the shared experiences, the joy of living each day with simple goals and aspirations that my friends had built their life around; the shared happiness and suffering that was inherent in life. If there was ever any doubt about my future, that Saturday night ensured I was here to stay, and ready to embrace my life, the life I needed to live.

As the party wound down, everyone hugged and laughed about our homily rendition of *Fox on the Run*, and Mark beating his mandolin half-silly trying to keep up. That was part of the fun. None of us were going to make a living playing music; we didn't intend to. We knew our place in life, simple mountain folk who found peace picking hand-me-down instruments in Mark's den. We were following our ancestors, who had gathered consistently to play music and congregate as family or extended family. Modern times hadn't changed the people in this room; hip hop music or contemporary country music was fun to listen to, but it wasn't bluegrass, it couldn't send a chill down your spine, nor elicit tears and laughter within the same chorus. We played songs that were older than our parents, accepting that the lyrics we sang were as applicable today as they were during the Great Depression, when our kin crooned lonesome sounds hoping for better times.

With the last holdout gone, I found myself not wanting to go home, to be alone. This was the most enjoyable evening I could remember; I didn't want it to end. Mark sensed my hesitation and said, "RJ, no need to rush off."

It was a kind offer, and I took him up on it, nestling comfortably onto the sofa.

Mark and I finished one last bourbon, quietly reliving the evening and the peace that comes from a perfectly balanced buzz. Finally, Mark broke the silence.

"RJ, listen, bud," he started.

"I hear you have been asking questions about Sue Ann's murder."

I nodded yes in response and stared at him, waiting for his next words.

"I understand why this matters to you, but as your friend, I think you should back off and let it go."

His tone was matter of fact and emotionless.

Mark's admonishment pissed me off and, unlike the other times I had been told to stop, I responded.

"Mark, I am not sure why you think it appropriate to say this to me, nor what your motivation is, but I am tired of being told I don't need to know what happened to my family."

I said in a high pitch, angry voice. I had been thwarted and managed for months. I couldn't contain my frustration.

Before Mark could react, I continued. "What is it, Mark? Why is everyone in this town so afraid of me knowing what happened?" I demanded.

Mark sat in silence, unsure what to say next. He was my best friend, and despite my angry voice; I knew he meant well. Finally, Mark said, "RJ, the mystery around who lynched the boy who killed Sue Ann holds dark truths that no one in town wants to revisit. Nothing good can come from the story being told of what happened on that night."

"Okay," I said.

"I guess I can accept that; the town in protecting its secrets and itself. What I don't understand I why I can't know? Why am I being specifically excluded from knowing?" It was a fair question.

It was also at the crux of the issue. Someone had decided the secret needed to stay buried. Even from me; but why? Now more than ever, the secret seemed personal.

I could tell Mark didn't want to answer my question. Reluctantly, he said, "RJ, people in this town aren't sure who you are. They don't know if you are still the guy you always were, or if New York changed you. Buddy, I am sorry to say this, but people aren't sure they can trust you."

His words were like a dagger piercing my soul; it hurt. Not sure what to say nor how to react, I set my glass down, crawled off the sofa and started walking to the front of the house. Mark didn't stop me. He knew I had heard enough, and I needed to process his words.

Mark's tough words and vehement rejection of my need to hear the truth stung. If he thought he was doing me a favor, he was wrong. The rejections I got from the sheriff and his replacement were inappropriate. Having my best friend act as my protector was too much for me to accept. Mark could say he was doing this because it was best, but no matter what, it wasn't better for me. It was my family and my history, and I deserved to know what happened.

PART V

27

No, it Ain't

I THOUGHT ABOUT LEAVING, PACKING UP MY THINGS, loading Winston in the car and driving away; if Johnson County didn't want me, I didn't need it. I had done it before, twice in fact, and although both times I thought I had found what I wanted, I hadn't. It took eight years in New York for me to conclude I didn't belong and had to get out. Could it be that after only a few months in Johnson County, the writing was on the wall; I didn't belong here either.

In New York, I was an outsider at first, but success removed that obstacle. My colleagues believed in me; they knew they could count on me. I would do what I said, be there in a crunch. If that meant spending the night in the office, or working all weekend, I would do it. To my knowledge, no one ever questioned whether they could trust me; in all my days, I never heard someone ponder my reliability. My need to leave my corporate life wasn't about a lack of trust. It was the nagging void that left me empty; the awareness I could achieve all the transactional measurements I pursued, and it wasn't enough. I needed more; I needed to settle with and live among people I valued and understood.

Now I was back home, ready to find my reconnection with my history, ready to contribute to the community, ready to live my life as a local, only to be told the people I grew up with couldn't trust me. It didn't seem fair. These people could trust me with their lives; I would do anything for Mark. How could he express doubt?

I don't think Mark's use of the word trust accurately reflected what people from my past felt. It wasn't about trust, the way I would describe it or my old boss, George, would use it. No, Mark suggested people were wondering if I was one of them. A remaining link to the generations of mountain folk who bonded together to solve problems, protect each other, sacrifice for the betterment of all. Mark's comment was deeper than trust; it highlighted what I already suspected: people wondered about me, what I wondered about myself. Had my time away caused me to put myself above everything, unable to put others' needs, feelings and lives first?

Confident that you are a part of something bigger than yourself, like a community, is reassuring. There is no need to question events or comments others make in your presence. I didn't have that previously working in an all-or-nothing environment; I was always aware someone was ready to take me down. New York taught me that when uncertainty creeps in, it is only natural you question whether you belong. Mark's parting shot opened a door to deep, dark doubts and allowed all my New York insecurities to bubble up. It also brought back thoughts from my childhood. As a kid, I felt detached from Momma, Daddy, and my brothers. To me, I was an only child. The family unit had already been raised and established before I joined them. This lingering emotion — that I was a bit of an afterthought — contributed to my notion I should seek a life outside Johnson County after college; an attempt to build my narrative.

Oddly, I didn't realize the impact my childhood had on my post-college decisions until returning to these mountains. But now I get it. I sought elsewhere what I was missing; to feel special and wanted. Obviously, New York didn't offer me a personal identity. I was a number, measured by the numbers I delivered.

Now I am back home, having failed to find the acceptance I wanted in New York, seeking to be a part of my old community, asking questions that are making people uncomfortable. I should know better; mountain folk get painfully quiet when they aren't comfortable. People guard secrets, and secrets protect people.

I was at an unexpected crossroads. Was I going to continue to push for answers, or let it go? Maybe in time someone would tell me, or maybe the truth would stay buried forever. Maybe it needed to stay hidden; until I showed up, the town was doing just fine without me meddling. My personal need to know was impeding a tranquil mountain transition; it was hurting my future. I was feeling selfish again.

Spring came early that year at Gizzard's Holler. After two memorable snowfalls, the farmer's almanac said it was time for spring, and true to form, spring arrived in mid-March. I was glad of the change. I needed to get out of the house, get active, and decide what needed to be done on the farm. Should I wind down the farm; sell the few remaining pigs and cows; and let the land return to its natural landscape, or invest in the farm and make a go of it? My emotions weren't the only driver. The savings I accumulated in New York were substantial, but not enough for me to fritter away doing nothing for the rest of my life. It was going to require a meaningful investment to recharge the farming operations, an amount I could cover. But if I pooled my resources to run the farm, failure would leave me starting over with no nest egg. I had done it before, but the thought of leaving the holler with no money weighed on me. It was time for me to decide what to do; I needed a plan that would work.

I had limited farming skills, but Momma's farmhand was still here, and he knew how to handle most things needing attention. His name was Billy Drake, and although only twenty-three, he was wise beyond his years. After graduating from Johnson County High School, Billy wasted no time looking for farm work. He spent most of his formative years on his family's farm in southern Johnson County. When he was sixteen, his daddy died in a tractor accident, leaving behind his wife and Billy. With little hope, Billy's momma sold the farm and moved to Kingsport, leaving Billy behind with her sister. It was Billy's aunt who demanded Billy graduate, and with her help, he did. Momma hired Billy to work with her former ranch manager, knowing she was going to slow the pace of the farm, and an experienced ranch manager wouldn't have enough to do. She hoped Billy could learn enough from the ranch boss to run the show when the manager left for greener pastures. The timing worked out, and after his boss left, Billy stayed on to manage what farming Momma wanted to maintain. Now, four years later, Billy could handle anything.

Living by yourself on a two-hundred-and-fifty-acre farm deep in Gizzard's Holler breeds a particular narrowness. If it hadn't been for Billy, I could have gone days without talking to a person. I tried carrying on many interesting conversations with four-legged animals. Despite my efforts though, they never spoke a word in reply. Billy was my primary outlet for human interaction, and he was a good guy. We became friends, and I learned to confide in him. In time, our friendship and my need to honor my roots convinced me to invest in the farm's growth. He was thrilled when I told him I wanted to add to our pig inventory, get more head of cattle, and grow wheat for sale. He and I agreed we would forgo growing crops; I would get my vegetables in town.

I owned the farm, but Billy ran it. He knew how to do everything, and if he didn't know how to solve something, he had a knack for figuring it out. Naturally welcoming, Billy encouraged me to join him during his daily activities. Billy enjoyed having me around. He also wanted to keep a close watch on me.

Billy knew I needed supervision if I was to attempt farming activities. Left on my own, I could cause problems.

A few months earlier, before I committed financially to the farm, I got more involved with the daily activities. Billy was keeping things afloat, and I was feeling sorry for myself. I needed something to do. Not thinking, I began doing chores, assuming I would be helpful. I should have known better. I grew up on a farm, but I wasn't a farmer. Daddy ran a well-run outfit; the farm didn't need me then and likely need me now.

My attempts to help seemed harmless enough until I made a mistake feeding the pigs. It didn't seem too hard; except I forgot to secure the gate. As soon as I was in the clear, the pigs made a run for it. Billy spent the rest of the day corralling those swine.

The next day, having not learned anything, without telling

Billy, I started the tractor and headed out across the meadow to see if I could clear some of the brush along the field's edge. Everything was working fine, that is until I forgot to put the parking brake on. As soon as I dismounted the tractor and walked over to admire my handiwork, I heard a pop. At that point, there was nothing I could do; the tractor was rolling down a slight grade and picking up steam. Its next stop would be a creek bed and a stand of trees. The tractor got stuck in the mud and wedged between two trees. Another afternoon wasted as Billy had to dislodge my handiwork.

From that moment on, I took directions from Billy. He was patient with me and, in time, I became helpful. The more I learned, the more I belonged.

Our friendship wasn't just for convenience. We developed a bond built on shared isolation.

Billy lived in the same small shed the McGinnis boys had shared over thirty years ago; he fixed it up a bit, but it was still spartan. Knowing he was alone, and I needed human connection, I frequently invited Billy to supper; he readily accepted. We talked about anything and everything, our favorite subjects being sports and travel.

Billy loved the Tennessee Vols and, more specifically, listening to games broadcast on his radio. Having never been to Knoxville, nor recalling seeing a game on TV, Billy's entire opinion of the team was based on what he heard on the radio; that and he knew it was the state school and he, like most everyone in the south, was proud of his state.

"RJ, did you ever listen to games on the radio?"

"Of course, I never missed a game as a kid." I remembered.

"My favorite part is when they start the broadcast and they say, 'From Mountain City to the mighty Mississippi, you're listening to the VOL Network'. I think that is really cool."

His pride showed on his face at being able to be a part of something as important as the state school's radio broadcast.

"Funny, Billy, I also love that moment. I get goosebumps thinking about it. The background trumpets play a song that sounds like a call to battle, while the announcer's deep voice reminds us that our state is connected from one end to the other for the game."

I paused. "That opening line always made me feel bigger."

"Yea me too." Billy agreed.

Billy didn't remember ever leaving the county, and he said he didn't want to leave, but he found exotic places and destinations fascinating to hear about. He asked about Texas and the ocean. He wanted to know if I had been to Europe; his granddaddy had served in Italy in the Second World War. I told him everything I had seen and about every place I had read about. I didn't have the gumption to tell Billy I hadn't traveled as much as he assumed. True confessions wouldn't have added anything to our evenings. He never doubted my stories nor whether I had seen the Amazon River; he just loved that with my tales, I could take him there in his mind.

One night Billy asked me about my family; it was a new subject for us as he never wanted to talk about his childhood, nor pry into my past.

"RJ, you never talk about your kin and this farm's history." He said as shoved another slice of ham into his mouth.

"That's true," I said as I considered what he said.

Unsure why, I started talking. I saw no reason to keep my life from Billy. I shared with him the happiness I had as a child living on the farm, the insecurity I felt at being the child with much older brothers that I barely knew, the shenanigans I pursued in high school, my feelings for Alice, and my decision to leave.

"Do you still care for Alice?" Billy asked.

"I do, more than I realized. I saw her recently and was as smitten as ever." Just thinking about her made me smile.

"Funny though, seeing her drove home the pain I have carried within my heart about my decision to run from home. I guess I now realize I hurt people I love, but it all pales compared to how I abandoned her."

Billy remained quiet, not sure what to say. And then he blurted out, "You need to see Alice and work it out with her. No reason to have one stupid decision lead to a lifetime of regret."

Profound words from a twenty-three-year-old farmhand; wisdom and common sense outlining what I already knew and feared, I needed to reconnect with Alice if I was to exist in my hometown.

At that moment I decided I was calling Alice and asking her on a date.

After our brief reference to Alice, Billy sat back and let me continue my family story. He didn't interrupt or ask questions; he was quiet, but he was paying attention. As I talked about coming home, I paused, not sure I wanted to give him my thoughts about the last year, what I learned, and my frustration with the secret that was known by all but me.

With nothing to lose, I forged ahead and shared everything with Billy; it was cathartic and freeing. I needed to release what I had trapped in my head. Until now, no one had allowed me to address my questions, or the feelings that were developing and impacting me. I was supposed to accept the secret and stay quiet. Billy never uttered a word, and I appreciated that. Sometimes a discussion is a shared conversation; sometimes, it is having someone listen.

When I was done, I waited to hear Billy's thoughts; all he said was, "That ain't right."

"No, it ain't."

28

The Last Letter

THE NEXT MORNING, INSPIRED BY MY SUPPERTIME conversation with Billy, I opened Momma's cedar chest and looked at the papers wrapped in the pink ribbon; it was the only item of Momma's left in the house for me to explore. It had been some time since I had last opened the chest. My earlier moments looking at the chest had proved emotional. Turns out, it was too emotional for me to look at all the contents at the same time. But I was getting stronger, I was working through my inner conflicts and accepting what I needed to do to earn my place in our community. I was ready for a final chapter with the unknown.

Not knowing what the stack held and with little sense of urgency, I reached for the first thing on top; no need to look ahead. Untying the laced ribbon binding the organized papers, I immediately noticed the first item was a greying envelope folded over neatly. The envelope was addressed to my grandparents, Betty and Thomas Warren. Inside the envelope were a few crumpled sheets, with lots of stains on them, discolored and ragged. They looked decades old; two short pages, written in a flowing style I hadn't seen before. I didn't recognize the handwriting. As I read the letter, I dismissed my initial assumption that everything in Momma's chest was related to Sue Ann. I didn't know what I was looking at, so I looked at the bottom of the second page and saw Uncle Bubba had written it to his Momma and Daddy. The date on the letter was March 1, 1945.

Momma and Daddy,

I know it has been a while since I wrote, been thinking about you. We are resting on an island somewhere in the Pacific Ocean. We have been here a while, and I am glad. Good to rest. Food is okay, but it ain't like home. Nothing is. I got your letter from before Christmas, and sure loved hearing about all the happenings in the holler. Sounds like the little ones are growing.

Daddy, how are things on the farm? How is my Heffer behaving? I hope she keeps calving. If you can, save her till I get home. I have been dreaming about having a steak to celebrate. Tell her it can be her part of the war effort. Any news from town? I hear most everybody my age is off somewhere fighting. Sure crazy to think about us spread all over the world. Have you heard from Alton or Tommy? I don't know where they are stationed.

Since the last time I wrote, I got a nick on my leg. I wasn't paying attention, and one of those guys on the other side got me good. I stayed holed up for a month, but I'm all better now. They gave me a Purple Heart; I'll send it him home next time I write. The guys I am with are good people. We are from all over the place, but we have each other's backs, like folks do back home.

Momma, how is the garden? It is amazing how much you miss vegetables when all you eat comes in a tin can. I can't wait to have one of your suppers. I tell the boys about your cooking all the time. I think they're tired of it; I don't blame em.

I hear tell we are moving on to another island in the coming days, hopping our way to Japan and then home. The Japanese are tough, but we are going to lick em. Shouldn't be too much longer; I think we are getting close.

Tell everyone I said hey and I love them.
Bubba

By this time in the war, Bubba had been gone three plus years, without seeing or talking to his family. He had witnessed and taken part in a grueling campaign to rid the world of the Japanese threat. The experience must have been life-altering. And yet, his last letter portrays a mountain boy who hadn't forgotten his family. He was eight thousand miles away on a tiny island, a small soul, invested in a big endeavor; trying to find some common sliver connecting him to the life he once knew. As for Mamaw and Papaw, receiving a letter from Bubba was a blessing. The boy was safe, at least on that day.

The words of a man I never met, who died long ago, brought a smile to my face; a simple note home that brought him and his loved ones together; if only for the last time. Bubba's letter was comforting; below it was a Western Union message that was a bitter reminder of his fate.

Dear Mr. and Mrs. Thomas Warren,

We deeply regret to inform you that your son, Master Sergeant Bubba Drew Warren, died in action on April

14th, 1945, on Okinawa Island while performing his duty and service to his country. Master Sergeant Warren was laid to rest in a Marine cemetery alongside other brave Americans. Please accept my heartfelt sympathies.
Major General Lemuel C. Shepherd, Jr.
Commander of the 6th Marine Division

Death wasn't new to the Warren clan, nor the people who settled the Appalachian Mountains; life was and always had been hard. However, a mountain upbringing didn't deaden the pain of losing a son.

They were proud of Bubba; he served his country. His letter back home and death confirmation notice had been passed down from my Mamaw and Papaw to Momma and now to me. It would stay with me until I could pass it to the next generation.

Several letters followed in the stack of papers that reminded me of the homespun nature of my family. A note from the time Momma's sister Margie went to Nashville to watch the Grand Ole Opry; and a ticket stub from the show.

Nita,

Having a glorious time in Nashville. You should see the clothes the women wear, so fancy. I have never seen so many people. On Saturday, we went to the Grand Ole Opry. It is beuutiful. Music brought me home to the front porch. See you soon.
Love, Margie

There was a letter from the high school principal pointing out the excellent work Momma had done writing her short stories.

"Nita is a very talented writer; her words capture your imagination…."

Momma had never shared with me she liked to write, but it was clear she did, and that she was talented. Included in the stack was a story Momma wrote titled, "The Case of the Curious Squirrel;" a playful missive about the squirrel who evidently took up residence outside Momma's window and made it a habit of watching Momma in her room. There were black and white photos from Momma's childhood; some people I could identify, others were a mystery. The photos showed simple people posing awkwardly; their faces offered stiff smiles, hiding the fatigue of farm life and the signs of premature aging. I sensed each person seemed to convey a story with their eyes that wanted to be told, but time and fate had prevented that from happening. My kinfolk had a rich history, even if it wasn't relevant to a quickly evolving world. My mind wandered as I considered what life must have been like in the hills before I was born, how those years influenced how people behaved in the future. Progress could change how things were done, but it could not wipe away the past and learned attitudes.

I had never taken a moment to look beyond my lifetime. To study the images of my extended family; to allow myself to consider that I wasn't far removed from the people I saw standing upright, overalls strapped across their shoulders. One generation separated me from folks who worried about getting through the day, not about next year.

After several hours of filling my cup with letters and writings that impacted Momma's life, I was ready to quit for the day and take Winston on a walk. He was growing anxious, and I needed to step away. Before I could move on to other things, there was one last letter I hadn't read; despite my desire to stand up, I read the remaining letter before calling it a day. I quickly realized that the letter would not be a feel-good letter about Momma's upbringing. Unfolding the paper, I immediately recognized the handwriting; it was the sheriff's hand.

Nita,

I appreciate your stopping by last week. It is always good to see you. I know you're still sick about the loss of Sue Ann. I wish I could say or do something more to help. I will always pray for you and Frankie.

As I told you, I see no reason to continue investigating what happened. Dillon did it, and justice was delivered. I think it makes sense for you and me to keep who delivered Dillon's fate to ourselves. Nobody is ever going to care. No need to make a fuss over this. What's done is done.

I am glad to have played my part in bringing this to an end. As I told you, if you ever need anything, let me know. Best to Frankie.

Willie Cogburn

Sheriff Cogburn, not surprisingly, lied to me. He knew what had happened to Sue Ann. He also worked with Momma to keep quiet about what happened after they buried Sue Ann. A brief conversation and subsequent letter from thirty-six years before had sealed the pact; no one was to talk about what happened on the farm in the fall of 1964. Evidently, over the years, the knowledge of who killed Dillon and the agreement to keep it private, migrated beyond those two initial conspirators. Everyone in Johnson County except me knew what happened and agreed not to share it with anyone deemed untrustworthy.

There was no stopping me now; I was going to discover the ultimate truth and cement my place as someone who may have left the county but never left my heritage. I had to know, and I had to prove to those around me, I was one of them; maybe this was a way to prove it to myself.

thing they didn't really want to do. I was using my Tennessee background to connect with them. Sadly, I was playing them, and they trusted me; a trust I misused. I am convinced that without my cajoling, they would never have proceeded, and despite forgoing the proceeds of the deal, they would have been happier. I internalized at that moment that our firm didn't measure the deal's success on what was best for our client; we kept count based on our collected fees and how fast we closed. That moment, though not initially obvious to me, ensured I would someday wake up and realize I didn't belong in the business world. I did not want to manipulate and position everything and everybody for my gain. I wasn't raised that way, and I didn't want to become like that.

Alice offered a comforting glance, telling me it was okay.

"Alice, pretending to be something you're not, or to care about something that isn't interesting, was easier than you might think."

I needed to share more; I continued. "Our firm had the best and brightest from the most acclaimed academic institutions; their credentials and family lineage were obvious. And if it wasn't clear, they wouldn't hesitate to let you know of their prowess. I could have reacted differently. I could have stayed hidden and just worked on my assigned tasks. But I didn't; I worked to fit in, to engage in conversations that were more suited for Yale than Tennessee. I remember the weekend all the junior associates stayed at the office preparing a presentation deck our senior team was going to use on an acquisition roadshow. There was a mountain of work to do, but you can't work non-stop without losing your mind. It was natural that we would divert our attention to other items. What I didn't expect was the never-ending conversations about money, trips they had taken or wanted to take, the cars they drove and the summers they spent in the Hamptons. I had nothing to offer, so I made stories up; stories like the time I sailed with my wealthy uncle in the Caribbean, or the embellishments I made about our family business and the wealth we accumulated."

Just saying that out loud to Alice made me laugh. Dismayed at my fibs, Alice shook her head in disbelief.

"It's true, I said that. I was a walking, talking fraud; not because I wanted to be liked, but because I sought to advance my professional career and standing. Looking back, my colleagues knew my truth; they knew I wasn't one of them. To them, I was another wanna-be angling to invade their destined path; it was easy to dismiss me, and they did."

"I didn't know you had a wealthy uncle," Alice joked.

"I need to meet him."

Alice listened to me and didn't judge. I knew then she was going to allow me to grow back to being a boy from the holler.

Special friends can pick up where they left off, even if it has been years since they spoke. That can be harder for lovers. Time and emotions can create scarring that blocks the natural process of restarting a relationship. It wouldn't be a problem for us. Alice and I were high school sweethearts who shared an intimate history. We were also best friends, and it was the strength of our friendship that was carrying the free-flowing conversation.

"RJ, do you remember how many kids we said we wanted to have?"

"I do. I think we said we wanted our own little basketball team. Three girls and two boys."

"That's right, maybe someday." Alice had never looked prettier.

Without thinking, I reached over and touched Alice's hand. It was the first time we had touched since I was home for the holidays in my senior year of college. This simple act stopped our banter, and we locked eyes. Years of pent-up emotion and shame for my departure roared forward, and my eyes became teary. Noticing my emotions, Alice smiled, leaned forward and gave me a soft kiss.

Her lips brought me back to the first time we kissed behind the football stadium. It was a kiss I will never forget. Despite the passion we once had for each other, our prolonged, touching kiss was innocent; full of the caring love a partner gives to another when they are showing acceptance.

A long hug followed the kiss. A welcoming hug that said, 'I missed you and I am glad you are back.'

That warm afternoon sparked the fire that had been dormant, waiting for ignition.

We spent the rest of our time silently watching the flow of clear water in the creek. Words weren't necessary. We had each other. We also had an unstated commitment to figure out how to strengthen our bond. I had hurt her and destroyed her trust in me. She was giving me a chance to earn it back. I would not fail. She sensed that, but she needed to experience it. Every day for the rest of her life.

As the sun fell behind the mountains, we packed our things and headed towards Alice's house. The short drive was quiet. We held hands, occasionally giving a squeeze to signal to the other person we were enjoying the moment. As I parked the car in the driveway, Alice looked at me and said, "I had a great time. Look forward to seeing you soon."

Before I could say anything, she leaned over and gave me a sweet kiss on my cheek. I have never enjoyed a kiss more.

30

Sis Was a Wildcat

I T HAD BEEN A YEAR SINCE I ABRUPTLY INFORMED MY boss, George; I was leaving my New York job, without a plan; without a sense of who I was or what I wanted to be. If measured through the prism of the corporate world I left, I had accomplished nothing in the intervening months. My time had yielded little productivity, no professional bounce back or positive step towards advancing my career. However, by the standards of Gizzard's Holler, I was doing just fine. Not only had I reconnected with family I hadn't engaged with in years, but my old friends' circle was intact. I was slowly rejoining the group; I was learning to cook, and Alice and I were once again a couple.

Our time together healed both of us. She found the strength to forgive me, and I found the courage to forgive myself. We talked for hours about life, our future, and the joy that each day brought. We didn't talk about my past, my doubts, or the mystery surrounding Sue Ann. Overriding my headstrong desire to find the truth about what happened before I was born was my need to belong. Alice was reminding me I belonged to her.

My personality was also changing. I no longer lived my life through a clock, hovering over my head holding me accountable for every minute of the day. If I wanted to pause and watch a robin build a nest, I did. In New York, people took classes to learn to meditate, to find inner peace and tranquility; meditation practitioners organized groups that would meet to find their solitude. In Gizzard's Holler one could find peace sitting on their front porch, watching squirrels bound from limb to limb in a playful game of catch. It is amazing how your mind frees when you allow it.

My heart rate had slowed in the intervening months; no longer did tension control my body; there was no lingering oppressive, unrelenting anxiety. Whatever "crisis" developed on the farm, I received the news with curiosity and eagerness to problem solve. If a cow needed tending to because of an issue birthing, I didn't become annoyed or worked up; I jumped right in, excited to be doing something that felt tangible. I realized I was fortunate to own a farm that I could enjoy. It hadn't always been that way; my ancestors, and many folks in these parts, toiled to survive and make ends meet; farming wasn't easy. My farming life was a luxury, not a burden. I existed comfortably, able to recapture my inner being and cast aside what I had previously sought and fought for in my professional career.

It didn't take long for my natural down-home accent to return; I first heard it when I told my boss I was going to Momma; now every word I spoke had the mountain drawl I grew up with and spoke until I left home. I started saying "reckon so" or "fixin" most every time I spoke. No longer did I feel shame for sounding country. I was country, and the people I loved were too. If I sounded like I fell off a turnip truck, then so be it.

My diet went to hell, but the food was too good to avoid; not Michelin restaurant level food that values presentation as much as flavor. No, it was down-home and familiar. Macaroni and cheese was once again a valued vegetable, with Pete's Diner offering it as part of their meat and three selections. Daily specials were Monday, fried chicken; Tuesday, meatloaf; Wednesday, chicken dumplings; Thursday, turkey and dressing; and Friday, hamburger patty and gravy. It was Pete's regular menu when I was in high school, and I don't see it changing soon; there is something comforting about routine. My frequent suppers at Mark's house reminded me of my love for chicken liver. Tammy put out a spread—fried chicken livers, mashed potatoes with gravy, and green beans — I ate till I couldn't move; that is until it was time for her apple pie, I couldn't pass on that. I was no longer skin and bones; Momma would be proud.

I became a regular congregant at church; Alice and I rarely missed a Sunday. It was the same rituals I experienced as a child, but my takeaway was different. Growing up, church attendance was a requirement, to be rejected whenever I could get away with it; you never look forward to doing something you have to do. All these years later, church became a planned part of my week I looked forward to, a chance to see folks, let my mind remember times with family members who have passed and consider the good word from Pastor Higdon.

My newfound joy in life manifested itself in every area of my day, no more so than with the opportunity that developed for me to grow closer to James. At fifty years of age, James now looked like the father figure I always considered him to be. Growing up, I am sure I was annoying to him. He did not want to be bothered by an eight-year-old. By the time

I became an adult, someone he could relate to, I bolted for New York, thus blocking any chance we had to establish a meaningful relationship. That changed when I came home, and James observed my transitioning back to holler life.

At first, we did nothing more than the occasional small talk so prevalent amongst Southern folk. We would see each other at church, say hello at Jesse's Barbecue, or chat a bit when we spent the evening picking banjos at someone's jam session; it was all superficial. And then one day James asked me to come out to his place after church for the day and an early supper. I don't recall the last time I had supper at Jame's house; certainly; it was before I went to college.

When the day came for my afternoon with James, I was excited and appreciative. I baked a lemon pie for the occasion. Aunt Emily had recently taught me her recipe, and I was eager to try it. Besides, any respectable person who comes for supper needs to bring something, and given it was a Summer Sunday, a pie was the right call.

James married his high school sweetheart, Tina, a year after he graduated. They were newlyweds still living at home and working on the farm. Knowing the arrangement wouldn't work for his new bride, he talked Daddy into helping him buy a small piece of property deeper up Gizzard's Holler; it was a few miles farther up Stinking Creek Road. James' homestead was such that he had to pass our farm to reach the outside world; a fact that no doubt made Momma and Daddy happy.

With his new piece of property, James set out to build a small house to raise a family. After a year and a half of building, and with supplies he could scrounge up, Tina and James moved into a one-story log cabin home with an expansive front porch. It was perfect, and the timing was right; two months after they moved into the new cabin, Tina gave birth to my niece, Mabelle. She was the only daughter James was to have; following Mabelle, over the next four years, Tina gave birth to two boys, James Jr. and Tommy.

James's life revolved around the farm, his family, Momma and Daddy, playing music, and Johnson County. There wasn't much else to it; he was fine with that and sought nothing more. I can't imagine James ever traveling to New York or any place with tall buildings; he simply wouldn't have found a reason to visit a place so foreign to his sensibility. The depth of his living compensated for what he lacked because of his sheltered existence. He understood and belonged to a community of people who had a shared experience; a commitment to serving God and protecting each other. If someone needed something, he was there along with everyone else; it is just the way it is. In James' mind, who needs flash and show when you have substance, and nothing is more substantive than unbreakable bonds?

After the initial Sunday supper at Jame's place, we visited more frequently; I would go to his house every other Sunday for the afternoon. The emotional comfort I gained from gentle afternoons rocking slowly on his porch, laughing and spinning tales infused my soul with warmth; Momma and Daddy weren't there, but it felt like they were. Cutting through years of detachment took time, so James and I started slow. Our conversations began with ordinary things and rarely went deeper. In time, however, we talked about his life with more honesty and feeling. James shared his past with me through stories; the stories that came to define him.

"Ya know, when Tina and I first bought this place, we

couldn't done it without Momma and Daddy," James began. "I didn't have a bucket to piss in, or a place to put it, but I was newly married, and Daddy knew I needed a place of my own. He drove up here and talked with old man Lester about his property and what he intended to do with it after he died; he didn't have no kids or a wife," James explained.

"After thinking on it and a few sips of shine, Daddy and Lester came to an agreement. Daddy would buy the land, Lester could stay in his shack until the end, and Tina and I would look after him. It was a fair agreement."

I didn't remember that part about Lester; however; I recalled, as a young kid, wondering why he was always around James' house.

"Old man Lester lived another ten years, and he wasn't too much trouble, except his constant flirting with Tina. Didn't bother her much, but I didn't care for it." He laughed.

As I observed James tell the story, I could see Daddy in his face; his mannerisms, chiseled chin, powerful eyes, and the slow pace he told the story, were all Daddy. As a child, I could listen to Daddy for hours telling tales of his life. With his perfect pitch at the right time to emphasize an important moment, he kept me spellbound. Now, years later, I was reliving those moments on the porch of my oldest brother, through his voice. The shared time was forging a bond between us; a connection I needed, and James wanted.

One Sunday afternoon, James randomly mentioned Sue Ann. James had just finished telling me about the time Momma got mad at him for teasing Ralph and how Momma had thrown a peeled potato at him to show her displeasure; it missed. Lost in the moment, with his laugh sliding away, James blurted out, "Ya know, Sis was one wildcat."

A little surprised by his unintended comment, James glanced my way to see if I had heard him. This was a subject we had steered away from since my initial questions after Momma's death. Even though time had passed, he knew I remained interested in hearing about the dark days in Sue Ann's life. And yet, in that moment, he was hoping I would set that aside and enjoy some memories that brought a smile. His hunch was right. Even though there were so many unknowns about my sister, I smiled and nodded a knowing acknowledgement of his intent, giving him freedom to talk of our sister without fearing the untouchable topic.

"I really loved that girl," he said.

"She had a spirit about her you don't see much. She was always a handful for Momma, and a worry for Daddy. Even though I was young, I could see she was going to be hard to hold back. I always thought she had Daddy's free spirit, the spirit that drove him to leave Cocke County and go out on his own."

"That's interesting," I said.

"Maybe that could explain my nature and early desire to explore the world beyond these mountains; maybe I was like Daddy."

I had never thought of that; the idea brought me comfort.

"What about Momma? Was Sue Ann like her?" I asked.

James laughed and shook his head. "Yup, she possessed all Momma's habits and her fiery attitude. That girl was a pistol, tough and unafraid. She was confident she could do anything, and left alone, she would have tried. Even so, she was as sweet as she could be. Even as a little girl, she had a way of looking at you that brought a smile."

"Oh, and one more thing," James continued. "She was a

rascal; she was every bit as wild as Uncle Tommy. Seems she came by everything honestly."

I could tell James enjoyed thinking of Sue Ann. It brought him happiness. You could see it on his face. "She was my little sis, and I will always miss her."

I learned a lot about James that day. I was so full of myself when I came back and heard there was a secret that everyone knew but me; I failed to realize the pain and sadness those who knew Sue Ann and lost her must have felt. It had been thirty-seven years, and even though her life stories were joyful, losing her left a massive void that time will never fill. In the years I was away, I had become someone who dismissed another person's perspective. I was about me and the deal I was closing; I was all transactional. Now, months after returning and throwing around my emotions to find answers, regardless of the pain it stirred, I realized people in these parts hold each other dear; but they don't let go; memories linger, and they are private. Outsiders aren't welcome to enter the hearts of those who live in the depths of small-town life.

James was sharing with me, in his own way, access to his world; a world I came from but failed to understand. Not that he was testing me to see if I would jump on the story and start asking questions; he wasn't testing me; he was trusting me. His trust was well-founded. I felt no inclination to pursue the only remaining open question I had. That would come another day, or maybe it would never come.

31

You've Done Good

TWENTY YEARS IN AGE SEPARATED ME FROM JAMES, BUT DNA and proximity in the holler wiped away two decades of time. No longer was I the annoying kid who wasn't old enough to matter. To James, I was now an adult; someone who could value James's life and experiences. The more I saw James, the closer we became. We were no longer kin from different eras. We were friends; with an extra bond derived from growing up in the same house. I sought James's advice, asked questions, and learned about life from his perspective. He was slow to offer his opinion. It wasn't his goal to be a mentor; he wanted to be family, and he knew how to do that.

James showed me how to live a life without regrets. This was new to me. In my career, I was constantly revisiting decisions, obsessing over the choices I had to make, or the ones I had already made. The never-ending, self-absorbed attention to every detail and every move I made left me unable to see beyond myself or the task in front of me. If something didn't go as planned, I would berate myself, or worse, I would have to debrief with the team, and we would unpack every single item until we could confidently blame someone or something. When you live your life with little room to accept failure, it is easy for your mind to fill with regrets; and I frequently had many. Funny, as I look back at my time in New York, my biggest regret should have been my failure to stay connected to my family and my roots; it should have been, but it wasn't. In fact, I don't recall considering what I was doing, or who I was becoming. I directed all my energy towards winning — no, towards beating the other side.

My New York attitude and investment banking demeanor were foreign to James; sure, he was competitive when coaching football, but that role didn't define him or any of the kids he coached. He didn't aspire to coach beyond Johnson County High School and none of the kids harbored any hope of playing beyond their high school days; for them it was a game on Friday night, followed the next day by chores and work to help their family get by. High school sports at a small mountain school were a release, a chance to step outside of normal life and work for something other than subsistence.

Regret was a luxury mountain folk didn't have time for. Things went wrong all the time; equipment broke; people came down with something and were laid up; the weather didn't cooperate; livestock died; plants closed; and plans that seemed thoughtful turned out not to work. It was all part of life. With the deck stacked against them, feeling sorry for yourself or revisiting the past made things worse. As James liked to say, "What's done is done."

The mindset James conveyed was exactly the approach Momma had to her cancer; there was no need to worry about what was going to happen, or fret over what she could have done; it wasn't her way. She accepted what was coming, faced it like she had everything else.

"Momma was tough," James said one afternoon on my front porch.

Finding it a random thing to say, I asked, "What made you say that?"

"I was just looking over at the headstones and was thinking about all she went through." He responded.

"As close as I was to her, I suspect there was a lot of pain in her life she never told me about. I know she never got over Sue Ann, the death of her brother Bubba, you living so far away — all were things that weighed on her." James offered.

"I can understand her sadness about Sue Ann and Bubba, but do you think my being gone hurt her too?" I asked.

"I do, Momma worried about you, but more than that she was certain you were gone for good and wouldn't be a part of her life. She was proud of you, but to her you might as well have been a million miles away."

It was an honest answer, and I appreciated it.

"I hate that."

That was all I could muster; truth is, I was ashamed. Ashamed, I had become so consumed with my ego that I failed to see what was in front of me: a loving family, with simple needs that weren't hard to meet. Unless of course you are so busy in your own world doing big things, trying to be big.

Days spent with James molded me, gave me the context I had been lacking. I saw those around me differently; they hadn't changed; I had. My slow adjustment to home, and my refined view of how I saw people, and their world made me happier, more fun, and more thoughtful. Putting people first became easier for me. I could sense when someone needed a pat on the back, or help; I was eager to jump in, roll up my sleeves and do my part. Life was more rewarding.

I grew closer to Billy, my farmhand. He exhibited all the characteristics I had known about Momma's siblings and their offspring; hardworking, honest, playful, even curious; not about things in my past life, but about the bubbled world he lived in. He wanted to know the names of all the trees on the property, was interested in learning everything he could about how to manage livestock, and could wax poetically about the habits of nesting squirrels and the pre-hibernation phase for local black bears. A sharp, common-sense mind, which rarely missed anything, and frequently showed a unique ability to empathize, made up for his lack of formal schooling.

I ate most evening meals at home with Billy; he was alone, and so was I. I also believed we were a lot alike. Had I not gone to college, I would have held the same youthful nature; possessing naivety about the world beyond, with advanced knowledge of my mountain surroundings.

It was Billy who once again rekindled my interest in the hanging of Dillon; I had thought little about it, having cast the mystery aside.

"RJ, I've been thinkin about the hangin of that boy in that tree over yonder, why you reckon it's such a big secret?"

Billy asked as he slopped up gravy with his cornbread.

"I dunno, Billy, why do you think it is a secret?"

I responded, enjoying the playful banter.

"I think its cause someone important hung him. Can't think of no other reason people would care and go to all this effort to hide something from thirty-plus years ago."

"Makes sense to me, Billy; you're probably right." I guessed.

"Well, then, who do you think did it?" he asked.

I didn't know, or at least I hadn't let myself remember the days when I was consumed by knowing. If our premise was right and it was someone of note, maybe the townsfolk were right, and it should stay a secret. I wouldn't gain anything from knowing who did it, and perhaps something bad could happen. Maybe my asking around would lead to the new sheriff or a future sheriff, who was an outsider, deciding he didn't want a hanging to go unanswered for.

"I really don't know Billy," I answered.

I wasn't completely honest. I had my suspicions, but I had decided they should remain with me. Maybe someday I will revisit this and put it to bed once and for all.

And that was my plan, until one evening on James's porch I blurted out, "Hey James, do you think I should care about who hung that boy?"

It was a break in our conversation about pig prices; James didn't see my question coming, but he didn't seem to mind.

"Why do you want to know that, RJ? I don't understand why it is so important to you."

He responded with little emotion. He wasn't mad; he really didn't get my obsession.

"It's a good question," I started.

"When I first learned Momma had cancer, followed by the revelation of Sue Ann, I was certain I couldn't know who I was until I knew the truth. I felt like I couldn't know myself if there were holes in my story. I even wondered if they had excluded me from knowing more secrets."

"Makes sense, I guess; were you right? Did you need to know about things not directly related to you to find yourself?" James asked gently, staring at me.

It was an unusual look; he was showing compassion, the same tenderness I received from Momma when she decided being tough wasn't the correct course.

James was right; it was at the heart of the issue. I didn't need to know everything from my past to connect me to who I was. I never lost contact with who I was; I just strayed a bit. James needed to hear that.

"James, I was wrong. I didn't need to know to find me, but just as soon as I got over that hurdle, I felt like an outsider who couldn't return to my home. I feared they wouldn't accept or trust me."

It was a vulnerable moment, and James saw my hesitation in exposing my insecurity.

"I was even told by Mark that the reason people were unwilling to tell me what happened is they didn't know if they could trust me." Saying it out loud hurt.

"That is not fair RJ, I don't think it is true. I have held back from telling you because I promised Momma I wouldn't. I have always meant to live up to commitments made to her, and I would really prefer not to break them now. She had her reasons for wanting the truth about Sue Ann's murder and the hanging of Dillon to die; I don't know if she is right or wrong, but it is how she felt."

He continued, "Momma made sure that everyone connected to that sad week promised to take the details to their grave. She had a powerful personality, and as you know, it was hard to tell her no. Obviously, she got her way, and until you reappeared, this was a mystery that stayed hidden."

"Thanks, James, for telling me that. I too will respect her wishes and let it drop."

I hadn't realized how the last remaining unsolved worry

had held me back until James shared Momma's wish with me. This wasn't about me; it never had been. Momma had her reasons, and that had to be good enough for me.

Free of the last residue of stress that had gripped me; I cast aside all thoughts of anything but growing old in Johnson County. My future was sitting on my porch with Alice by my side and thinking about what was right in front of me. Any attempt at learning about my past, and that of my family, was a search for more examples of the heritage I had grown to love; my days of annoying queries were over.

The farm operation grew, and Billy added two more helpers; we were a bona fide outfit. We now had a dozen pigs, three dozen head of cattle, a hay meadow that covered one hundred acres, and more chickens than I could count or eat. I spent every day with my hands in the dirt, working the land and building an existence that I could understand. I wasn't making money; I was making do; I was also living to the fullest each day.

I took up writing and found I enjoyed penning short stories about the folks I lived with. Most of the time, I took liberties with what I described, but that was okay; the stories were for my eyes only.

At the start of my second fall in Gizzard's Holler, the high school principal asked me if I would teach a general business class; I really didn't want to do it. I was certain it would reintroduce the anxiety I felt when business was my existence. Reluctantly, I said I would give it a go; surprisingly; I enjoyed my time in the classroom. I was teaching students with whom I could connect. Thirteen years ago, I was in their shoes, hoping for a future that would excite me, but anchored in a world that filled my soul with a foundation to be proud of.

My time in the classroom expanded after hours into mentoring sessions. To my surprise, I easily connected the two disparate worlds, Johnson County and everywhere else. I think I offered the first actual view of what awaited people who left this valley. I was credible; I was honest; I was happy.

On the two-year anniversary of Momma's death, I leaned against the poplar tree silently thinking about how my life had changed. I missed Momma and Daddy; you can never replace the void that is felt when you lose your parents; there is an emptiness that is always present, even if I lived in the house they spent their lives in.

This wasn't the first time I had spent an afternoon next to the graves of my family members; I was a frequent visitor. Today was different, though. Today, I felt Momma; she was there with me.

It was a chilly day, but Momma's love wrapped me in an emotional blanket. What started as a routine moment for me to pay my respects shifted when I sensed Momma's spirit was next to me; my tough exterior faded, and I once again became RJ, the youngest of four Burnette kids born in Gizzard's Holler.

I told her I missed her and loved her. Updated her about Gizzard Holler and townfolk since she had passed. I told her about the farm, my friends, my teaching, and Alice. I told her everything. I'm not sure how long I sat under that tree talking to Momma's spirit; it didn't matter. She was listening. I felt like a child coming home to tell my parents about the fish I caught in the pond; I was so excited I barely took a breath. In time, the pace of my words slowed, and my intensity faded. I had said everything there was to say. In that moment, I closed my eyes and sensed Momma holding me tightly with her strong, bony arms; when I was completely immersed in her touch, I heard her say, "I love you, RJ, you have done good."

Nothing compares to the joy of receiving affirmation from your Momma; to hear she is proud of you exceeds anything that can ever happen. Looking back, I didn't need to hear her say those words; I knew I had made something out of my life and was living a life that would make my family proud. It was nice to hear, though.

32

Where Are We Going

IT WAS THE FRIDAY BEFORE THE FOURTH OF JULY weekend, and I had plans. Alice and I, newly engaged, were going to spend Saturday boating on Watauga Lake with Mark and Tammy. Everything was ready. We had recently agreed to marry. As is the case, things move slowly around here; it took me months to get the nerve to ask her for her hand. Even though we had been dating for a year, in my way of thinking, Alice still needed time to confirm who I was.

Preparing for tomorrow's lake day, I was a ball of energy; sparked by the energy of our relationship and the idea of spending the day with her, Alice consumed most of my thoughts. Funny how love can make you act silly. Winston had never seen me dance around the room, bellowing out country love songs with a voice that was best suited for picking a banjo, and now here I was. It had been three years since Winston and I had packed up and come home; in those few years, Winston had grown old. He didn't want to move unless he had no choice. My singing was all the motivation he needed, and he slowly stood up, disapprovingly shook his head at me and gingerly walked onto the porch.

My improved kitchen skills led me to try more things. However, for tomorrow's occasion, I only needed macaroni salad and coleslaw. Mark was bringing hot dogs and burgers for the grill, and Alice volunteered to make dessert. Having thrown together what I was contributing; I went out front and see if I could stir Winston to take a small walk.

As I opened the screen door, I noticed James off to the left rocking in the chair, content to wait for me to come outside. Winston was lying by his side, pining for a back rub.

"Good morning, why didn't you tell me you were here?"

"Awe, no hurry. I was enjoying the tranquility of my favorite front porch." He replied.

And why wouldn't he? This was his home before it was mine. Time and distance couldn't block the peacefulness of the home you grew up in.

"What's up?"

"Say, do you have an hour? There's something I have been meaning to do with you."

"Sure," I responded, uncertain what I had agreed to.

"Okay, come on then. I'll drive. Bring Winston. It's a quick trip."

Driving to an unknown destination, I didn't consider what I was about to walk into. It seemed odd for James to do this, but he was my brother, and if he needed me for something, I was all in.

Leaving my farmhouse, we turned left towards James' place. I instantly concluded my surprise had to do with his house; that wasn't to be. Without saying a word, James drove past his place heading deeper into the holler.

I couldn't contain my curiosity. The only thing farther up in the woods was Ralph's shack. Why would we be heading there?

"James, where are we going?" I asked.

"We're going to see Ralph. We have something to talk about."

"Okay," I said, unsure how to react.

It was only five minutes until we reached the end of the road and Ralph's home. Fully in tune with his surroundings and able to hear an approaching car way before it could see his house, Ralph was standing in front of his porch; a structure that looked more dangerous than secure.

Ralph recognized James' truck, but it didn't cause him to smile. He didn't look disturbed; he looked uninterested.

James parked the truck and said to himself, "This should be interesting."

As we approached, I reached out to shake Ralph's hand. He looked aged, much worse than the last time I saw him. It didn't look like he was taking care of himself, nor was anyone helping him. I felt sad to see him that way.

"What's going on, fellas?" He said in a gravely, soft voice.

"We have something to talk about," James said. His voice carried a more serious tone than when I asked the same question.

"Is there a place we can sit?"

Sitting down implied we were staying more than a minute; a thought that didn't seem to sit well with Ralph. He didn't like visitors, even if they were family.

"Sure, I guess." Ralph reluctantly replied.

He pointed over to a cleared section that had a few tree stumps loosely aligned close together. It looked like a place where he built fires. It was an odd setup, given that it suggested a welcoming fire pit arrangement. But to my knowledge, no one ever came around Ralph for a communal fire to take place.

I followed James over and sat down on a well-worn stump. An awkward silence followed.

"Ralph, RJ has learned about Sue Ann and how she died. He also knows about the Dillon boy. He's been asking questions damn near since he got home, and no one has told him what happened."

I didn't know what to say. I had moved on from this, come to peace with not knowing. The thought of what happened didn't live in my mind, nor did I wonder why things turned out the way they did. And now, my oldest brother, who I had grown close to and had previously talked to about this many times, was suggesting he wanted me to know what occurred.

I wanted to stop him, get up and walk away, but I didn't. I sat there and blankly stared at James. After a moment, I said, "Okay, what happened?"

Ralph looked at James, disbelieving what he had just heard. His mouth opened and displayed his blackened teeth and tobacco-stained lips. It was a grisly sight. I couldn't tell whether he was smiling or disgusted.

"Why do you think I should do this? If you want the boy to know, you tell him."

It was a good question. Why had James chosen to suddenly reveal the secret, and why had he chosen Ralph to be the storyteller?

Ralph remained unconvinced. "James, this is silly. I ain't got no interest in talking about what happened. That's been buried a long time ago, and I don't think about it no more. Seems to me you should let it go too."

James sat quietly considering what to say next. He looked like he was trying to decide whether Ralph was right. If stirring this up now made sense.

After several minutes of silence, James looked at Ralph and said, "Ralph, RJ has become one of my closest friends. He is family. He is your family. Momma wanted us to keep this secret in the family, and we have. Now it is time we accept RJ is one of us. I think Momma would want him to know."

James' words infused me with pride. Nothing anyone has ever said meant more to me than expressed his feelings. I was part of the family. A family that protects its truths and secrets. The three of us had taken different paths to get here, but now we sat in front of this ramshackle cabin that Ralph called home, united as one. We traveled our own unique paths, but we started at the same place. It was only fitting that we ended up together, not over five miles apart.

Strengthened by the love James expressed, I looked Ralph in the eye and asked him, "What happened, brother?"

Ralph paused, processing the words he had heard in the last few minutes. Finally, he said, "It was me. I hung the bastard."

Stunned, I didn't know what to say. Finally, I weakly replied, "Ralph, why?"

"That's what Momma and Daddy asked me," he said.

"I told them what I had done the morning after I had hanged him, and they wanted to know why I did it." He stopped himself and grew quiet.

We all sat in silence. I didn't know what to say. The mystery of what happened was laid bare for me to digest. I know knew what happened. My brother, at fourteen, killed the boy who murdered Sue Ann, and everyone covered it up.

Sheriff Cogburn knew what happened, my family knew,

I guess the whole county did. In a fleeting moment, the Sheriff agreed with Momma it was best if they shut down any further investigation. Sue Ann was murdered, and the boy who did it was dead; no need to talk about it anymore. Since Dillon was a transient, insignificant to his brothers, and another name that nobody would care about, the sheriff could ignore Ralph's actions. Dillon was like so many before him, a soul whose death didn't matter to anyone.

It was a lot to process. I can imagine the anger Momma and Daddy felt towards Dillon. I understand the sheriff not wanting to hurt them anymore. Holding Ralph accountable would have added to the Burnette suffering; it would have been too much. What I kept getting hung up on was the mindset of the entire community that embraced the hidden story, the conclusion, and the desire to forget. The need to protect those who hold shared values and experiences was powerful. My family was a part of the community and had been for decades, so if we were in trouble, it was natural for those who could to rally around and figure it out. Here, "figuring it out" meant whitewashing the death of a murderer that no one cared about and who, it would have uniformly believed, deserved to die.

The slow flow of the small unnamed stream was the only sound for several minutes. The rhythmic movement of mountain water flowing over smoothed rocks pulled me into a trance. I became frozen with emotion.

Much of my feelings had nothing to do with Ralph, what he did, and the events of 1964. I am not sure I would have acted any differently than he did. If someone attacked my family, I would strike back. I was raised this way. It was how we were all raised. Despite that fact, I couldn't help but remember, the entire community felt compelled to keep this from me: Momma, Daddy, James, Sheriff Cogburn, my best friend Mark, Mr. Porter, everyone I asked. Maybe even Alice. They all followed the plan. After what I learned, I couldn't get mad at them anymore. I understood they executed Momma's unwritten pact. I know they were trying to protect Ralph. It was the right thing to do; but didn't they trust me to protect him? It was obvious they didn't. I hurt people by leaving and becoming New York's RJ. I turned away from them, and they hadn't forgotten. In their mind it was only fair to assume the secrets of these mountains are the property of the mountain folk who live here. People have lived their lives by a code that has existed since the valley was settled. We take care of each other, above all else.

That cultural trait was to be admired — self-reliance. But I couldn't help but consider the contradiction my community had embraced. In my search for honesty and truth, I had uncovered a vigilante system of justice that was accepted and protected. It was a far cry from the peaceful, simple ways I believed existed here and the harsh black and white expectations the rest of the country would apply to home-grown accountability. It was a moral code that applied its own standards of how to deliver justice.

This information was an unexpected detour in my under-standing of my home. It was a detour but not a roadblock. In my mind, I could bridge the gap between the outside world's expectations and the protected confines of Johnson County. It didn't alter my opinion of Ralph or of the people who held the secret. To them, they had done nothing wrong. Dillon was the culprit, and they made him pay for his actions.

I had come full circle. Early in life, I focused on leaving, but then I discovered the thing I left for was hollow, lacking the bond Johnson Countians built. I became an empty box with nothing inside to protect. In the three years since returning, I learned to appreciate the value of belonging, of being a part of something that defines your being, that guides your path. Not an isolating journey, but a shared road to be walked with people who will stand beside you, behind you, and for you. I found my home, and for that, I am blessed.

Comforted by what I had become, I smiled at Ralph, put my hand on his shoulder, and repeated, "Brother, why did you do it?"

With a tobacco-stained grin, Ralph raised his head, his eyes meeting mine, and said, "I reckon it made sense."

Acknowledgements

Saying thank you is never adequate; I will try. I could not have completed this book without the guidance of Kumud Srinivasan, Courtney Wainner, and Colin Martin. Their insight, advice, and patience with me are laudable and much appreciated. Every time I received their feedback, it made the book better. I will forever be in their debt.

Special thanks to Ashley Fields for her tireless support of my work. We should all be so lucky as to have someone that valuable in our lives.

I would be remiss if I didn't acknowledge the impact of the people in my life who have lived the Appalachian experience and stand tall. I hope *Lost in the Holler* brings you joy.

About the Author

In 2023, Michael published his first book, Mom's Diary. In the spring of 2024, he launched *I Was Just Thinking*, a twice-a week blog on Substack. Michael devotes his time to writing, cooking, and his two grandchildren. He lives in Bristol, TN, with his wife.

29

The Kiss

ALL THAT I HAD LEARNED ABOUT MY PAST, MY FAMILY, and their secrets filled my head with constant thoughts. What I needed was to fill my heart. It was time to call Alice.

"Hello."

"Alice, this is RJ. How are you doin?"

"I'm good, RJ." Her tone was welcoming.

I immediately felt sixteen again, struggling for words to ask her out on our first date.

"Alice, I was wondering if you and I could go on a date. Maybe a picnic out on Laurel Creek?"

Without hesitation she said, "I would like that."

"Great, how about I pick you up Saturday around eleven?"

"That works."

Friday night I couldn't sleep. I stared at the ceiling, reflecting on my life with Alice and the loneliness without her. It was a long night of anticipation.

Saturday was a gorgeous June day. I had waited for this day for most of my adult life. Alice was giving us a chance.

A chance to recapture the center of my existence; a chance to recapture Alice's heart.

Laurel Creek offers many isolated places for a picnic, and we knew the perfect place. We had spent many afternoons tucked along the east side of the stream below Adams Waterfall; it was a spot that held many memories.

After we settled on the blanket, I quickly noticed Alice's commitment to rebuilding our relationship. The conversation was comfortable. We laughed at how our friends had turned out. Retold funny tales from our early dating. I told stories about times in New York when my hayseed upbringing was obvious. It was good to laugh at myself.

As the hours passed, I noticed I was comfortable being me. I hadn't felt that sensation in years. Alice brought out the best in me. I didn't need to perform. I could express myself and show my vulnerabilities.

"Alice, wonderful as New York can sound, I lost who I was. Without you, I couldn't get my anchor to hold."

Sensing her receptiveness of my vulnerability, I shared my darkest moment as a banker with her, a moment I will never forget and will always regret.

Two years before I quit, our firm represented a mid-size company with headquarters in Jackson, Tennessee. It was a family business, with the second generation of boys running what their daddy had built from scratch. Without the next generation interested in stepping up, they considered selling their business; it was a hard choice, and they were reluctant. That's where I stepped in. Our firm had tasked me with convincing them to work with us, pushing them to proceed, and when the time came, pressuring them to take the deal. It never felt right to me; I was leading them to do some-